# EVIDENCE

## *OF*

# REVENGE

**KnightGuard
Security
Book 5**

# Lila Ferrari

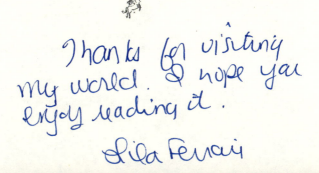

*Thanks for visiting my world. I hope you enjoy reading it.*

*Lila Ferrari*

Paperback ISBN: 978-1-7330210-9-8

For more information on books by Lila Ferrari, or to subscribe to her newsletter, visit her website here: https://www.lilaferrariwrites.com

## PRAISE FOR LILA FERRARI

danger, and a stalker to look forward to in this story. The characters are likeable and different but good together; their chemistry is amazing! Definitely recommended! — *Reader review*

 **Sexy and exciting**
Loved this book. Best one of the three that I have read. Sexy, exciting and suspenseful from start to finish. —*Reader review*

 **A great romantic suspense story**
*Evidence of Lies* is the third book in the KnightGuard Security series and is a great romantic suspense story. I really enjoyed this book. The characters are well developed, intelligent, and likable. The storyline is well crafted and engaged my interest from start to finish, with secrets, deception, a stalker, danger, intrigue, and a chance for romance. —*Reader review*

 **Assuming**
Assumptions make for a wonderfully emotive edge in this thrilling romance. The characters are excellently written to draw the reader into their lives. The connection the reader gets with the storyline is enhanced by an addictive plot that make putting the book down almost impossible. A brilliant romance written by an author whose superb talent with words builds a whole world that you do not want to leave. —*Reader review*

PRAISE FOR **EVIDENCE OF DECEIT**

 **Really enjoyed this book**
I've read all the books in this series and I honestly loved every one of them! Lila Ferrari has the ability to keep the reader enthralled by keeping the story

moving along and making you want to keep reading and wanting to get to the next page as fast as possible. — *Reader review*

★★★★★ **Fantastic**

The story line caught my attention at the very beginning and kept me interested throughout the entire book. I loved the characters. — *Reader review*

★★★★★ **Romantic Suspense has NEVER looked Sooo Good!**

I found this to be a superb storyline that grabs you right from the start keeping you engrossed and on edge throughout the whole book! Great characters that will keep your interest extremely well. The chemistry, sweetness, and twists in plot kept things interesting. — *Reader review*

# ACKNOWLEDGMENTS

I can't thank enough everyone who has read my books, made suggestions, and given me the encouragement to continue writing.

A shoutout to my writing mentors. The enthusiasm and knowledge this group has shared has been invaluable and an inspiration to me. Also a big thank you to the members of Florida Star Fiction Writers who have encouraged and applauded my successes. Thank you.

Extra special thanks goes to Ray Ferrari. You have been my rock and best friend. Your edits, while sometimes painful, have made this book even better.

And a huge thank you to Chris Kridler of Sky Diary Productions for editing my rough drafts, keeping my story on track, giving me valuable suggestions to make my books better and for designing my cover.

Thanks to all who took the time to review my books. I thank you from the bottom of my heart. Reviews are appreciated. It helps new authors get recognized.

Any errors, blunders, or inaccuracies made are all mine.

# EVIDENCE OF REVENGE

## Courage, Redemption, Second Chances

**Protecting the innocent is easy.**
**Protecting her heart—not so much.**

*This is Sam Knight's story. Many of you have expressed an interest in her and how KnightGuard Security came about. I hope I've answered your questions.*

## WHAT WOULD YOU DO FOR LOVE?

Samantha "Sam" Knight should be on top of the world. Her business, KnightGuard Security, is thriving. She has great girl-friends and a boyfriend who loves her.

But something isn't right in her life. A nagging suspicion that someone is gunning for her has thrown her off her game.

Mark Stone left the SEALs to settle down and start his construction business. He loves it and Sam. She's a warrior, a great lover, and they have a strong relationship. She's everything to him, but he can't get her to commit to marriage.

After the unexpected death of his sister, their lives are turned upside down. Amid new challenges and new dangers as their friends fall under attack, one by one, Sam is pulling away from him, and he doesn't understand why.

Sam knows that whoever is pursuing her wants to ruin her life. Does she have to walk away from all that she loves to protect Mark, or can they destroy the threat together?

*For Ray,*
*Always*

# CHAPTER ONE

Samantha Knight walked along the shoreline of Moon Beach, ignoring the seagulls' antics and avoiding the lightly rolling waves drenching the sand. It was quiet this time of year. The seasonal visitors, "snowbirds," as the locals called them, were trickling down. In another month, the beach would be crowded with a swarm of pale bodies. Most would leave red as lobsters.

There were a few white, fluffy clouds on the horizon but lots of blue sky. The sand felt cool on Sam's feet as she dug her toes deeper. She zipped her sweatshirt higher and stuffed her hands into the pockets.

Black Pointe, Florida, was usually warm this time of year. A cold front had come in.

The beach was her special place for solitude and peace, but both were eluding her today. Something was tugging at her memory, and she couldn't grasp what it was. But it was unsettling.

Sam inhaled the salty air and laughed as a couple of seagulls competed to steal some food from an unoccupied blanket.

*Silly birds.*

Several little kids in bathing suits gleefully made sandcastles. Their moms looked on as they raced back and forth, refilling their buckets with water. She couldn't understand why they weren't cold.

Actually, she could. A similar beach scene from the past on this same beach with her brother Danny and her parents flitted through her mind. She sighed. So long ago. She missed her parents, and their deaths still hurt.

She watched several couples walking hand in hand, laughing or jumping back to avoid the waves. A woman walked by with a black lab on a leash pulling her whenever he saw a seagull. They didn't allow dogs on the beach, but nobody was there to enforce the law.

A man was going up and down the shoreline with a metal detector, bending when he thought he struck something of value. She envied his optimism.

The quiet and solitude gave her time to reflect on her life.

Her business, KnightGuard Security, was doing well—too well.

There wasn't a lot of downtime for anyone on staff, and she was on a hiring spree. No complaints there.

For the past month, though, she'd felt uneasy. Her intuition told her someone was watching her, and her gut never let her down. After her friend Grace Winslow's freaky stalker incident a while ago, she imagined stalkers everywhere.

This felt different.

No one had approached her, sent her messages, or dialed the phone and hung up. No pizza deliveries or dead cats.

There was none of the usual nonsense that stalkers do, but Sam felt—no, she knew—she was on someone's radar.

Sure, she was in the protection and security business, but

without proof of harassment, she didn't want to involve the staff, especially since everyone was flat-out busy.

"Hi."

Sam yelped, and her heart slammed across her chest. She was so lost in thought, she hadn't seen the little girl with the huge brown eyes walk up to her.

"Hi."

"Whatchadoing?"

Sam sighed. "Thinking."

"Okay, bye."

Sam's goodbye got lost in the wind.

What was wrong with her that she wasn't paying attention? This wasn't like her. Her mind was cluttered with so many things. She hoped her time on the beach would help, but it didn't.

The tide was going out, and she walked to the edge of a dune and sat down. Sam watched the waves receding, exposing seaweed and whatever else was on the beach. She couldn't help reflecting how the ocean was like emotions; it could build you up but also leave you bare and exposed.

*Enough!* She was thinking too much.

Her brother Danny and Hailey, one of her best friends, were getting married in two days.

Tomorrow, she would put her party face on and engage in the pre-marriage celebrations. She was beyond happy for them.

She was standing up for Hailey. Something she was proud to do. Danny's best friend and her boyfriend, Mark Stone, would stand up for him.

The upcoming marriage, however, was causing her unwanted feelings of guilt and angst.

Mark wanted to marry her. They had been together for three years, and Sam loved him. But not enough to marry him —not yet.

Her business was expanding into other security areas. Mark's construction company was taking off, and he was hiring more employees.

These were not insurmountable issues. So what was her problem? If she was honest with herself, they were just excuses.

The possibility of giving up her independence and maybe her business was terrifying. Although truth be told, Mark had never asked her to. Even more frightening was thinking about giving her heart and soul to Mark. The fear he would die and leave her alone both overwhelmed and scared her. Irrational, sure, but she couldn't get past the feeling.

Not to mention she was sure someone was watching her and probably watching her friends, too. She couldn't, wouldn't, let her troubles hurt them. Whoever was watching her was like the wind. You knew it was there, could feel it, see it in action, but it was still invisible.

Then there was the problem of kids. Mark wanted children. She didn't know if she was ready or ever would be.

She and Mark both kept weird hours. They rarely saw each other as it was. Who would take care of kids if they had them? And how would being married be different from the relationship they had right now?

Why was love so complicated?

Why couldn't her life be simple?

Questions she didn't have answers for. Everywhere she turned, her friends were getting married or working odd hours. They were having kids and still making their relationships work. Why not her?

The wind picked up. Sand peppered her eyes, and she shivered.

She glanced to her left. The metal detector guy had left, as had most of the people who'd been walking on the beach.

It was quiet, too quiet—a deathlike quiet.

*Death.*

*Oh my God.*

Today was the anniversary of her high school friend Suzie Shaw's burial.

How could she have forgotten? She never forgot.

Suzie—sweet, kind, beautiful Suzie. Suzie always had something nice to say about everyone, unlike Sam. Suzie believed everyone was redeemable and deserved a second chance. And look where that got her.

A shallow grave by the side of a path. Her body exposed by dogs who dug her up. Sam shuddered.

Sam didn't know her best friend in high school was killed the week after graduation. Killed just a week after they hugged each other goodbye and promised to get together at the end of summer to party and celebrate.

Sam and Grace learned about Suzie's death after they returned from their summer vacation in Europe. That summer when everything looked brighter until it didn't.

Was that what was bothering her? Maybe. But something bigger was going on. Her Spidey senses were in overdrive.

Someone was spying on her.

She glanced around the beach again. Could feel eyes on her.

Her gun! She slowly reached for her purse, dragged it to her lap. Opened the clasp.

There was a whisper of wind at her back. Her hand was in her purse, grasping the gun.

Her pulse quickened. Would someone actually attack her out in the open? Why not?

She was now the only one on the beach. Damn.

"Hey, sweetheart," a soft voice whispered in her ear.

Sam jumped when two arms wrapped around her. Then the familiar scent of bay surrounded her.

"Mark! Sam willed her heart to stop frantically beating.

"You scared me." She shook her head, "You're lucky to be alive."

He chuckled. "I'm sorry. I thought you knew I was back here."

"No, why would I?" Sam had been so busy thinking about who could be watching her, she wasn't paying attention. Not paying attention could get her killed. What was her problem?

# CHAPTER TWO

Score!

Colin Woods pulled his baseball cap farther down on his forehead and slowly guided the metal detector to the next spot closer to his car. It was time to leave. The small, thatched-roof concession stand was closing. No customers. The beach was empty, and he didn't want to call attention to himself.

His scalp itched from the wig, and the damn waves had soaked his pants, but they were small inconveniences.

He had been only a few feet from Sam Knight, but she didn't see him, although her head was swiveling, looking for a threat. His heart had thumped wildly with excitement. Would she recognize him as the threat?

What would he do if she did? He had a gun hidden in his belt behind his back; he hoped he wouldn't have to use it.

He had other plans for the bitch.

She looked so small and inconsequential sitting there. But he knew Sam had already checked the beach for danger hiding in the bushes. Little did she know that her threat was in plain sight.

Splurging on the metal detector may have set him back a few bucks, but it helped him blend in on the beach. He looked like an ordinary man hoping to find treasure, but in reality he was a man looking to get revenge.

Sam was smart enough to suspect someone was watching her but not the reason.

Colin would keep that fun fact to himself until he had Sam where he wanted her—ready to kill.

His plan to destroy her had been in place for a month, and he was ready to strike.

The woman was a magnet for trouble, a fearless warrior, and an advocate for the downtrodden. None of that mattered to him. Unfortunately for Sam Knight, she'd made one too many mistakes—mistakes she'd pay for.

After her friend's body had been found, Sam went on a mission to find out who killed her. She just couldn't leave anything alone. She chased down the two bitches who lied about Tony and convinced them to testify in court.

Tony was convicted and sent to jail for ten years. The drug business that Colin hoped to take over, and Tony had groomed him for, was almost destroyed. Now he was practically penniless because of that bitch. Tony died in prison a couple of months ago, but before he did, he'd made Colin promise to take care of Sam Knight. It was a promise he would keep.

For the past month, Colin had been careful, going out of his way not to call attention to himself while spying on Sam and her friends.

Disguises were wonderful distractions. He looked like a businessman one day and a beach bum the next. He'd filled in his cheeks, wore different hats, changed sunglasses and outfits. He liked to think of himself as a chameleon.

He knew from following Sam these past few weeks that

she liked this beach, volunteered at a shelter, lunched with friends, and had a lover.

Her life was perfect. His, not so much—but it would be.

Following Sam Knight was a gift that kept on giving—giving him pleasure, giving her grief. Watching and planning her demise consumed his life. Soon he would take hers.

What was that expression? Oh yeah. Tit for tat. Soon it would be.

# CHAPTER THREE

S am stood at the entrance of First Church's sanctuary, waiting for her cue to enter. The bridesmaids were halfway down the aisle, walking in step to Pachelbel's Canon in D Major—one of her favorite pieces. Danny was standing at the altar surrounded by his groomsmen, his hands visibly shaking. He finally tucked them into his pockets.

Her brother and her best friend, Hailey, were getting married, and her heart was bursting with joy. What could be better than that? It was a small wedding—about eighty people. Neither of them wanted a big wedding. Sam was fine with that. Danny and Hailey were getting married in the same church as their parents had so many years ago.

The same church where she and Danny had been baptized and where they held her parents' funeral.

*Sam held Leonardo tightly as the minister droned on and on. Why couldn't he shut up about Mommy and Daddy? They were gone. Gran said they were in heaven, looking over her and Danny. Everyone around her was crying, but she had no tears. She missed them terribly.*

*If she and Leonardo had been home, they would've saved Mommy and Daddy. But she was at Gran and Pops.*

Sam and Danny were staying at their grandparents' while her parents had a special date night. Turned out her mother wasn't feeling well and they left the restaurant early to return home to find two burglars ransacking their house. They were shot as they walked through the door. Shot like they didn't mean anything to anybody. It took the police about a month to solve the case and put the two men in jail. The two men could rot in hell for all she cared.

Hailey cleared her throat. "You're up, Sam."

Realizing it was her turn to walk down the aisle startled Sam out of her dark memories. She smiled at Hailey and walked slowly into the sanctuary.

The music played in the background, and Sam prayed she wouldn't twist her ankle or worse. High heels were not part of her dress code, but she would do anything for Hailey.

She reached the altar and stepped to the left.

Danny's eyes glistened as he watched his bride and her uncle walk down the aisle. Hailey was ecstatic that her uncle could step in because her father died a while ago.

Her girlfriends had made a big deal of helping Hailey pick out her gown: a simple off-the-shoulder dress with a sweet-heart neckline and embroidered lace and sequin detailing. She looked radiant in it. Danny and Hailey turned toward the minister and repeated their vows. They were perfect for each other. Sam knew Danny would do anything for Hailey.

Did her parents feel the same happiness when they got married here? Did they have a good marriage? She thought so. Heavy thoughts for a festive occasion.

She barely remembered her parents. Pictures of them were the only way she could recall their faces. Yet so many happy times were etched in her memories, at least until there were no more happy times.

She wanted, no, needed her mother. Needed her advice and comfort. But Mom and Dad were dead. Thank God her grandparents had taken her and Danny in and given them a good home with lots of love. It didn't make up for losing their parents, but it helped them keep ties to the community and their friends.

It had been a while since she'd visited or talked to her grandparents.

Thank goodness they could make it to Danny's wedding. They no longer had grandparent duties or lived in Black Pointe. The two of them traveled, visiting friends and places they thought they would see so many years ago before fate stepped in.

They would be here for a few days after the wedding. She wanted to drive to Grace's parents' house on the island where they were staying. The wedding stirred up so many memories. Sam needed to talk with Gran and Pop.

Beethoven's "Ode to Joy" was playing. Hailey and Danny kissed each other and started walking down the aisle. As Danny's best man, Mark would escort Sam out. She straightened Mark's boutonniere, and he winked at her. His black tux accented his dark hair. He was already handsome, but dressed up, he was sex on a stick.

He smiled as he held out his arm for her, and his eyes twinkled, promising a good time later.

She'd already forgiven him for scaring the crap out of her at the beach the other day. He said he'd been worried about her.

However, she didn't miss the hint of sadness in his brown eyes. She'd put the sadness there, and guilt consumed her.

Mark hoped to be married earlier this year, but she'd turned him down—again. Why? He was a good man, had her back, made her laugh, and she loved him with all her heart.

Sam gave him a small smile. At some point, she either

needed to say yes or let him go. It wasn't fair to either of them for her to string him along.

----

Colin sat in his battered Toyota truck and fiddled with the radio. Static. The old jalopy only worked sporadically, but he wasn't wasting his money on a new one. He'd get a brand-spanking-new truck with all the bells and whistles when the drug money started rolling in.

He thanked the weather gods that the day was sunny and not too warm. It would have sucked to be stuck in the truck if it was raining or too humid. He'd parked on the street a block from the church so that he could see what was going on but far enough away the guests couldn't identify him. Not that anyone in that crowd knew what he looked like.

Good fortune was certainly coming Colin's way. Last week, when he went to Stone Construction to fill out the employment forms, he'd overheard Mark telling a guy that Sam's best friend and her brother were getting married today. It took a little searching to find out where the wedding was taking place, but he lucked out. Colin didn't care about weddings. Weddings were for losers. He just wanted to spy on Sam and her friends, watch them experience some joy. It wouldn't last long.

Besides, why marry a woman when you could get the sex for free?

You never had to worry about paying for a divorce or getting stuck paying alimony for the rest of your life—no little bastards running around looking for your attention, either.

Lord knew his father never married his mother, and that had been a good thing, because dear ol' mom disappeared with another man when Colin turned ten.

On his birthday, no less. No cake, no card, and no happy birthday, son. She never said goodbye, never looked back. Never cared that he needed her.

Colin's father didn't care, either. He'd already hooked up with another bitch by then. The first of many who would flit in and out of his life. None of them caring about the young boy.

The only man in his life was his mother's brother, Uncle Dale. He spent many summers at Dale's fishing camp learning woodworking. It was the one thing he excelled at.

Dad was living in some beat-up trailer in South Carolina with the last woman that he connected with. Good for him. He claimed to be happy. Not that Colin cared.

But that wasn't his life. He wanted more.

Christ, he had more until Sam Knight got his cousin Tony arrested based upon the lying testimony of two bitches that he and Tony fucked with at the fishing camp. So what if they became a little rough with them? A slap here, a slap there, it wasn't enough to really hurt them, just enough to keep the bitches in line.

When Tony died, all the plans Colin made went up in smoke. His schmoozing with druggies and dealers—all for nothing. All the money he thought he would make was in someone else's pocket. He was a minor cog in a big wheel instead of the man in charge and it was all Sam Knight's fault.

Nothing would happen to Sam today. He wanted to see who she talked to and what the bride looked like. He would file that away for future reference. Hurting her friends was one way he intended to get back at Sam. She hurt his family and ruined his life. He would hurt hers. Then he would kill Sam just like prison killed Tony.

Bells pealed. Showtime. He pulled his cap farther down his forehead, then put on a pair of sunglasses and scooched down in his seat.

The bride and groom walked out, happy as could be. Well, they wouldn't be happy for long. Sam followed next, looking pretty in pink on the arm of a tall, muscular man. They were laughing and kissing the guests. Just one great big happy family. *Enjoy it, bitch. Because soon you'll be mine and you won't be happy.*

Colin fingered the tracker in his pocket that would be placed on Sam's car. Soon he would know all the ways to torment Sam Knight before he killed her.

## CHAPTER FOUR

**M**ark Stone leaned down and whispered in Sam's ear, "You're gorgeous and so sexy," just before he carefully twirled her on the dance floor.

Sam was a small, self-assured, kick-ass woman. She owned KnightGuard Security, kept her staff of ex-police officers, special operatives and retired military personnel on their toes. Too bad she was born with two left feet. Mark made sure he had a firm grip on her, especially after an embarrassing incident a year ago.

Sam smiled brightly as she safely made it back into his arms. He saw the moment of panic pass through her eyes, and he held her hand tighter. *Success.* When Sam realized he wasn't letting go, the tension left her, and she gave him a small smile. She had to know he would never let her down.

So many people packed the dance floor that he had to sidestep to avoid several dancers as they passed by.

By all standards, it was a beautiful spot. Thousands of twinkling lights sparkled from the ceiling and on the palm trees outside. Candles flickered from the tables. It couldn't be more romantic. The DJ knew what music to play to make it even more festive.

"Danny and Hailey look so happy, don't they?" Sam asked as the wedding couple waltzed by. Hailey gave them a brief wave as Danny leaned in to kiss his bride and winked.

Mark tucked Sam in a little tighter. "Yeah, it's been an interesting year for them. Good to see Melanie is out of rehab and could make the wedding."

Sam nodded into his chest. Mark remembered how hard it was on Danny when searching for Hailey's sister. Melanie had been prostituting herself for drug money. They were all happy she'd completed rehab and was getting herself back on track.

"What a difference a few months make," he said.

"So true," Sam said.

The music ended. The DJ announced the bride and groom were leaving and Hailey was going to throw her bouquet. They stood on the sidelines as all the single women lined up. Anne, one of Sam's best friends, noticed Sam wasn't in the group and yelled at her to join them. Sam shook her head.

Mark leaned over and murmured, "If you join them, I'll make it worth your while."

Sam shook her head and sighed. "You'll make it worth my while anyhow, but I suppose I better get over there. Hailey's giving me the evil eye, and I don't want to ruin her day."

She grudgingly walked over. Mark knew the other side of Sam, the side she only showed to close friends. She would never let Hailey or any of her friends down.

His heart thumped as she joined the group.

All the women looked terrific, but Mark only had eyes for the small, red-haired woman in the long, pale pink, glittery gown. Sam looked stunning.

He appreciated the plunging *V* neckline held up by thin

spaghetti straps and the open back that dropped to her waist. Sam complained it showed too much skin, but Mark had told her he loved her "too much skin." He prayed she wouldn't twist her ankle in the high heels she hardly ever wore.

Hailey turned her back and was in position to throw the bouquet. The girls pushed and shoved each other, laughing and angling for the best spot. Sam's eyes were on the bouquet as she nonchalantly eased herself toward the back and side of the reception area.

The men counted down. Three. Two ...

One.

All the women stepped aside as a group, leaving Sam standing alone with the bouquet aimed straight at her.

The look of panic on her face when she realized the women had moved out of the way of the flying bouquet, leaving her to catch it—priceless.

But damn, his woman stepped up to the plate, caught the bouquet, all the while giving her friends the stink eye. They laughed as they gathered around her.

Hailey rushed over and exclaimed, "I knew you would catch it. You're next to get married."

"Not happening," said Sam.

Turning to the other women as she clenched the bouquet, she squinted her eyes. "I swear I'm so getting even with you guys." The women laughed. Sam shook her head, then hugged her new sister-in-law.

It hurt Mark to see Sam clutching the bouquet. He didn't want to ruin the event, but he'd hoped he and Sam would have been married by now. They'd been together three years, and he'd asked twice before. She turned him down each time, saying she needed to build up her business or some other excuse. KnightGuard Security was thriving. So he wondered why she wouldn't say yes.

He would ask again soon and hope she would say yes.

If not, well, Mark didn't know what he would do. Leaving Sam was not an option. Staying and hurting every day wasn't either.

# CHAPTER FIVE

W hat was that incessant buzzing?

It sounded like a horde of gnats was dive-bombing toward his body. Mark opened one eye and groaned. Damn.

It was his watch. He closed his eye and pulled a pillow over his head. But the stupid watch kept beeping. He wanted to stay in bed and continue where he and Sam left off last night—him licking every inch of her delectable body, listening to her moan his name as she came, and finally inserting his cock into her sweet pussy and having her come again.

Mark reached over to touch her.

Empty. Her side of the bed cold. Crap. Mark knew it would be, but he was still disappointed. He turned and brought his nose close to Sam's pillow and inhaled the scent of their lovemaking.

Their conversation began and ended at midnight. He'd just finished making love to her and was sniffing the lavender body cream—cream he'd rubbed all over her luscious body.

"Mark, I've got to go."

"Go?"

"Yes, sweetheart. Go. I have an early morning meeting at the office."

"Stay." All the sex had reduced him to one-word sentences.

Sam laughed. "No way. We'd never get any sleep, and this is a really important meeting with new clients."

He tried to kiss her, but she avoided his lips and jumped up to get dressed. "Uh-uh. If you kiss me, it's all over and I'll never leave."

"Call me after you get back from Fort Lauderdale. I know it'll be late, but that's okay," said Sam as she kissed him goodbye.

Mark brought the pillow with her scent to his face again, pressed it to his nose, inhaled, then got up. No sense torturing himself anymore. He threw on a pair of sweats and walked barefoot into his kitchen, yawned for the umpteenth time, and made a pot of coffee, a big pot.

He had a huge construction job starting this week that he needed to be sharp for, but he was still exhausted from Danny and Hailey's wedding two days ago.

He could never get enough of Miss Sam Knight. He knew it the minute he saw her at Salt & Sea three years ago.

Laura Clark, the owner of the bistro and one of Sam's best friends, had been dating one of his friends.

When Laura heard Mark owned a construction company, she asked him to draw up some plans to update the restaurant.

It was an easy renovation for his company.

He was checking up on progress late one day when he saw a man attacking Laura and another woman in the parking lot.

He raced over to help, but by the time he got there, the small woman had tackled the man, wrestled him to the ground and tied his hands behind his back. The man was face down on the cement, yelling and squirming while Laura struck him with her handbag. Mark chuckled. It was quite a sight.

He remembered staring at the vision of this petite dynamo taking down a man twice her size. She startled him when she shouted, "Don't just stand there. Call the police!" then shook her head and rolled her eyes. Rolled her eyes!

"Yes, ma'am," was all he could say.

Sam had taken the man down fast and hadn't even taken time to think about it or call for help. Just did it.

Good lord, she was a warrior if he ever saw one, and he had seen plenty of them in the SEALs. Not many women were as brave as she was.

The minute he met the snarky Sam Knight, he was in love.

It made no sense to him, but he wasn't stupid enough to let the feeling go.

Sure, he'd been in relationships before, well, a lot of one-night stands, and over the years there had been a couple of women he'd developed strong feelings for . This time it felt different. It was as if he'd met his soul mate.

Sam didn't agree with him at first. They'd danced around each other for a while until he finally won her over. She didn't know he was an ex-SEAL and always had a plan B or C or whatever. Sam never had a chance.

She was everything to him. Too bad she couldn't see it.

Mark poured himself a cup of coffee and walked out to the back deck. The sun was breaking through the clouds, and the humidity was rising. It would be another hot one, and he didn't relish running around in the heat all day. Unfortunately, that was the nature of the construction business.

Two new employees were starting Tuesday. He needed to make sure they knew what they were doing. He had no doubts about the ability of his first female employee, Mia, the new office manager. He knew she'd get control of supplies and cash. Things he didn't have extra hours for. The company was growing too fast and taking too much of his time.

He wasn't so sure about the guy, Colin Woods. He was a little squirrelly but provided good references. Maybe he was nervous when Mark interviewed him. Some people were. Mark wasn't too concerned yet. Woods was filling in for an employee who'd gotten hurt after a hard night of drinking and wouldn't be back for at least a month. A stupid accident. That was why he never got drunk outside of his house. Too many things could happen.

He was also down a few entry-level workers. The project would get behind if he didn't hire the extra people. He'd built his business upon fair prices and on-time delivery as much as possible.

On top of that, something was bothering Sam. She didn't mention any problems, but several times, she appeared lost in thought, and when he asked her what was going on, she just shook her head. He couldn't help noticing that she was searching the shadows looking for something. He didn't know what she was concerned about. He hoped that she would confide in him soon. He wanted to help.

His watch beeped again—time to go. Mark sent Sam a quick text telling her he missed her, got a smirking emoji back. He snorted, got dressed, tried not to worry about the new employees, and left the house.

# CHAPTER SIX

S am had an early-morning meeting with new clients at her office. The convenience of having her living space above the office made time more manageable even though she knew that she'd disappointed Mark when she didn't stay over. He had to leave at the crack of dawn for Fort Lauderdale, so this was easier for both of them.

They'd been together for three years but never lived together. Oh, Mark hinted several times and then outright asked her to move in with him or marry him, but she'd hesitated. She claimed she wasn't ready, that her business needed her, or used some other excuse not to.

He'd laughed it off the first couple of times but wasn't laughing now. Sam knew they needed to take their relationship to the next level, but she wasn't ready. Would she ever be?

Walking down from her loft into the KnightGuard Security offices with those thoughts running through her mind, she heard grunts and groans as she passed the gym where employees were exercising. She made a mental note to get there later. After stuffing herself at the wedding, she needed the exercise. Whiffs of freshly brewed coffee circulated in the air; she'd grab a cup later. First, she needed to check in with Aunt Marcia and then prepare for her meeting. As she walked toward the front office, something felt different.

The voices in the background were the same. The office noises were the same. So what was off?

The front desk! Instead of her gray-haired aunt sitting there, a young woman with black hair was bent over the desk. Sam stopped short and tried to remember what week it was. Oh, right. Vacation time. Aunt Marcia was taking a well-deserved vacation. Okay then, this was the temp that the employment agency sent.

"Hi. Welcome to KnightGuard Security."

The woman startled, dropped the papers she was holding. The blank look in her brown eyes meant she hadn't recognized Sam. "Hi. Can I help you?"

"No. I'm Sam Knight."

"Oh, my God. Ms. Knight, I'm so sorry I didn't recognize you." The woman picked up the papers she dropped and struggled to stand. "I'm Jenna Payton."

"Please, call me Sam, and welcome," Sam said. "Let me know if you need help with anything. Most employees have worked the front desk, so they're familiar with the phones or anything else you might need."

Jenna nodded. The phone rang. She put her finger up and sat down to answer it.

Sam waited for Jenna to get off the phone. "I have a meeting with the staff right now, and two clients are coming in at ten. Have them sit out here and then call me." She turned to go. "Oh, offer them water or coffee, please. Both are available in the kitchen."

She started to walk away and then turned. "I hope someone showed you around."

"Yes. Danny showed me around when I arrived. I also have a detailed list of instructions from Marcia."

"Great."

Leave it to Marcia to leave detailed instructions; her aunt was nothing if not thorough. Sam headed for her office, then glanced at her watch. Fifteen minutes until her meeting with the staff. She needed coffee. No sense checking her calendar. It was packed with appointments.

# CHAPTER SEVEN

Colin adjusted his tool belt as he prepared to climb the stairs to the second floor of the new office building. He'd gotten to the job site early. It was a decent job; the pay and the hours were good. Spying on the boss was a bonus.

He brushed away the beads of sweat running down his neck, then concentrated on his tools and the other paraphernalia strewn across the floor. No sense having an accident before he ruined Mark Stone and destroyed his bitch, Sam Knight.

Colin mentally thanked the gods in heaven that he went to trade school and learned woodworking. Too many people looked down on trade schools. But it made sense for people like him, who didn't do well in English and history and didn't get along with snobby kids who made fun of him because he went to a trade school. He wasn't good at many things, but he was very good at fine cabinetry; his uncle was a master carpenter who taught him everything he needed to know.

Stone Construction was almost finished with the small

commercial building that would house a successful insurance company.

The owner of the company insisted on custom wood paneling and built-in cabinets in his office..

Another carpenter had started the job, but in Colin's estimation, his work was not up to par.

He could do much better.

He looked at the half-finished project and imagined what it would be like to have all the money in the world to spend on your own business and have high-end finishes. It was something he would never know, unless something big, like a pile of money, fell into his lap. Otherwise, he'd be working his butt off for other people until he could get his cousin Tony's business up and running again.

Good luck for him. But not good luck for the previous carpenter, who had a little accident that would keep him out of work for several months. It was bad luck that the man had a run-in with an automobile after consuming a few beers. Good for Colin that he followed the carpenter a couple of weeks ago and bonded with him over drinks. A person had to be careful with whom they drank. And Colin, the carpenter's new friend, had made sure he had too many drinks.

Colin had his souped-up resume, minus the year in jail, on Mark Stone's desk the next day.

His background check was spotless, thanks to a friend who was a talented hacker. He met the guy in prison when he was serving time for check forgery. They got out of jail at the same time. Who said crime didn't pay? It sure did for him. The contacts he'd made in prison were invaluable.

"Woods. Hey, Woods."

Colin whipped his head around. Mark Stone was bearing down on him, and he put on a big smile.

"Welcome." Mark put out his hand, and Colin shook it. "Have you looked over the plans for the built-ins?"

"Yeah. It should be an easy job." Oh, it would be but not only this job—everything, if his plans went well.

Mark was about two inches taller than him but bulkier and very serious looking. Colin wasn't intimidated by the large man standing in front of him. He didn't know much about Mark's background, just that he'd been in the service. Colin had held his own in prison against men a lot tougher than Mark.

"Good. Any problems, let me know. Mr. Roy is a good customer, and I've promised him the finishes would be top-notch."

"No problem, boss. The cabinets and paneling will be perfect."

Mark looked him up and down and nodded. He turned and called out another worker.

This job would be perfect, and if he had his way, all his preparations for getting Sam and Mark would be too.

He'd given himself three months to even the score with Sam Knight.

A life for a life with some fun thrown in along the way.

Colin smiled to himself and got to work on the paneling for the private office.

Things were looking up in Colin's life, and he liked it—a lot. Revenge would be his. He would rebuild Tony's drug business, and he would be the next drug kingpin.

# CHAPTER EIGHT

S am brought the pot of coffee to the table.

It was the weekend. Neither she nor Mark had to work. It didn't happen often, so it was a treat not to rush off.

Mark fixed bacon and eggs and placed the plates in front of them.

They could finally catch up after not seeing each other for a week. It was unusual that she hadn't spent even one night at his place, but early meetings and new employees were consuming her time.

"How is that new carpenter working out for you?" she asked as she poured him a cup of coffee.

Mark leaned back in his chair and nodded. "Surprisingly well. He's very talented."

"He completes the team?"

"Yeah. I've hired a few new laborers to replace those that left, and we're all set for my next project off Route 40." He beamed with pride. "A four-story building for a new law firm with all the bells and whistles."

"That's terrific," said Sam.

Mark reached for the pitcher of orange juice and poured some in a glass. "How's Marcia's vacation going? Have you heard from her?"

"No." Sam laughed as she reached for the glass of juice Mark was handing her. "I made Marcia promise not to check in when she left. She's somewhere in the Atlantic right now, hopefully, having the time of her life." She scowled. "At least she's supposed to be."

"Who'd you get to fill in?"

"Jenna Payton. She's new in town and came from the temp agency. I like her. She's observant, smart, and keeps track of where everyone is so I don't have to do it." Sam picked up a piece of toast, spread jam on it, and took a bite. "It's like Marcia cloned herself."

Mark laughed. "Don't tell Marcia that. She'll never go on vacation again if she thinks someone can take her place." He winked at her. "It'll be our secret."

He scooped up some egg and put it on his toast. "You still going out with the girls tonight?"

"Yeah, everyone is around, so it's a good time to catch up. I'm bringing Jenna since she doesn't know anyone here. I think the girls will like her."

"How about I join you?" Mark's eyes crinkled.

Sam stared at the man she was in love with.

Their lives were far from stress-free, but when they were together, everything was perfect except for the marriage proposal that was still hanging in the air like a black cloud.

Mark kept his promise not to ask her again until she was ready, but it was out there all the same. Should she say yes and get it over with? Or say no—she wasn't getting married, ever. She couldn't handle losing another person in her life.

Yes.

No.

The words were playing like a ping-pong game in her head. What to do? She couldn't keep him hanging. Mark deserved an answer.

"Riiight." Sam picked up their dishes and brought them to the sink. "Don't you have poker tonight?"

"Yep, and I'm hoping Hank comes," said Mark as he rubbed his hands together. "I'm ready to take him down."

"Does he know everyone knows his tell?"

"Nope, and we're not telling him."

Sam snorted.

Hank was a big, muscular guy. Well, all the guys who worked for her were big and muscular, but Hank carried a little more weight, had a serious face, and loved to win. The only problem was that when he had a winning hand, he had a slight tick above his left eye that gave it away. Everyone knew it except Hank.

Mark got up, kissed Sam on the cheek, and turned to leave. He did an about-turn, stalked back and pulled her in for a bear hug, then kissed the life out of her.

The cool air hit her face as he pushed away and smirked. "Later."

---

THE MUSIC at Neptune's Navel was blasting. Sam could hardly hear Jenna above everyone talking at the top of their lungs. That was the problem with going to the bar on a Saturday night. It was always busy—and noisy. She led Jenna to the outdoor patio and spotted her girlfriends sitting in a quieter corner.

The girls all moved over to provide room for the two of them. Laura was working as usual and couldn't make it.

Maybe she'd bring Jenna over to the Salt & Sea to meet Laura sometime.

She was introducing Jenna to everyone just as the server came to take their drink orders.

"Get the Zombie Surprise. You'll love it," gushed Marlee as she took a long sip of a drink with skewers of fruit, barely missing her eye with a skewer. Sam winced as Marlee put her glass down and smacked her lips.

Sam glanced at Marlee—still sober. Marlee was a small woman like her and didn't hold her liquor well. She'd keep an eye on her, as would the other women. Two drinks, and Marlee would keel over or worse. Marlee wasn't a drinker and generally watched herself, but when she was having fun, all bets were off.

Ben didn't appreciate the last time Marlee got drunk on Sam's watch.

He sure wasn't going to like it if it happened again.

"So, Jenna, are you from around here?" asked Hailey.

Jenna's eyes narrowed, and she hesitated before answering. Sam imagined it odd, but maybe Jenna was uncomfortable giving out personal information to strangers. "No, I'm from a small town in Georgia, but one of my mother's friends has a fishing camp near here, and I used to visit on the weekends."

"How do you like working with all those hunks at Knight-Guard?" asked Marlee.

Sam shook her head. Jeez, Marlee was on a roll tonight.

"Maaarlee," said Claire. Marlee gave her an innocent look that fooled no one.

"You don't have to answer," said Sam. "Marlee likes to tease. She has her own hunk."

Jenna looked from woman to woman and grinned. "It's okay. There's some nice eye candy working there, but I'm not looking. Besides, I don't think my boss wants me ogling the employees while I'm on the phone."

"Damn straight," said Sam. Everyone laughed.

"Do you have a boyfriend?" asked Anne. Anne never looked better. She was happy. She loved her job as a kindergarten teacher and was dating a nice guy, one they all liked, after a dry spell of not dating anyone.

"Hmmm." Jenna tapped her fingers on the table. She was hesitating again. "Yes, but I don't see him often; he's working a complicated job right now."

"That sucks," said Marlee. "I know how much I miss Ben when he's away on the job."

"Amen to that," chorused all the women.

Sam glanced around the table. Somehow her friends, old and new, had found their special someone.

It seemed like most of their men worked at KnightGuard Security, except for Mark, but he was as close to the guys that worked there as any of them.

They spent the next hour eating, drinking, and catching up. She was happy to see some of the girls and Jenna exchanging phone numbers. Jenna could use some friends. It was hard enough moving to a new area when you didn't know anyone. Sam was glad she could help.

Sam looked around at all her friends' smiling faces.

Marlee, Anne, Claire, Grace, Julie, Hailey—they all found love. A couple had kids. All worked full-time and made their relationships work. What was holding her back? What was she so afraid of?

---

MAN, this restaurant was cool.

Jenna's head swiveled like a Chucky doll at all the unique

elements—the thatched roof over the bar, the nets falling from the ceiling, the music, the parrot in the corner, the yummy-looking drinks, and all the hip-looking people drinking and laughing. And in the corner was a waterfall with colored lights and she heard the soft tinkle of water hitting the bowl. A water-fall! Who has one of those in a bar? Apparently, when you owned an upscale establishment like this, you could and you did.

Neptune's Navel was night and day from the places she was used to. Her feet weren't sticking to the floor. No one was fighting in the corner or feeling up a woman, no drunks stumbling around or throwing up in the bathroom. The clientele was well-dressed and having fun. She bet the bar was nice-looking in the daytime, too.

Sam had taken her arm and led her to an outside patio overlooking the river.

Holy crap! Could this place get any cooler? Twinkling lights, soft music, a few couples were dancing, there was no rancid smell of food, and in the corner was a group of good-looking women waving to them.

If she mentioned this place to her boyfriend, would he bring her here? Nah. He was a beer and burger guy. No frou-frou drinks or hippie food for him. He'd probably complain about dressing up, paying the higher prices for food and drink, then he'd make fun of the cool-looking people.

Sighing, she shook her head.

This could have been her in another life but certainly not the life she had now. Fuck this. She would not wallow in self-pity. Now was the time to seize the good life.

She was smart. Her past was not going to stop her from getting ahead and enjoying all that life had to offer.

"Jenna?"

Sam had been talking to her, and she wasn't listening.

Not listening could get you hurt or worse.

Crap, she needed to get out of her head.

"Sorry, just taking in the view."

Sam nodded and introduced her to her friends.

It was nice of Sam to bring her here, though.

She enjoyed working at KnightGuard Security. However, she had plans for her future that included lots of money. Enough money to come to a place like Neptune's Navel and order anything on the menu, regardless of cost.

# CHAPTER NINE

S am sat at a window seat in the Roasted Bean.

The quaint coffee shop was around the corner from KnightGuard Security and one of her favorite places to frequent. It had been raining, but now it was just drizzling sporadically. Puddles covered the road, and the occasional car would drive through one and splash a pedestrian, who would curse at them. It made for great entertainment while she waited.

Grace asked to meet her here.

She'd been surprised and pleased because Grace was supposed to be taking it easy at home. Being pregnant with a surprise baby, caring for a toddler and another baby, besides holding down an almost full-time job, had to be tiring. She was tired just thinking about it.

Wafts of coffee scented the air. The whirring sound of the espresso machine and the jazz playing in the background lulled her into recent memories.

After Hailey and Danny's wedding, she'd visited her grandparents, who were staying at Grace's parents' beach house.

It was the same beach house where a stalker had tried to kill Grace.

Grace's parents wanted to sell the house because of the terrible memories, but Grace persuaded them not to. The location was perfect—right on the ocean. Grace grew up there, loved it and didn't want to hide behind the painful memories, so her parents renovated the rooms and let friends and family stay there. Grace believed you had to confront the past to get on with the future—a sentiment that Sam agreed with.

She and Danny had stayed with Gran and Pops, who lived next door to Grace and her family after their parents died. It helped that Grace was her best friend since they were babies. It helped that the ocean had always been her comfort place.

"Hey." Grace slid into the opposite chair. Sam's body tensed. Grace had surprised her, and that didn't happen often. She needed to be alert and on her toes.

"Hey, yourself," Sam answered. A server came over with menus and told them about the daily specials. After they ordered, Sam looked at her friend. At seven, no, seven and a half months pregnant, Grace looked beautiful. Her brunette hair was loose on her shoulders today. The rust-colored short-sleeved shirt complemented her brown eyes. She paired the top with a blue-striped skirt.

"Pregnancy becomes you."

"Humph. I look like the Goodyear blimp. I can't see my feet. Besides, they ache if I stand too long." Grace groaned, "I can't wait for this little guy to be born."

"How long now?"

"Less than two months," said Grace.

"The boys must be beside themselves, waiting for their little brother."

"Not just them but Luke too. The three of them are

driving me crazy." Grace laughed. "Aiden just rubs my belly crooning 'baby, baby' while Connor asks every day if this is the day his baby brother will be borned—his words, not mine —plus Luke won't let me do anything. Insists on cooking, cleaning, and bringing me tea while I put my feet up."

Grace wasn't exaggerating. Luke had turned into a dictator after the scare they had a month ago when baby McBride tried to make his presence known early.

Sam smiled. "How did you escape today?"

"Luke had an early meeting. I brought Connor to school and Aiden to the babysitter. I'm going into the office. I still have interviews to do, so I thought a change of scenery would be nice."

"Luke's going to hunt you down when he finds out. You know that?"

Giggling, Grace said, "I know. He's going to be mad. I hope I get home before he does. Otherwise ..." She tilted her head and smirked. The corners of her eyes crinkled. "There'll be some great makeup sex."

"Eewww. TMI."

The server interrupted just then and placed their food and drinks down. He asked if they needed anything else and left when they said no.

"So how did the discussion with your grandparents go?" Grace took a bite of her salad and put her fork down. "Gosh, I love them. I'm so glad they could attend the wedding and weren't in the middle of the ocean somewhere."

Sam contemplated Grace's question.

She had a pleasant conversation with her grandparents, and they discussed the church where her parents got married and their marriage. Sam was grateful to hear they had a wonderful marriage and surprised it hadn't been perfect.

It stunned Sam to hear that her mother had resisted

marrying her dad for a long time. It was a situation similar to her and Mark's relationship. Her gran filled her in on details she hadn't heard before.

"Well, Gran told me my mother was a wild child and stubborn, always was from the time she was born. She stared at me and asked, 'Something I think you can identify with. Right?'"

"Ha, she knows you so well."

"I know. Right? Anyhow, it turned out my mother was pregnant."

"Pregnant? Before they got married? Wow. That surprises me," said Grace. She added sugar to her iced tea, stirred and took a sip. "Yum."

Sam couldn't believe her mother had been pregnant and not married. Whoa, that had changed her whole perspective. What would she do if she were pregnant with Mark's child? Marry him? What if he wasn't ready for a child? Would she go it alone? Who knew?

"Me too. Apparently she was pregnant with Danny. My dad asked her to marry him, but she said no. Mom didn't want to burden him with a baby. He had just graduated from law school, and she didn't want him to settle for just any job because she was pregnant."

"That sounds like your mom." Grace smiled at Sam.

"Gran said Mom had just started her teaching career, was overwhelmed and confused. My dad was upset with her and left for a month," said Sam. She fiddled with her fork and finally took a bite of muffin.

"Oh, Sam, your dad must have been so distraught."

"Yeah, he was. Mom finally begged him to come back and said she would marry him."

"Holy crap. Why did she decide to marry him?"

"She told him it was better to live a life with someone you loved than regret not doing it."

Grace winked. "And isn't that what I've been telling you?"

"Wiseass. Anyhow, Dad told my gran that he hadn't left the area, only pretended to. He told her that he would always watch Mom's back but he was thrilled she agreed to marry him."

"That is so romantic." Grace waved her napkin in front of her face. "I love a great love story."

"Me too." Sam thought about her and Mark. Their relationship was strong even if she hadn't accepted his marriage proposal.

"Sam. Sam." Grace rubbed her hand. "Sweetie, where did you go? You were far away. Is everything all right?"

Well, wasn't that embarrassing. For the second time today, her mind went elsewhere, and all the while, someone could be watching her. They weren't right now, but they could have been. Her face flushed. Sam closed her eyes and exhaled, then glanced out the window when she heard a police siren. The sidewalk was full of people walking by laughing, talking, or shopping, but thankfully, no one paid attention to the siren or her. The black and white whizzed by in a flash of light and shadow.

"Yeah." She nodded. "I was thinking about my gran and Mark."

"Mark?"

"He's asked me to marry him, and I said no." Sam sighed. "Gracie, I don't want to lose him. I love him, but I'm so afraid he's going to die and leave me alone. It would break my heart."

There, she admitted it. Why was honesty so hard? Why couldn't she say that to Mark? He'd understand. Maybe. Mark thought she was so strong. How could she ever admit how weak she was when it came to love? Would he think less of her?

Grace reached for her hand. "Sam." She stopped and

released a deep breath. "Mark is not David. David was termi-nally ill. Neither of you knew how sick he was when you started dating. I know it was a scary time and it reminded you of losing your parents and Suzie."

"Ya think?" Sam swiped a tear from her eye. Wasn't this turning out to be an embarrassing day? First, Grace sneaks up and surprises her, then mentions David, Suzie and her parents. No wonder she teared up.

Memories of sweet, kind David threatened to reduce her to a slobbering fool.

David was the first man she'd ever fallen in love with. The first man she'd ever made love to. They met during college, and they planned to spend the rest of their lives together. They planned to get married, have lots of children, and laugh through life. David taught her that the world wasn't black-and-white and he believed in second chances. Though he was a mild-tempered man, he charged in like a bull if he saw anyone being bullied.

Most importantly, David loved her idiosyncrasies. He always said that he loved her more because of them.

Too bad life had other changes in mind. David died a year after they met. Cancer—the scourge of mankind. It had devastated her.

"Oh, hon, none of us knows when our time is up." Grace rubbed Sam's arm. "You deserve happiness. Mark makes you happy, and he's so in love with you. You've kept your heart safe, but life isn't about being safe."

"Damn, that's what my grandmother said." Sam fiddled with her food.

What was she going to do?

They finished lunch in comfortable silence.

After paying the bill, Grace waddled off to her office, and Sam walked the block to KnightGuard Security.

She loved the two-story brick building that had been a day away from demolition when she saw it. She fell in love with the large-paned windows, the concrete columns at the front door and the red-bricked exterior. The real-estate agent tried to steer her away from buying it, claiming it would cost a fortune to renovate—if the city even let her. There was something about it that beckoned her. The large double doors screeched in protest when she'd opened them.

It was dusty, dirty and had broken pieces of equipment strewn about. In its heyday, it had been a silent film studio, then a casket company until it went out of business. Wiping cobwebs from her hair, Sam felt like she almost heard the many voices of people who worked there.

She put a lowball offer in, and to her and her agent's surprise, it was accepted. Between what Sam's parents left for Danny and her and what her grandparents added in, she managed to buy the building and get a loan for the rest.

Sam hired contractors, and they spent six months getting it in shape. Under the cobwebs, broken beams and dirt, they found the interior was in decent shape. The outside took a little longer. KnightGuard Security hired its first employee eight years ago, and she never looked back.

It never ceased to amaze her that the company was hers, that the former warehouse housed such talent and she enjoyed continued success. It had been her dream. David and Otis Hood, her mentor, encouraged her to become who she was today and to build the business. A tear dripped down her cheek, and she wiped it away—no time for sentiment.

Sam had scheduled a staff meeting in an hour. She had new clients and needed to catch up on finished cases. She liked to be on top of things. It helped that Jenna was putting together a packet of information for everyone. One less thing to worry about.

She'd been a godsend since Marcia left on vacation. Prompt, intelligent and able to see the big picture and follow through. Sam needed a person like that in the office. Maybe a job offer was in the future—something to think about.

# CHAPTER TEN

Laura reached for her umbrella and got out of her car. It was threatening to rain, and with her luck, probably would while she and Sam were eating.

Always be prepared, her mom used to say.

It helped to remember that mantra with her restaurant. She always had to be one step ahead. Trouble and problems were everywhere and surfaced when you least expected them.

She was meeting Sam at Neptune's Navel. She hoped Sam got there first to grab a table. If not, Jake was sweet on her and would find them something.

She opened the door, and a rush of cool air caressed her body. It was a humid day, and the cool air felt great. Looking around, she was dismayed to see every table filled. And every seat at the bar, too. Jake waved to her from the far end of the massive bar, and she walked toward him.

"Pretty girl. Pretty girl."

Laura shook her head and giggled. Petey, the parrot, really liked that phrase and used it on all the women who entered. Walking toward the bar, she waited for Jake to finish serving a drink. Jake's restaurant was more casual than hers, and the bar was packed. Not for the first time, she wondered if she should install an outside bar. She already had some outdoor dining, but a bar by the Riverwalk would bring in more customers. Something to think about.

She passed the stone waterfall in the corner. The soothing sound of water made for a pleasant atmosphere. Maybe she should install a fountain, too.

Gah. What was wrong with her today? She didn't have the extra money, and the fiasco in the parking lot would have her dipping into savings even though the insurance would pay for most of the damage.

"Hey, pretty girl. What's up?" Jake gave her his megawatt smile, and his blue eyes crinkled. With his sun-streaked hair, muscular build, and strong jaw, he reminded her of a surfer dude even though she knew Jake had served in the air force and had never gone surfing in his life.

She also knew he wouldn't kiss her here, even though she saw the desire in his eyes. It would be unprofessional, and Jake was nothing but professional when it came to business. In his private life ... well, that was a different story.

"You know I hate that bird, don't you?"

"Maybe so, but he has good taste." Jake winked and wiped down the bar in front of him. "What brings you here? Besides me, of course."

"I'm meeting Sam. Have you seen her?"

"Sam?" Jake stared blankly at her and tapped his fingers on the bar. "I've been flat-out busy and didn't notice her come in. Have you tried the patio?"

"No, but I will." She started to walk away but turned back. "Are we still on for tonight?" she asked in a low voice.

Jake leaned over the bar and whispered in her ear. "Wouldn't miss it for the world."

A flush radiated from her face down. Jake looked her up and down and smirked.

"Humph."

She heard Jake chuckle as she walked out to the patio.

It was still overcast, but the large striped umbrellas covering the tables were up. She hoped the rain would hold off. It was quieter out here, even though all the tables were full. She glanced over at the marina. Boats were bobbing up and down with the waves. The marina was full too. She guessed not too many people wanted to chance being on the water and getting stuck in the storm.

"Over here." Laura turned towards Sam's voice and noticed she'd grabbed a corner table. Good. It was nice to catch up with a good friend, be out of her restaurant and its problems for a while. They didn't get to see each other often.

"Hey, stranger." Sam stood and hugged her.

"Hey yourself. Have you been waiting long?"

"No, just a few minutes."

Laura gave Sam a once-over. Something was different.

Sam had pulled her red hair into a ponytail, which wasn't unusual.

But the sparkly top? Whoa, sedate Sam in sparkles? No way.

"Sparkles?"

"Guilty." Sam sighed. "I went shopping with Marlee, and she told me I was in a rut. So I bought sparkles."

Laura giggled. "Remind me never to go shopping with Marlee."

She felt a whisper of air, then a hand holding a pink-colored drink came into view. Jake leaned in and smiled. "Today's special, the Blushing Navel. Sam, can I get you one?"

"Sure," said Sam.

Jake walked away, and Sam lifted a brow. "Hmmm, something you want to share?"

Laura laughed. "No. But I have a feeling you'll get it out of me."

"You know me so well." Sam grinned.

"Well, Jake and I have been seeing each other on our days off. Not that we get many days off."

"Wow." Sam leaned back in her chair. "Didn't see that one coming."

"I know." Laura took a sip of her drink. "Yum." She pushed it around the table in a little circle. "It was unexpected. I've come over here. He's been to my restaurant. We'd see each other at the farmer's market." Laura shrugged. "You know how that goes."

"Actually, I do. Well, congratulations. Jake is a nice guy. Are you two serious?"

"Nah. We're both too busy. Plus, I don't want to hook up with another restaurant owner, especially with the hours we keep. We're only friends enjoying each other's company."

A waiter came over, took their orders, and Laura and Sam caught each other up on their lives.

Jake returned with Sam's drink and leaned in. "Has everything at the restaurant been resolved?" he asked Laura.

"Yes. As much as it will be." Damn, she hoped Jake wouldn't bring that up. She should have warned him. Sam would want to know what was wrong. It was a series of little things. She didn't have a handle on them yet and definitely didn't want to waste Sam's time.

Jake left. Sam raised her brow. "What's going on at the restaurant?"

"Oh, silly things." Laura sighed. "I've hired several new waitstaff and bartenders. Training has been difficult. Oh, and someone called the health department and told them they got food poisoning when they ate at the bistro. We checked everything in the kitchen and couldn't find a source. The person had no phone number listed, just an email, so I responded to them, and it bounced back. Then the other night, about ten cars were scratched in the parking lot."

"Whoa." Sam's eyes widened. "Those aren't accidents. Any idea who's behind it?"

Laura shook her head. "No, it was probably kids thinking it was funny. If you remember, I had a similar incident a couple of years ago."

Sam nodded.

"However, it's still going to cost me about $500 to $1,000 a car."

"Ouch."

"The insurance will cover most of it. I think. But I'm outraged it happened. If people don't feel safe, they'll stop coming to eat down here."

"I'm so sorry that's happening to you." Sam's lips thinned and she shook her head. "Let me send Hank over. Get his assessment on what you need, and KnightGuard can install cameras in the areas you don't have adequate coverage."

"Branching out?"

"Yeah, business is good. I'm hiring more people with different skill set and adding security installation for when business is slow." Sam cocked her head. "Actually, installation is always a moneymaker, not just in slow times."

"Great. Will the cameras be expensive? If it's in the thousands, I can't afford them right now." Laura grimaced. "Although, if I don't do anything, it won't matter because I won't have a restaurant to worry about."

Sam reached for her hands. "No worries. I can't afford to give you the cameras for free, but I'll charge you my cost, and the labor will be free."

"Oh, Sam." Laura placed her hands over her heart. "I appreciate that. Meals will be on me when they do the installation."

Sam laughed. "The guys will never leave."

They finished lunch, talked a little more. Sam looked at her watch. "Damn, I'm going to be late for my next appointment if I don't leave now." She pulled out her phone. "Just in case, I'll call Jenna to schedule Hank to set it up."

Sam finished her call.

"How's Jenna working out?"

"Much better than I expected. I'm thinking of offering her a job in the office after Aunt Marcia gets back. We could use a couple more people."

"It's so hard to find competent employees. I'm glad she's working out. If she doesn't stay, send her my way. I need help in the office."

"Will do." They air-kissed and walked out into the humidity.

Laura hoped having the security cameras in the lot would help, but other squirrely things were happening and needed to be investigated as well. At some point, she would have a long discussion with Sam about investigating. Right now, dealing with the car owners and paying for more cameras was all she could handle.

# CHAPTER ELEVEN

Colin gagged as he opened the door to his uncle's fish camp. It smelled like dirty socks and rotten food. He tried to remember the last time he was here. Wasn't it just a few months ago that he and his girlfriend, Chrissie, were here? Yeah, that sounded about right.

He placed a chair by the door to hold it open and let in the fresh air. After Chrissie arrived, he'd get her to clean the place. That's what women were for—that and sex.

The fishing camp had been his uncle's favorite place for as long as he could remember.

He looked around the small living room with the wood stove in the corner. They hardly used it, although Cypress Lake got cold in the winter. His uncle paneled that room first when he bought the cabin. However, the kitchen was the pride and joy of the cabin. It took all summer for him and his uncle to build the oak cabinets, but they were magnificent.

After his mother left and his father hooked up with his sluts, Colin spent every summer here. As he got older, his uncle came to the cabin less often. His cousin Tony, on his father's side, was two years older than him and would bring friends to party with on the weekends. And boy, did they party. Sex, drugs and rock and roll. Bitches hanging onto both of them. Good times.

When he and Tony got tired of them, they passed the women on to their friends.

Except for that last girl. Tony got a little too rough with her. She was already dead a day when Tony asked him to bury her. That was a bummer. It was a good thing Tony had wrapped her up in a tarp. Yuck. Carrying her to the trunk, he almost lost his breakfast.

Such a shame, too. She was too innocent. She never belonged there with Tony's crowd. Tony knew she loved him but treated her like shit. Those are the breaks—you play with fire, expect to get burned.

He remembered that she was tall and willowy, pretty if you liked that kind of woman, always willing to forgive Tony and give him a second chance to redeem himself —as if.

Clingy, though. Tony didn't like clingy women. She thought he would marry her. Well, that didn't work out so well for her.

But those were good times. He was ready to have money and party hearty again.

He and Tony liked free-wheeling bitches with big boobs who didn't mind getting kept in line. Big boobs—Chrissie had big boobs.

Damn if he wasn't horny now. No, he was way beyond horny. His hand wasn't doing it for him, and he needed pussy.

As if on schedule, Chrissie pulled up in her compact car.

He watched her open the door and walk up the path to the porch. It was hot outside, and she had on a tight pink sleeveless top that revealed her assets and tiny, white short shorts that would show off her ass, plus a big smile on her face—he knew that smile.

"Clothes off now," he growled as she walked through the door.

He sounded like a caveman, but she reduced him to that. He didn't love her, but he loved her body and the sex she put out. Sure, he could get pussy from any of the other bitches hanging around. But Chrissie was the one he liked the most and the one that he confided in. Well, sometimes confided in.

Chrissie stepped in and shook her ass as she walked over to the bed, stripping as she went.

Man, she was built—built for the pounding he was going to give her—big boobs, a small waist, long legs, and a booty that wouldn't quit. He slapped her ass. "Bed. Now. Get on your hands and knees and show me that ass."

Chrissie winked at him as she turned her back, climbed on the bed, and wiggled her ass.

Colin didn't bother taking off his pants, just unzipped them and pulled them down, along with his underwear. He didn't need to prep Chrissie; she was always wet for him. Didn't have to worry about condoms either; she was on the pill.

In one fluid motion, he was in her, pumping away while she screamed his name. The pressure built up in his cock, which was growing harder and longer. His heart pounded in tandem with his cock plunging into her. Sweat rolled down his face. Colin thrust and thrust, releasing what felt like a gallon of cum.

He rested a moment and pulled out. He wasn't one for endearments. Why should he be? He already had her. If Chrissie didn't like it, she would have left him by now. He didn't care. She was convenient. Besides, there were plenty of other bitches who wanted a piece of Colin Woods.

Chrissie collapsed on the bed and lay there for a minute before turning over. "Well, hello to you." She gave him a big ol' smile.

"How's work?" he asked.

She gave him a Cheshire Cat grin. Tapped her fingers on the bed as she stared at the ceiling.

"Work is good. I like it there. Best part is I hear everything."

"Do you know if Knight has said anything?"

"Like?"

"Oh, I don't know. Maybe Sam feels someone watching her. Maybe she thinks the scratches on the cars are related to her? Maybe she's looking for another dick."

Colin pinched her tit and smirked when she squeaked. "Anything at all?"

Chrissie glared at him but had the common sense not to back-talk again. "I know Laura told Sam about the scratches on the cars. She thinks it's just kids fooling around. I was told Sam volunteered one of the KnightGuard employees to put security cameras on that part of the restaurant's parking lot."

The cameras didn't bother Colin. He wasn't going back to the restaurant.

That had been a test to get Sam thinking. Apparently, she wasn't thinking hard enough. He needed to up his game a little. Not too much yet.

# CHAPTER TWELVE

Sam sat on Mark's patio in front of the fire pit, staring into the flames, enjoying the late evening. Although the weather was warm, a cooling breeze kept the outdoors comfortable and perfect for a fire. Mark had the large brick patio built a year ago and added an outdoor kitchen with a grill. Then he splurged on a rattan sectional sofa and side chairs. And if that wasn't enough, he had some of his contractors build an open-air gazebo, which was lit up with hundreds of twinkling lights.

It was everything she would have done if it were her house. But it wasn't, although Mark had asked her several times to move in with him. She'd resisted so far. Why?

She wouldn't lose her freedom. She loved Mark. He loved her. She just wasn't ready.

"Here you go, sweetheart." Mark carried out a tray with wine for her and a beer for him, plus some of the fish dip Jake made that he was famous for.

He placed the tray on the table and handed her the glass of wine. Then he sat on the sectional close to her.

He stared at the fire. "Boy, it doesn't get much better than this, does it?"

"Nope."

The fire pit created a romantic atmosphere. Mark placed his arm around her shoulders, and she settled into his shoulder. He nibbled on her ear. Sam started giggling. Her ear was ticklish. However, he usually did that when he had something serious to discuss with her. Uh-oh.

"Sam, can we talk?"

*No.* "Of course. What do you want to talk about?"

Mark hemmed and hawed for a minute. "I love you."

"I love you too."

He took his arm off her shoulder, picked up the beer, and took a gulp. He exhaled softly. "I ..." He bit his lip. "I want us to get married. It's time."

Sam's heart jumped. They had this conversation once a year. It wasn't fair to Mark that she kept saying no, that she had a business to run or this or that. She was running out of excuses.

"Mark, we've been over this." She turned to look at him. He looked so hopeful. Her gaze went lower. She could see his arousal pressing against the zipper of his shorts. He smirked.

"I know you want to get married. I do too. But we're both so busy with work and growing our businesses," said Sam.

"Au contraire, mon petit chou."

"Whaaat?"

He shrugged his shoulders and grinned. "Just trying new nicknames for you."

She shook her head. "Don't."

He smirked then got serious. "Our friends are making it work. We can make it work."

"I know, but I just"—Sam swallowed hard—"can't commit to that right now."

Mark scrubbed his hand over his chin. "Sam." He blew out a huge breath. "We ..."

His phone rang. He pulled it out of his pocket, looked at the caller ID and told her it was his mother. He put up a finger and answered it. Sam couldn't decide if she had been saved by the bell or not.

"Hi Ma. How are y—"

Silence.

"What! No. Oh my God."

What happened? Mark closed his eyes and a tear fell. Oh, sweet Jesus. Was his mother in an accident? Had his father died?

"When? How?"

He listened intently. Sam's heart leapfrogged in her chest. Mark was close to his parents; a death would devastate him.

"Let me know the details."

He hung up. Bowed his head in silence. Huffed once. Looked at Sam and rubbed his eyes.

"Tell me."

"My sister was killed in a car crash this morning."

"Oh, Mark, that's horrible." Sam reached over and pulled him close. She felt wetness on her shoulder. He wasn't close to Amanda, but Sam knew he loved his sister and tried over the years to help her.

"That isn't all. I'm my niece's guardian."

## CHAPTER THIRTEEN

" . . . Greener pastures. We will miss Amanda Teresa Stone ..." The minister's soft drawl droned on. Mark would bet his life that the minister didn't know his sister, Amanda, from Adam, and for sure, she hadn't set foot in a church in a long time. Oh sure, they went to church when they were young, but it had been a long time since either of them had spent any time in church. Besides, funeral services were a balm for the living. The dead didn't care.

Thunder clapped as the soloist began to sing. It would be a rainy day in Georgia for sure. The stained-glass window behind the minister darkened as the storm approached. Some might consider it an omen of bad things to come, but Mark didn't believe in that crap. He didn't need a darkened window to tell him shit was coming. He shook his head. *Think happy thoughts. Think happy thoughts.*

The service was for his parents. This last goodbye was for his mom.

He stared at the shelf in front of him, holding a hymnal and bible.

The Bible preached forgiveness. How could he forgive himself for not trying harder to help Amanda? He tried, lord, he tried, but he hadn't tried hard enough. Too late now, but he would make sure his niece was safe.

A sniffle beside him brought him back to the present—a present he'd rather not be in—so many new responsibilities.

How would he run a business, raise a five-year-old, and maintain a relationship with Sam?

She never signed on to parenting a child. Did she even want kids? They never talked about having them. He never saw her hold a baby, even though her friends had children.

What if she didn't want kids? He was a parent now. He couldn't give up Alexis. How would having her affect Sam and his relationship? His heart sank thinking about all the issues. Yet this was his life now, and he would figure it out.

He put his arm around his mother's shoulders. She gave him a small smile that didn't reach her eyes. Parents shouldn't have to bury their children. This moment shouldn't be happening. His sister was dead—sweet, funny Amanda. Sure, he'd seen his share of death in the SEALs, but that was to be expected. You put your life on the line every day. Dying young shouldn't happen to ordinary people.

Amanda was trying to do something right in her life. She'd lost her way for a while but was on the road to making a good life for her and Alexis.

*Drunk driver.* If the guy weren't already dead, Mark would have found and killed him. Thank God Alexis, her five-year-old, wasn't in the car.

The memory of Amanda at her lowest made him shiver. He'd found her once after several days of looking in every dump in a rundown neighborhood inhabited by drunks, dealers, and pimps. She was on the floor, emaciated and stoned.

*"Mark, stop interfering in my life. If I want to do drugs or fuck every man who comes around, I will. You're not my dad. You're not*

*my husband. Heck, you're not even my boyfriend. I know you want to help, but this is my decision. Go back to your SEAL buddies and leave me alone."*

She wouldn't listen to him then.

Somehow an angel from one nonprofit organization had connected with her, encouraged her to get clean, get a job, and get on with her life.

Amanda was smart and had the courage to embrace a second chance. She'd never asked for it, but he sent money to her every month. Thankfully, it was never returned.

His sister had come so far in the past six years.

She'd gotten off the drugs, had a decent job, and then got pregnant. He didn't know who the father was. Amanda wasn't telling.

All he knew was that her spunky five-year-old was with the babysitter right now, not understanding what it meant that her mother was dead, that her uncle was now her guardian and that she would leave the only home she ever knew to live in Florida with people she didn't know. His parents would have taken her in, but Dad was confined to a wheelchair, and his mom couldn't take on the added responsibilities of a small child. God only knew how he would.

Sam's soft hand reached for his. She was his rock, his light in the darkness, his comfort when things went to shit, as they sometimes did.

He covered her small hand and patted it. His life would be more difficult if she wasn't by his side. He loved her so much and wanted to marry her, but she kept refusing. Why? Bah, he couldn't think about that right now. The pain in his chest was cutting off his breath.

Mark looked around the small chapel at his family and friends.

They'd held the service here, not knowing who would show up, but the chapel was full.

Joe, Claire, and her parents arrived with Danny and Hailey. Some friends from KnightGuard Security were there. His poker buddies. A few people from Amanda's work and some parents of Alexis's classmates also came. He was happy that Amanda had made friends.

"Amen."

A bell tolled. The service was over, but Mark didn't want it to end. If it ended, it meant he wasn't connected to Amanda anymore and reality was going to set in. He wasn't ready. He loosened his collar. It was tightening like a vise around his neck. The contents in his stomach threatened to make an entrance. He swallowed hard. He could do this. It wasn't the first funeral he'd ever attended. Taking a deep breath, he escorted his mother and Sam out through the chapel doors.

The minister shook hands with the family, and the small group made its way through the sanctuary to the community room for a reception.

Mark had ordered food from a local caterer to be delivered.

He'd eat, stay for a week with his parents and then drive home.

He held his mother's arm, handing her a clean handkerchief when tears rolled down her face. She wiped her eyes, bowed her head, and then looked up at him, her blue eyes glistening. "I miss her."

"I know, Ma. I do too. But we have Alexis, and I promise to do good by her."

His mom nodded. "I know, son. I know it's a lot of responsibility to take on, but you'll do fine. Just promise you'll bring her around occasionally so we can see her."

Mark bent over and kissed her tear-streaked cheek. "You know I will."

A TEAR SLIPPED DOWN Mark's eye and over his cheek.

Sam reached out to wipe it away but pulled her hand back. Did he even realize it had happened?

She wasn't sure Mark would want her to acknowledge how much this affected him.

His body was rigid, and his hands clenched tight to his side. Amanda's death was devastating. Her heart hurt for him.

He was a protector, and he hadn't been able to protect his sister.

Burying a child was probably the most painful thing parents had to do. Sam wondered how her own grandparents had handled losing their only daughter. They spoke lovingly about her, missed her, but never discussed the pain. She never asked.

She glanced over at Mark's mother, Evelyn. Mark mentioned Amanda had their mother's delicate features, dark hair, and blue eyes. Evelyn was still beautiful, even though her hair was gray and there were lines of worry on her forehead. The stress of taking care of an invalid was hard on a body.

Mark looked like his dad.

Same dark hair as his mother, but he got his brown eyes and a strong jaw from his father. His father's hair had turned white, and his eyes were rheumy, but Sam could see a younger Mark in him.

Thank goodness Amanda lived close to them and visited often with Alexis.

Mark was going to spend the rest of the week with his parents so he and Alexis could bond.

As for Alexis, the red-haired, green-eyed doll must take after her father. Mark didn't think there were any redheads or green eyes in his family.

All Sam knew was that a series of unfortunate incidents set Amanda on the path to self-destruction.

Mark told her a set of lucky events gave Amanda hope and a change of heart.

How would Mark handle this new situation? Most likely, the same way he went through SEAL training, where the motto was "the only easy day was yesterday." Mark had about as much experience as she did in the childcare department. Grace wasn't much of a help when she'd asked her for advice.

"Grace, what am I going to do?" Sam asked. "I know zip about five-year-old girls, Mark even less. What if I make a mistake and Alexis gets hurt or worse?"

"Oh, Sam, you're smart. You and Mark will figure it out. Besides, kids are resilient," Grace had said.

"But. But ..."

Grace rubbed her shoulder. "Sam, nothing's going to happen. All your friends will help. It's easy-peasy. You'll see."

"What if ...?"

"Sam." Grace sighed heavily. "You run a kick-ass security company. You deal with thieves and murderers. You employ people who could kill with their pinkies. I think you can handle a five-year-old girl. Just give her lots of love. That's all she needs right now."

Then Grace called her a wuss and told Sam to stop worrying—as if.

There were other things to worry about. Like how would a child affect her and Mark's relationship? Would Mark feel he had to choose between her or Alexis? Where did she fit into this little family now?

And what about her uneasiness that someone was watching her? So many questions. No answers.

# CHAPTER FOURTEEN

S am opened the door to Neptune's Navel, stopped, and looked around. Not at all what she was expecting in the middle of the afternoon. Of course, she'd only been here for lunch or dinner.

It was quiet—almost too quiet. Sam assumed the bar was busy all day long. She needed the noise to quell her thoughts.

It was disappointing to see so few people sitting at the tables chatting. She saw a couple of men drinking at the bar, keeping to themselves. Surprise, even Petey the parrot was napping. And the music. What was going on with that? She would have appreciated the soft guitar music in the background another day. Today, she wanted to feel the pounding beat of drums course through her body, buffeting her angst.

The beach was her favorite place to think, so why did she come here? And why Jake's bar? Good questions. She wanted to be alone but needed something familiar. She didn't do bars by herself and wasn't a big drinker, but today's quiet time alone with her doubts scared her. Her girlfriends were busy with their lives, and Sam didn't want to burden them with her problems. Although they would be upset if they found out she was nursing her thoughts alone in a bar or anywhere.

She grabbed a barstool at the far end, close to the open kitchen and away from the other patrons. The spicy odor of onions and beef cooking wafted out, tantalizing her tastebuds.

But she wasn't hungry.

"What can I get you?"

The bartender interrupted Sam's thoughts.

He looked familiar; she'd seen him before, couldn't remember his name.

His name tag stated he was Mike. He was young, well, younger than her, and very cute—too cute—and self-assured, almost cocky. Bet the young women loved him, but she had her own hunk. Or did she?

"Bloody Mary, please," said Sam.

"Anything to eat?"

"No. I'm all set. Thanks."

The bartender busied himself with making her drink. A man slid in next to her. Sam turned to get rid of the interloper and realized it was Jake. Damn. She'd hoped to avoid him. Hell, she'd hoped to avoid anyone she knew.

"Sam Knight. I can't believe my eyes." His eyes twinkled. "You realize it's the middle of the afternoon?"

"Yes, Jake, I realize that." She gave him a small smile. Hoped if she didn't say much, he'd leave or magically disappear.

He looked around, surprised. "Are you by yourself?"

She thought about not answering.

She had no energy to tell Jake to harass some of his other customers, although he probably wouldn't listen.

"Yes, Jake, I'm alone. I needed to get away from life and my problems for a while."

"So, you thought ... what? You'd come to a bar and drink your problems away?"

The bartender came over and nodded to Jake. He placed a coaster and her drink on the bar in front of her, then left to help other customers.

"No, I came here to contemplate my life and solve world peace."

"Ha. That's what they all say." Jake looked her up and down. "You look like you've lost your best friend. Please tell me you've left that frogman and want to experience a real man."

He was kidding, of course. Wasn't he? Mark would eat him for breakfast if he thought Jake was coming on to her.

"As if." Sam shook her head and gave him a small smile.

She swirled the drink around the brushed copper counter-top. If she said nothing, maybe Jake would take the hint and leave.

Pointing his finger at her, Jake said, "I knew it. Man problems. How can I help?"

"Can't." Sam sighed.

There was no way in hell that she was discussing her man problems with Jake. Nope—not happening. Not in this life. She was the rock, not needing anyone's sympathy or help. She was the one who helped everyone else, not the other way around.

"You know what happens here, stays here." He waggled his brow.

Sam shrugged, sighed again and stared at her hands. *Was that a new mole? When did that vein get so blue?*

How long could she stare at her hands and avoid talking to Jake? He was one of Mark's best friends, but she didn't go around discussing their personal problems with his friends.

Why, oh why had she come to Jake's bar?

"This has nothing to do with Mark, does it?"

She took a sip of her drink. "Yum."

"You're deflecting. I have ways of making you talk." Jake lowered his voice and tilted his head. "Seriously, though, you've both had a major change in your relationship. I have a feeling Mark becoming a new father is overwhelming for both of you."

Sam bit the inside of her lip. How did he know?

Alex was a great kid, and Mark was doing his best to adjust to unfortunate circumstances.

She was helping as needed. She wondered if Mark felt he was putting her in a position he thought she didn't want. Could she walk away? Would she walk away? Never. Mark had to know that she was committed to him. And this problem was a minor blip in their relationship.

"Mark talk to you?" she asked. *Please say no.*

Mark had been quiet, pulling away ever since his sister's funeral and coming back from visiting his parents.

What was he thinking about? Sam didn't know. She hadn't asked. Maybe she should, but somehow she was afraid of his answer. He'd asked her to marry him once months ago, and then just before his sister died, but that was before Alex came to live with him. Did he think she wouldn't want to be an instant mother? Or did he think taking on the responsibility of raising a child was too much to ask of her if they weren't married? Or even if they were married. Good questions that she had no answers for.

"No. You're both my friends, and I know what it's like to deal with a new parent, a new life, and the unfamiliar."

"Hmmm." Sam hesitated. "Sounds like you've had some personal experience."

Jake tapped his fingers on the bar. "Yeah, my mom remarried a couple of years after my dad died. His death devastated us. My mother catered to my every whim, so when she remarried, I was a spoiled, only child, thrown into a family of over-achievers."

"I bet that went over big."

He blew out a breath of air and gave her a small smile. "Oh. Yeah. It was a challenge for all of us. At least my stepfather was patient. His kids were older and not so forgiving. It took a while, and my life was uncomfortable until we all adjusted to each other."

Boy, did she know that feeling of being lost and alone.

After her parents died, everyone looked at her and Danny with pity or sympathy. It hadn't bothered Danny as much.

At least her parents hadn't spoiled them. Her grandparents hadn't either.

"Alex is a great kid; I love her to bits." She hesitated, blew out the breath she'd been holding. "I'm sensing Mark is pulling away from me, and I don't know why or if we can fix it."

Silence.

"Oh, Sam." Jake rubbed his chin. "Of course, you can fix it. You've been together, what? Three years now?"

Sam nodded.

"You both have jobs you love and friends who will stick by you?"

"Yes."

"I bet if you let them, your friends would step in and help with Alex. You have a strong relationship with Mark. Talk to him." Jake closed his eyes for a second and chose his words. "Talk to him. I know that most men don't like to talk about relationships ..."

"And you do?" Sam smirked. Receiving relationship advice from Jake was getting weird.

He flinched in mock indignation. "Hey, I own a bar. People come in with problems. I listen and give advice if they ask.

Besides, I think you've just insulted my feminine side." Jake laughed. "As I was going to say, you need to talk to each other. You're both strong people who look out for others. But you complete Mark. He was blowing in the wind before he met you."

Well, she wasn't sure about that, but she'd take the compliment.

Jake rubbed her shoulder. "Relationships are hard, but you and Mark are good for each other. You can make it work."

Easier said than done. There had been only two men in her life that she loved—David and Mark.

She didn't date much through high school and college. David and Mark were warriors in their own right. David never backed down from a fight. He stood up to bullies with his words. Mark never backed down from a fight either but used skills he learned in the SEALs. She felt safe with both. They were protectors like her, and she knew both had her back.

Damn. She'd already lost one man through no fault of her own. She wasn't losing another. She needed to fight for him, even if he'd given up on her.

"Determine what concerns you both have and figure out a game plan. Alex is a kid and resilient. You won't screw up with her as long as you love her."

She bit the inside of her cheek. Isn't that what Grace said?

She and Mark had a lot of talking to do, and today was as good a time as ever. At least before she chickened out.

Mark had taken a few days off from work to acclimate Alex to Black Pointe, so he was home.

It was now or never. She'd wait until Alexis went to bed and go over.

She asked for the check.

The bartender brought it over, but Jake grabbed it.

"I'll take care of this. You go home and take care of your

problems. And if the big guy doesn't want to talk, tell him I do house calls."

"Oh lordy." Sam shook her head. "What am I going to do with you?"

Jake winked at her. "Anything you want, sweetheart." Then he got serious. "Sam, you've never avoided a problem. You can do this."

Shrugging, she picked up her purse. "I hope you're right."

---

"Uncle Mark?" Alexis's voice startled him. They'd been eating in silence, each lost in their thoughts.

"What, sweet pea?"

She giggled. "I'm not a pea."

Mark looked over at his niece. Her red hair was pulled back in a ponytail, pieces of which had fallen out already. Best he could do.

He knew nothing about little girls. Big girls, women, he was an expert at. He was so out of his league here.

They'd just finished lunch. Mac and cheese. He hadn't had that in years. But Alexis had a limited palate, and this was the one thing she loved.

"No, but you're sweet."

She giggled again, then her brows knitted together. "When am I going to go to school?" School? Crap, it was on the list—the long list of things to do.

They'd only been back from Georgia for a week, and the list kept growing.

He'd requested the transcript from her old school. He scheduled an appointment to tour the new school for tomorrow. It was a crappy time to enroll her. No chance to find her new friends or interview the teacher before she started.

But he learned Alexis was a resilient kid, so Mark thought

she'd be okay. She had to be. He couldn't stay home and babysit.

Next on the list was to find a pediatrician and have Alexis's records transferred.

Oh, and he couldn't forget finding an after-school babysitter.

And then there was his sister's estate. Not that there was much, but still ...

A hearing for guardianship was planned for next week, and he prayed no one would come forward and challenge him for custody.

Not that he thought anyone would, but the unnamed father was still out there. His sister had told him she didn't know who it was, and a father's name wasn't on the birth certificate, so he felt secure that there wouldn't be any surprises there.

And the most important item after taking care of Alexis's needs was repairing his relationship with Sam. They'd been at odds since he got back from Georgia, and it was his fault.

He was overwhelmed and scared. He hadn't been this scared—ever. Well, maybe on some missions but never in a relationship.

Sam and he hadn't spent the night together since the funeral. They were both busy or pretending to be.

Sam already indicated that she didn't want to get married. She probably didn't want a child in her life, either. But that was his life now.

His heart was torn between the niece he inherited and the love of his life.

He needed to resolve the issues with Sam. But what if she said it was all too much and she was leaving him? Could his heart handle that? Would she make him choose between her or Alexis? He hoped not. He was a parent now, and Alexis had to come first.

Damn, he was in an impossible situation.

He had responsibilities now.

The SEAL in him said, "Suck it up. The only easy day was yesterday."

The man in him wanted to look to the future with the woman he loved with all his heart.

Mark leaned back in the chair and sighed.

He could see only two options, and neither one was perfect.

He had to talk to Sam, and for the first time in forever, he was afraid.

# CHAPTER FIFTEEN

After putting Alexis to bed, Mark grabbed a beer and turned on the TV, hoping for a game or a mind-numbing program to watch. But nothing good was on.

He turned off the lights and the TV and sat in the dark, thinking dark thoughts. The lamppost threw shadows across the living room. It was quiet except for the occasional car passing by.

He missed Sam. Missed her snarky comments. Missed her sweet body. Missed her loyalty to her friends. Missed her commitment to justice but most of all, missed her.

She had softened his edges and soothed his soul. He always thought someone saying that they'd found their soul mate was bull, but the minute he'd met Sam, he knew she was it for him.

Mark closed his eyes and wished Sam were cuddling in his arms. He snorted. Sam never cuddled when they were with friends and wanted no one to know her softer side. The side that craved romance, hearts, and flowers. The side that cried his name when she orgasmed.

An alarm beeped. He jolted awake and reached for his gun. His hand slipped on the smooth leather. Not here. Shit, where was it?

He remembered that he'd hidden it in his bedroom because of Alexis. It didn't matter. He could kill someone in a dozen different ways. The alarm beeped again, signaling it had been reset. He watched as a small, slender woman walked by.

"You just couldn't stay away from all this manliness, could you?"

Sam let out a little scream. "Jesus, you scared me. Why are you sitting in the dark?"

Good question. He sighed. It was time to talk.

"Why are you here? It's late. I thought you had meetings all week."

She walked over and sat next to him, slipped off her shoes. Silence. The light from outside reflected off her face and emphasized a sadness in her eyes.

"I ..." She stared at her hands. "We need to talk."

Oh boy, here it comes. *She's breaking up with me.* He slumped back on the sofa. He reached out a hand to touch her but pulled it back. If he touched her, he wouldn't, couldn't stop, and Sam's rejection would make it worse. His chest tightened, and he prepared himself for what was to come.

Sam turned to look at him; a tear glistened in her eye. "If you're going to break up with me, do it fast. Rip off the Band-Aid. Don't make me suffer."

*Break up with her? Make her suffer?* What the hell was she talking about?

"What?"

"You're going to break up with me. Right?"

Mark's mouth opened and closed. Now he knew what a fish out of water felt like. He couldn't get enough air in his lungs. He had a problem that needed to be handled delicately.

Sam was hurting, and it was his fault. His fault for not manning up when shit happened. For hiding like a pussy in the house, not talking to her. His fault.

He wiped her tear away with his thumb. "Sam." He sighed. "Sweetheart. I would never break up with you. I know I've been distant, but a lot has happened that I had to make sense of."

The pain in her eyes almost undid him.

He reached over, pulled her into his chest, rested his head on top of hers. "I love you. I will always love you." He relished how she fit perfectly into his arms, and he'd missed this intimate connection for the past couple of weeks.

"I know you don't want to get married right now and especially don't want to raise a child." He drew in a breath and exhaled. "I was avoiding everyone because I haven't figured how to make this right for all of us."

He felt the hot tears before he heard the sniffling. Wanting to look into her eyes, he tried to lift Sam's head, but she slipped her arms around his waist and held on tight. He wrapped his arms around her. This was all his fault. Sam didn't cry, ever.

Big sobs wracked her body as he murmured sweet nothings into her hair. Hair that smelled like coconut and vanilla.

It was a while before he felt her catching her breath and the crying stopped.

"Crap, I'm so sorry," she said as she lifted her head, her eyes red and swollen. "I haven't cried like that since my parents and David died."

Mark exhaled the breath he'd held. He knew about her parents and a little about David, the only other man she'd fallen in love with, who had died young.

Sam was always so strong for everyone else. But sometimes even the strongest people needed taken care of.

"Aargh, what a fool I am." Sam looked at the floor and shook her head.

"Sam, look at me."

She continued to stare at the floor. Oh no. Not on his watch was she ever to be embarrassed by her tears. He lifted her head and stared into her eyes. She was beautiful, even with red, swollen eyes.

"This is on me. I pushed you away while I was sorting things out. I was wrong. My only excuse is that I was overwhelmed with my sister's death, becoming Alexis's guardian, wondering how to ask you to be part of my changing life and wondering if you wanted to be. Terrified that you would say no and leave me." He took her hand and kissed it.

Expelling a huge breath, Sam turned away, closed her eyes, and turned back toward Mark.

"Mark, I may not want to get married right now, but I would never walk away from you or Alexis. She's part of you. Together we can make this work."

Mark saw only the truth in her eyes. He did a mental fist pump. "*Yesss.*" He wasn't losing her.

"Can you forgive me for pushing you away?" He kissed her forehead.

She nodded.

"Can you forgive me for not confiding in you better?" He kissed her cheek.

She nodded.

"Can we have make-up sex?"

He kissed her mouth.

Sam pushed him away and started laughing. "You are such a dork."

"I know. But can we?"

Sam didn't say a word. She got up, took his hand, and led him to the bedroom.

Mark didn't want to rush things, but he needed to make

love to her like yesterday. He needed to make her his again. He reached over to remove her top, but she pushed his hands away. Mark cocked his head and opened his mouth to ask why. She put her finger to his lips and shushed him.

"We have all night, and I want to undress you first."

Okay then. That worked for him. She usually let him have control in the bedroom, which always surprised him, but if Sam needed to be in charge right now, he was all hers.

She pushed his T-shirt up and off, rubbed her hands over his chest, then tweaked his nipples. When he yelped, she kissed them to make it all better. His cock was aching to be released. Could she keep teasing him all night? God, he hoped so or maybe not. He loved feeling her hands on his body, but he ached for her.

"Woman, I'm not going to last if you continue doing things like that."

Grinning, Sam unbuckled his belt and unzipped his pants, bent down to pull them off, one leg at a time. He was glad he was barefoot. It wouldn't take as long to get naked. She stood back and stared at him, licking her lips, teasing him.

Inch by inch, she pulled down his boxers, humming the entire time. Sweet Jesus, if she didn't get to it, he definitely wasn't going to last. She stopped when his boxers were halfway to his knees and leaned in to rub his cock. If his cock was hard before, it felt like cement now.

"You're killing me here."

She gave a little smirk and ran her tongue around the tip of his penis, licking the pre-cum. He closed his eyes. Heaven. Then she plunged down with her mouth, sucking up and down. His cock nodded with pleasure. He groaned. *This must be what heaven felt like.* She rimmed his cock, then pulled away.

He felt the absence of her mouth as cool air shocked his cock. She grinned as she removed his boxers, looked him up and down, squinted her eyes and proclaimed, "You'll do."

Laughing, he grabbed her, tossed her gently onto the bed, and followed her down. "I'll do?"

She giggled and tried to get him off her but to no avail.

They were face-to-face. Mark leaned down to kiss Sam, and when their eyes met, he saw need, lust, and love in her whiskey-brown eyes.

Nothing else had to be said. They were meant to be with each other. He needed to show her how much he loved her.

Mark twisted to the side. "Your turn. Upsy-daisy. Take those clothes off."

She stood up and inched her top off, shook her shoulders and licked her lips.

"I'm going to come before we even get started with you looking like that," he whispered.

He took in the red lacy bra that barely covered her glorious breasts, groaned, and lifted his chin. "More."

She smirked as she shimmied out of her pants, showing off the tiny, matching red panties. *Be still my heart*. She was a vision of sexiness.

"More."

Her fingers rimmed the top of her panties, pushing them down and off, followed by the bra. Dear lord in heaven, his woman stood there showing off the most magnificent body he'd ever seen. It always amazed him to see how feminine yet toned she was. Perfect-size breasts with pink areolas. Her pussy was glistening.

"Take the elastic out of your hair."

She did and shook her red mane.

He lay on the bed and beckoned to her. She walked over, got on the bed and straddled him as she made small circles on his chest.

"Bring those beauties down here."

She bent over. Mark took one peaked nipple in his mouth and sucked. She mewled. He sucked harder, and she groaned.

She was humping him now. He let go of the one nipple and latched onto the other, sucked hard and pulled his mouth away. He put his hands on her ass and pulled her down so she was lying flat on top of him. His cock was so hard, it hurt to have her lie on him, but he knew how to fix that.

"Condoms, side table."

Sam leaned over, got the box, looked at it and then him.

"Was there a sale on ginormous?"

"Hey, I have big plans for you tonight."

"Oh, dear lord. Gotta love a man who plans ahead." Sam laughed, took a condom out, unwrapped it, and slid it over his cock. He reached down between her legs; she was dripping. In one movement, he twisted, and she was beneath him.

"Open for me, sweetheart."

She opened her legs and wrapped them around his waist. He couldn't wait to make love to her. This was his Sam, his woman, his heart, his everything. He plunged into her with a heat that consumed him, and they both groaned. Faster and faster. He couldn't stop now if he wanted to. Sam matched him thrust for thrust.

His balls contracted. His heart was pounding. Sam cried his name, and as her pussy clenched around his cock, he came. And came.

After he softened and reluctantly pulled out, he kissed her. "I love you, Sam Knight. You are mine forever."

"I love you too, Mark Stone. You are my everything."

He leaned in to kiss her.

But just like that, she had fallen asleep. He watched her chest rise and fall with each breath. Felt her supple, warm body snuggle into his. Inhaled the sweat and sex of their coupling. She was his warrior—his haven, his home, and no one or anything would stand in the way of their happiness.

He would kill to keep Sam and Alexis safe.

But first, he had to make it all work.

# CHAPTER SIXTEEN

Why did everything bad have to fall on the same day?

Rain fell from the sky in buckets. Thunder roared. A lightning bolt hit a tree next to Sam's car.

Her friend Anne taught kindergarten and was Alexis's teacher. No, not Alexis. The little girl informed she and Mark that she wanted to be call Alex. Anne had called to tell her Alex was in the principal's office for fighting. *Fighting?*

What was Alex—about three and a half feet tall, maybe forty pounds wet? And why was she fighting? She'd only been at the school for a couple of weeks.

Mark couldn't handle this situation. He was in Georgia buying specialized equipment for a new construction project and would be staying overnight.

Sam left an important meeting at KnightGuard Security to pick Alex up.

But first, she had to stop by the babysitter's house for Alex's car seat. One of these days, she needed to buy one for her own car.

The car seat was in Joyce's front hall. Sam grabbed it and ran out into the rain.

Holy crap, the car seat was heavy. Mark had ordered the super-size one with all the bells and whistles, including a cup holder—for when Alex got thirsty, of course.

Kids today! What did her mother put her in when she was small? It was something a lot simpler than this. The car seat didn't become complicated until years later.

She opened the back door and hoisted the car seat in on the third try. Then stared at the complexity of it.

Where did the seat belt go?

She finally found the hole in back to thread the seat belt through, then accidentally pressed a button and the headrest shot up. Too high. She tried to push it down, but that didn't work. *Damn it all hell*.

It was just a car seat. She could take down grown men, shoot with the best of them, run a security protection company, and she couldn't handle a stupid car seat?

Kicking the back tire hadn't helped. Well, it never did. She pressed another button, and the headrest finally dropped down.

The front straps were loose, but she'd worry about them when she got to school. There were other adjustments she needed to make, but she forgot what they were. Rain was dripping down her back, causing her clothes to stick to her.

For a moment she thought about running back to ask Joyce to show her what to do but decided no one else should have to get drenched. It was late, she wasted too much time on the damn car seat, and she had to leave, but first she removed her rain jacket, hoping to dry off before she reached school.

Not for the first time since Alex arrived, she thought it took a village to raise a child. Something she wasn't ready to do yet. Or maybe it was because she was afraid. Didn't matter. There were no little Sams or Marks in her immediate future.

She pulled into the visitors' parking lot and parked as close to the door as she could. Then finagled herself into the rain jacket, her wet clothes making it difficult. Looking in the mirror, she almost didn't recognize herself. The ponytail that looked so neat when she left her house looked like a rat's tail, and her supposedly waterproof mascara ran down her face, making her look like a raccoon.

Sam took a deep breath. Oh God, not only did she look like a drowned rat, but she also smelled moldy, like a wet dog. She shivered. Couldn't do anything about that now. She opened the car door. The rain jacket would provide some protection. But the rain was coming down so hard, she was going to get soaked again by the time she reached the principal's office.

Sam ran up the walk, avoiding puddles and barely noticing the flower garden the children had planted.

The office buzzed her into the building.

There was no need to follow signs to the principal's office. She was intimately familiar with it.

Everything from her elementary-school experience flooded back.

If it weren't for her best friend Grace interceding with the other kids, she would have spent a lot more time in the office.

The principal's name had been Mrs. Hart, and she and Sam had become fast friends.

Well, not fast friends, not even friends. Mrs. Hart tolerated her. The wooden bench she sat in every time was friendlier than the staid principal. Mrs. Hart believed children should be model citizens, never speak up or fight. That had never been Sam.

Sam took a deep breath. *Please don't let Mrs. Hart still be here. Please don't let Mrs. Hart still be here.*

Lunch was over, but the lingering smells of tuna and pizza wafted through the halls.

The floors were worn down the middle from the thousands of small feet moving about over the years. At least the gray walls had been repainted in bright primary colors.

Sam spied Alex by herself outside the principal's office, swinging her legs back and forth on the wooden bench.

Sam's heart ached for the little girl.

It wasn't as if she hadn't spent most of her recess sitting right where Alex was. She looked so small and lonely.

Alex looked up when she came in but avoided her eyes and pursed her lips.

Sam scooched down and touched her arm. "Are you okay, hon?"

Alex nodded.

"All righty then."

Sam glanced at the nameplate on the principal's door.

Damn. What were the chances?

It wasn't Mrs. Hart but her son, Drew. Could this day get any better? Drew Hart had been in her homeroom and constantly teased her about being sent to the principal's office. On more than one occasion she had bopped him on the head for being a dick. Sam hoped he wouldn't remember that.

"I need to talk to your principal, and then we'll leave." Sam walked toward the door but turned. "Don't move."

Alex nodded.

Sam popped her head into the office. Drew smirked when she mentioned her name.

Great. Now she *and* Alex had a reputation at Black Pointe Elementary School.

After some pleasantries and catching up, Drew said he didn't know why Alex had hit the other girl.

Neither Alex nor the girl would say what had started the fight.

The other girl wasn't hurt, and she confessed that she started the fight with Alex.

Her mom had already picked her up.

A few minutes later, after talking to the principal, Sam left the office.

"Come on, pipsqueak. Let's get you home."

Sam picked up Alex's backpack and shook out her raincoat. She helped Alex put it on. They stood under the portico for a minute. Sam took a deep breath, looked at Alex.

"Ready?"

Alex nodded, Sam took her hand, and they ran out into the deluge.

Sam opened the back door, and the bane of her existence was still there, taunting her.

She helped Alex into the car seat and spent a few minutes with the contraption. Finally, she could strap Alex in.

Her day was shot, so she called the office to reschedule her appointments.

The ride over to Mark's house was quiet. Sam turned on her favorite classical radio station and wondered what five-year-old kids could get into a fight about.

Oh yeah, it could be anything. She'd been in a few fights at that age and grounded more than a few times. The fights seemed important, but looking back, they were usually over silly things. But sometimes, it was over someone getting bullied and needing a friend. She hated bullies then and still did. She would quiz Alex about what happened when they got into the house.

*Mommy got behind the steering wheel and turned to Sam. "Samantha May Knight, I want to know what's going on. Why are you fighting?"*

*Uh-oh. When Mommy called her by her full name, she was going to get in trouble.*

*"The boys were picking on Gracie."*

*"Why?"*

*Sam hesitated. "Because Gracie and me are bestest friends, and they don't like me."*

*"Oh, Sammie, when are you going to learn that you can't protect everyone, and you certainly can't go around beating up every person who disagrees with you."*

*"I know, Mommy. I don't beat everyone up, only the ones who deserve it."*

*Her mother sighed. "You're grounded for a week."*

Parking as close to the house as she could, Sam grabbed the backpack and opened the back door to let Alex out.

She stared at the car seat straps. The two of them got them attached before, but for the life of her, she couldn't remember how to unhook Alex.

She tugged on the set of straps—nothing.

Pulled on another—nothing.

Good lord, she was in the security business and she couldn't get one small child out of a seat belt.

Alex didn't say a word, looked down, and pressed a button. She was free.

"How on earth?"

Alex shrugged—wiseass. Sam laughed and took her hand as they dashed for the front door. Sam plugged in the alarm code, they took off their wet things and hung them in the small front hallway.

"How about a snack?" Sam asked.

Alex looked down at her feet and then up at Sam.

"Okay," she said in a soft voice.

They walked back to the kitchen. Sam got some juice and cookies and sat across the table from Alex.

"Want to tell me what's going on?" she asked the little girl.

Alex vehemently shook her head.

Sam stared at the little girl, whose lips were clenched—stubborn. She was so out of her league with children.

"Well, something happened. If you don't tell me, I'll have to tell Uncle Mark about the fighting, and he won't be happy. Right now, it's between you and me."

Alex's eyes watered. Her shoulders drooped, and her bottom lip quivered. "Please don't tell Uncle Mark," she whispered.

"I won't." Sam took her hand and stared into big forest-green eyes. "As long as you tell me what happened."

Alex hemmed and hawed. "Kaitlyn pointed her finger at me and laughed."

Okaaay. That didn't seem like enough of a reason to hit someone.

"Why not walk away?"

"She called me poor. Said I didn't have a mommy."

Crap. Sam's heartstrings clenched, and she bent down to hug Alex. "You have a mommy, and she loves you. She's in heaven with my mom watching over us."

"Your mommy's in heaven too?"

"Yup."

Alex mulled that over. "I'm glad they're together."

Sam nodded and swallowed hard. The pain of losing her parents still hurt. She knew how Alex felt. A conversation with Mark was needed to handle this situation.

But first, she asked, "So why did Kaitlyn call you poor?"

Alex's lips trembled. "My clothes don't fit."

What the hell?

Sam asked her to stand up. She looked Alex up and down.

Mark had dressed her in blue pants that didn't reach her ankles and a long-sleeved striped pink top whose sleeves didn't cover her wrists. Her sneakers fit, but they were worn. Mark had obviously never dressed a little girl.

Sam closed her eyes.

Alex looked like a poster child for poor children everywhere.

Why hadn't she noticed this before?

Had Mark? Probably not. He'd been thrown into this mess with no instructions.

Sam took Alex's hand, walked down to her bedroom, and looked in her closet—not much there. She spotted two dresses and a jacket. Pulling out the dresser drawers, she saw a couple of pairs of pajamas, a few tops, some shorts and three pairs of pants. She held them up. All looked clean but used and too small.

"Well, now. It looks like you need a new wardrobe. And it just so happens, I'm a fantastic shopper. What do you say we go shopping?"

Alex's eyes lit up, and she clapped her hands. "I say yes!"

Sam bent down to Alex's level. "I'm curious why you said nothing to Uncle Mark."

Alex looked down at the ground, shuffling her feet, and then into Sam's eyes.

"I don't want him to give me away."

# CHAPTER SEVENTEEN

*ive her away?*

Sam swallowed hard. She stood up but felt dizzy and reached her hand out to the table to steady herself.

She looked at the little girl who'd never met her dad, lost her mother, lived with an uncle she didn't know, had no one to confide in, and was enrolled in a new school where she knew no one. And Alex was the one who felt ashamed?

It never entered Sam's mind that Alex had to make so many changes because she seemed to fit right in.

And all the while, Alex was alone, scared, and had said nothing to anybody because she was afraid of being given away.

Sam's heart broke. It felt like yesterday when she was five, her parents were dead, and she and Danny went to live with their grandparents. The circumstances were different because she had her friends and knew love, but she was still scared. It helped that her grandparents lived in Black Pointe and that she continued to go to the same school with the same friends.

She couldn't fix all the problems tonight, but buying

clothes was something she could do. Tomorrow, when Mark got home, they would have a serious talk about the other issues.

Okay then. Nothing to be done until he got home.

Sam glanced around Alex's room. It was a perfectly pleasant guest room. Not too big, not too small. There was a queen-size bed and a dark blue chair with a reading light behind it. The walls were a dull beige. Great for adult guests—not so great for a little girl. They needed to fix that.

"Alex, finish your juice and cookies, then we're going clothes-shopping."

Alex's green eyes popped open. She stuffed a cookie in her mouth, jumped up from the chair and proclaimed she was ready.

Sam laughed. "Sweetie, I didn't mean this second. Swallow."

Alex gulped down her cookie.

A few minutes later, Sam picked up the remains of their snack and cleaned the table.

She helped Alex with her rain gear, and they were on their way.

The mall was about fifteen minutes away, and Sam hoped there were kids' stores there. She never had to check before.

They parked in the covered garage and walked into a cacophony of noise.

Sam figured the rain had a lot to do with all the people milling around.

They walked close to the stores to avoid bumping into giggling teenagers and harried workers.

Wafts of popcorn and Chinese food vying with Italian food, undercut by the smoky scent of coffee and cloying sweet-smelling candles, assaulted her nose. Her nose and stomach were at odds with each other.

All the colors and sounds mesmerized Alex, her head whirling around at each store.

Had Amanda ever brought her to a mall? Probably not if they were strapped for cash and Amanda was working a lot.

Straight ahead was a map of the mall, and Sam steered Alex to it. She found half a dozen kids' stores and plotted her way to the first one.

Two hours later, Sam carried two full shopping bags. Her feet hurt, she was sweating, and she wanted to leave. The mall was hot and noisy.

Alex clasped two smaller bags and was chattering on about the different stores and how she loved her new clothes and how she couldn't wait for Uncle Mark to see them and ... and ...

*And please save me,* Sam thought. Who knew shopping for and with kids could be so tiring and challenging?

They had one more important stop to make.

Build-a-Bear was on their way to the car. Sam had seen lots of happy kids building their bears and thought Alex would enjoy it.

Alex stood at the entrance, her eyes wide, her mouth open.

"I thought you might like to build your very own bear," Sam said.

Alex pressed her small face to the glass. "Ohhh. Look, Sam, they have abliens and monsters and dogs and cats and lambs and tigers."

*Abliens?* Aliens. Sam laughed to herself.

What would Alex choose?

"Take a big breath," said Sam.

Alex inhaled deeply and held the breath.

Sam laughed. "You can let it out, sweetie. Give me your bags, and I'll put them behind the counter. Look around. What would you like to build?"

Alex gave Sam her bags and wandered around the store, stroking each finished creation. Then she walked around again, stopping occasionally to think. Finally, decision made, she came back and announced it to Sam.

"I want to make a teddy bear."

Well, that was unexpected.

*Mama, Mama." Sam tugged on her mother's skirt. "Can I build a bear? I want a teddy bear." They had passed the Build-a-Bear shop, and Sam watched all the excited little kids running around stuffing bears, choosing outfits, and showing them to their friends. If she didn't get a bear now, she thought she would just die.*

*Her mama looked down at her. "Oh, Sammie, not today. I'm in a hurry. But we'll do it soon, I promise."*

They never got the bear. The following month, her parents were killed. Sam swallowed hard, not letting the tears that threatened to spill down her face scare Alex.

"Great idea. A bear it is," said Sam, putting more enthusiasm in her voice than she felt. She shook off her memory and smiled at Alex, who ran over to the bear section. With all the choices, Alex surprised her by choosing a traditional brown bear.

"Have you ever had a teddy bear?"

Alex scrunched her nose and shook her head. "No, mama didn't have a lot of money."

That thought made Sam sad. But they were here now, and if Alex wanted ten teddy bears, she could have them.

They brought the bear body to the woman operating the stuffing machine, who instructed Alex to put her foot on the pedal. Alex stood there enthralled as the beaters turned the stuffing, which looked like cotton candy, round and round to fill the bear. Kids' happy voices mingled with the *whoosh, whoosh* of the stuffing machine and the adults talking in the background. Excitement filled the air as the children found their stuffed animals and outfits.

The last thing to do was insert the heart, and the bear was live. Sam's heart melted when Alex reached for her bear and kissed it.

Then it was on to the computers to fill in the bear's name, date of birth, and whatever else one needed for a birth certificate.

"So, what do you want to name this bear?" asked Sam.

Alex clutched the bear to her heart and bit her lip, thinking hard. "Sammiedoodles."

"Sammiedoodles?" *Oh crap.* No. No. No. She would never hear the end of this.

"How about Snugglebug?"

Alex shook her head.

"Baby Bear? Fuzzball? Buttons?"

Alex shook her head.

Damn. Alex stared at Sam, her little body stiff, and biting her lower lip.

"Sammiedoodles it is."

Alex clapped her hands.

Then it was on to fill out the form, choose a couple of outfits, pay, and leave, with Alex holding Sammiedoodles and her new outfits on one arm and her two little bags on the other.

"Thankyouthankyouthankyou," said Alex. She swung around with the bear and the shopping bags—both threatening to be sent flying.

Sam watched the happy little girl as she skipped down the aisle.

Mark wouldn't be home tonight.

Tomorrow, they had a lot to discuss. The first being renovating the guest room. Second, Alex needed a woman in her life. Not a sleepover-one-night-and-leave-the-next-night kind of woman, which was what she was now.

Mark was a great uncle, but he knew nothing about little girls. It was time to take that step and make a commitment.

"Alex, why don't we have an overnight at my place instead of Uncle Mark's house? Just you and me." Sam looked at the bear. "And Sammiedoodles."

Alex's eyes got wide. "Yes. Yes. Yes."

"Okay then, let's go."

"Can we play Fish and eat ice cream and stay up late?" Alex stopped in the middle of the aisle and looked at her with wide eyes.

Crap. Well, now she was going to have to break Alex's happy bubble. "No to Fish, yes to ice cream and no to staying up late. You have school tomorrow."

Sam watched Alex's mind process what she said. "What kind of ice cream do you have?"

"What kind do you like?" Sam remembered an ice cream shop in the mall. Buying it here would mean not stopping on the way home.

"Chocolate chip."

"Chocolate chip it is. We'll stop at the ice cream parlor and get some."

A half hour later, they were on their way to Sam's loft with the packages, Sammiedoodles, the clothes and ice cream— lots of ice cream. Turned out Alex didn't just like chocolate chip.

They finally made it to Sam's place.

Alex was over the top, thinking she lived in the big warehouse. Well, she did, but as she explained to Alex, she only had a loft upstairs.

Through the glass doors, Sam waved to Steve, who was manning the phones. Then they got into the elevator that would take them upstairs. When the doors opened, Alex stood there looking around in wonder.

"It's like a fairyland." She ran to each long window and

looked outside at the glimmering lights of the lampposts and surrounding buildings.

Sam put the packages by the door and the ice cream in the freezer.

"I don't have Fish, but I have a checkerboard. Have you ever played checkers?"

Alex shook her head.

Well, this was going to be fun. Sam hadn't played in years and couldn't remember why she even had the board.

They ate chocolate chip, cookie dough and rainbow ice cream topped with whipped cream and sprinkles, lots of sprinkles. Then played checkers for a while until Alex started yawning.

"Come on, sweetheart. It's time for bed."

In one of the shopping bags were the pj's Sam had bought.

She had an extra toothbrush and paste in the bathroom and told Alex to change and brush her teeth.

"I'm done." Alex walked out of the bathroom in her new pajamas and holding Sammiedoodles in its new pj's. And wasn't that adorable. They had matching pj's.

"How would you like to sleep in my bed?" asked Sam. "It will be a special treat."

"Yeah." Alex ran up the stairs to Sam's bedroom.

Sam pulled the covers down, and the little girl jumped into the bed.

Alex lay down, snuggling the bear. "Tell me a story about when you were a little girl."

Damn. A story. Sam didn't have many stories to tell a little kid. She sure wasn't going to tell Alex about spending all her time in front of the principal's office. Or why. She wasn't going to talk about guns and murder. Those things gave her nightmares.

Maybe something in her box of keepsakes would inspire her.

Sam opened her closet door and bent down, pulling out a small painted wooden trunk. It had been her mother's keepsake trunk and was one of the few items Sam kept. She caressed the scarred wooden top, remembering all the times her mother would open it and tell Sam stories about each item as she pulled them out.

"What's that?"

"It's where I keep my memories."

She opened the lid, and a picture of her parents lay on top. Sam took a deep breath. It was her favorite picture of them. Her mother was pregnant, probably with Danny, and they were smiling sweetly at each other, both touching her stomach. Her heart ached to hold them again.

However, she was on a mission. She pulled out journals, pictures of her and Danny as kids, her taking self-defense lessons, Danny sailing. So many memories. Finally, she got to the bottom and saw Leonardo. The memory of receiving him still took her breath away. As weird as it sounded, she felt like she had received her soul mate.

*"Mama. Mama." Sam screeched as she ran into the kitchen, holding her latest prize. Her mama was standing at the stove, her hair pulled back in a ponytail, so like her own but redder. She turned towards Sam and scooched down.*

*"Sammie, what's wrong? Are you hurt?" Her mama patted her down.*

*Sam looked at her mama. She thought she was the prettiest woman alive—and nice. Her mama was the nicest woman she knew, except for her best friend Gracie's mama.*

*"No." Sam grinned and pulled out a miniature figurine. "Look what Gracie gave me. She got Leonardo for a present but hates him." She hugged the little green Ninja Turtle figurine tight to her chest. "I love Leonardo. He's the bestest."*

*"Why do you say that Sammie?"*

Sam's heart ached for her mother. She looked over at

Alex, who was looking at her with big eyes, and could imagine how lost the little girl felt. Sam touched Leonardo, who was looking a little used from being so well-loved. His emerald-green skin was faded, and his katana sword was wobbling. However, Leonardo had been her hero until she turned eight and didn't believe in the Ninja Turtles anymore.

*"'Cause he's bravest and strongest and protects his brothers and hates bullies." She let it out in one breath. "And I want to grow up and be just like him."*

*Her mama smiled, held out her arms and pulled Sam in for a hug. "Sammie, you are the bravest and strongest little girl I know."*

*Sam gave her mama a kiss.*

*She was brave. And strong. Mama and Papa and Gracie always told her so.*

*Gracie could talk her way out of problems, but she liked to make a point—with her fists. The bullies didn't like that.*

*She might be the smallest one in the class, but Gracie said she was the bravest. Sam just wished her teachers at school understood that. She was constantly being punished and made to sit outside Principal Hart's office during recess.*

*Sam shrugged. She didn't care.*

*Someone had to be brave and strong and stand up to bullies.*

This was the perfect time to tell a story with a message about fighting. Although Sam wasn't going to mention the detention or the trouble she got in fighting. She wanted to encourage and empower Alex to use her words.

Alex had lots of questions about Leonardo.

She'd never heard of him but loved Sam's story and promised not to hit—so much. Then the little girl blinked a couple of times, closed her eyes and seconds later was lightly snoring.

Sam smiled to herself, covered Alex, and went downstairs to watch TV for a while. She was almost ready to head up when Mark called.

The conversation was brief.

She hadn't mentioned renovating Alex's room or that maybe she should move in. Moving in now was the right thing to do.

She loved Mark and Alex. Her heart was thumping loudly over the TV that played in the background. Some silly game show and she was making life decisions. Moving in was a long way from getting married. All in due course.

She spent a few minutes going over her week, her upcoming schedule, the clients she had to meet, and the scheduling of employees.

These were all tangible goals, but that feeling that someone had her in his sights wasn't.

It was still just a feeling.

No one had made a move against her, but she didn't want to bring trouble to Mark's doorstep, especially with Alex there.

The one thing Sam knew for sure was that she would protect the little girl with her life.

# CHAPTER EIGHTEEN

*ould this have played out any better?*

Colin pulled into a quiet street dotted with ranch-style homes. It was early Saturday morning, and the weather was perfect, with lots of blue sky and white puffy clouds.

In his wildest dreams, he'd never imagined he'd be invited into a mark's house. Mark's house. The irony wasn't lost on him.

Mark had a project he wanted done and asked Colin if he would like to earn some extra money. Hell, yeah.

The extra money would come in handy. Getting into Mark's house even handier. It turned out Mark's niece was living with him, needed bookshelves and other things built in her room. It was a win-win for him.

Colin backed his truck into Mark's driveway.

The house was in an established neighborhood with lots of live oaks and palm trees dotting the yards. No bushes surrounding Mark's house, though. Smart man. Someone could try to get in unnoticed but probably wouldn't get far.

Mark had an unassuming ranch typical of Florida houses

with a colorful flower bed underneath the windows. He never thought of Mark as a gardener, but hey, he wasn't here to talk about plants, sing "Kumbaya" and bond over a cup of tea.

Holding his toolbox in one hand, he rang Mark's doorbell with the other. It echoed in the house.

His heart was racing, and he wet his lips. Then he patted his pocket. Yep, the mics were still there.

Between the mics, and what he could find out at work, he had Mark and Sam covered.

Let the games begin.

A woman yelled, "Coming," and he heard multiple locks disengaging and wondered what kind of security Mark had. It sounded like good security. He wouldn't be trying to get into this house, but there were other ways of hurting people.

"Hi."

Colin almost dropped his toolbox. Standing right in front of him was Sam, the object of his desire and schemes. Mark mentioned that either he or Sam would here. But to see her in real-time?

Sam Knight was a short one, all right, but he'd never discount her ability to hurt him.

He knew she was more than proficient in martial arts and had a keen shooting eye. She was slender, but he saw the well-defined muscles in her arms.

She didn't smile, just stared at him like he was a bug that she wanted to squash right on the doorstep.

Had she recognized him? *Nah*. His stomach flip-flopped. If she had, it would have thrown a wrench into his plans—not a big wrench, though. And why would she have recognized him? They'd only met once back in high school for a second, and back then, he was a pimple-faced skinny kid.

"Hmm. Hi. I'm Co-Co-Colin." Terrific, now he was stuttering like a fool. "I'm here to do some work." God, he sounded like a dope. He cleared his throat and pasted on a big smile. "Mark asked me to come over."

"Oh, right. Mark told me someone would be by." She smiled at him and opened the door wider. "Mark's out with his niece right now. He wanted her room to be a surprise."

Whaaat? Mark was out. Say it wasn't so.

He could take Sam Knight out right now and disappear.

But no, he had big plans for her friends. Plans that would hurt Sam long before he physically hurt her.

"Well, that's great. Just show me her room. I have a general idea of what to do."

As Sam led him down a short hallway, he couldn't help noticing how fit she was. Not his type, though. Her breasts were too small. She was too small. He liked big-breasted, tall women. Women with some meat on their bones.

Shaking his head, he chastised himself and got back to the present. He wasn't doing Sam Knight, ever. The only thing he would being doing to Sam Knight besides kidnapping her would be deciding her fate. Fire or water? He hadn't decided yet.

Colin looked around the comfortable house. Mark did all right for himself.

The place wasn't pretentious. Mark had few pictures or pillows thrown around. The living room had two large sofas and two leather chairs facing a big-ass TV. A dining room that held a table and six chairs was off to one side, and behind that was the kitchen—all off-white walls. A little boring for his taste, but he wasn't here to redecorate, just do reconnaissance.

They passed the master bedroom where Mark got his rocks off with Sam, then another guest room, and finally the kid's room. He thought the house was nice enough, certainly nicer than where he was staying and heaps nicer than the trailer he grew up in.

The girl's room wasn't big.

Lingering fumes irritating his nose indicated the room had been recently painted.

Pink—definitely the girl's room.

There was a white cast-iron bed all gussied up with pillows and a small brown bear. Someone had painted a mural of trees with assorted birds in shades of pink, green, and white behind it. A dollhouse and a little rocking chair completed the room.

"Mark probably told you what we needed. The wood is in the garage. But over here"—Sam gestured toward the double window—"is where we'd like a window seat and bookshelves."

Colin nodded. "No problem. I can have this done in no time. I'll double-check the wood to make sure I'll have enough and set up in the garage."

"Perfect."

He followed Sam back through the house and into the garage. She opened the garage door for him. "I'll be around if you need anything."

*Oh, sweetheart, I won't need anything more from you right now, but soon ...*

"Thanks."

A couple of hours later, he'd finished the bookshelves and window seat. They looked great, but then he was a master carpenter and took pride in his work. He'd scoped out the house and placed mics in the bathroom and under the kitchen table.

Sam was working on her computer in the living room and didn't know he was casing the house.

He cleared his throat. She looked up from what she was working on.

"I'm finished if you'd like to look at the room."

"Great." Sam got up and followed him down the hall. She stopped at the little girl's room and looked at his work. "Oh, it looks terrific. The only thing left is to paint it, and her room will be complete."

Colin picked up his tools and walked out; he'd already put his saw away. Sam followed him to his truck.

"Thanks again for coming over so quickly. Mark's niece is going to love the window seat and bookshelves." She put out her hand to shake his.

"Oh, it was my pleasure."

Sam had no idea how much this was his pleasure, but she'd find out.

He shook hands with her, not squeezing as hard as he wanted. Then he got in his truck and drove away.

He hadn't figured a niece in his scenarios, but now that he thought about it, she was another way to torment Sam and Mark.

He would never hurt a child, but he could kidnap one. Smiling to himself, he nodded.

Things were looking up.

# CHAPTER NINETEEN

After a brief cold spell, the weather turned balmy and a light breeze was blowing. Instead of their usual last Friday of the month lunch at Salt & Sea, the girls decided to get together at Neptune's Navel for dinner.

Sam and Grace arrived first and garnered a corner table outside.

Boats bobbed in the water, and the waves gently lapped at the patio. Jake had covered the outside deck in twinkling lights. A jazz band would play later.

Grace leaned back and took a sip of her virgin Zombie Pacifier. "Oh my God, this is so good."

Sam laughed. "Jake makes the best drinks. I didn't ask, but is everyone coming tonight?"

Grace tapped her fingers on the wooden table. "Yup. I don't know how Laura got away from her restaurant, but I'm glad she could. She works too hard."

"That's for sure." Sam dipped a chip into the smoked fish dip Jake was also famous for, popped it into her mouth and groaned. "Best dip ever."

She looked up to see a petite dynamo heading their way.

Marlee Burns was Ben Green's fiancée and one of Sam's favorite people.

She was Ben's first case with KnightGuard Security, and the petite woman had stolen all their hearts. She was fearless to a fault, outspoken, and loyal to her friends besides being funny as all get-out.

"Hey, you two." Marlee plopped herself next to Grace.

Julie, Laura, and Hailey followed behind her.

Air kisses all around. "Okay then, we're only waiting for Anne and Claire," said Sam.

No sooner were the words spoken when Anne and Claire walked in and sat down.

"Wow, I'm surprised that we got everyone here tonight," said Anne. "After the day I've had with this new group of kids, I could use a stiff drink."

After knowing Anne for years, Sam couldn't believe Anne was still teaching. Sam knew she would go crazy chasing after kindergarteners all day, but Anne loved it.

Jake, the owner of Neptune's Navel, appeared at their table as if conjured up by magic. "Ladies, good to see all of you. Snuck out on your men, I see. Are they behaving, or do I need to have a talk with them?"

The women laughed.

"I'm surprised you're not playing poker with the guys tonight. Didn't you get the invite?" asked Sam.

Jake smiled. "Yeah, I got the invite. Unfortunately, two servers called out sick." He spread his arms. "So I'm it tonight. What can I get you?"

They gave Jake their drink orders and caught each other up on their lives.

"Laura, I'm so glad you could make it," said Hailey.

"It's been a while, hasn't it?" Laura looked sad for a moment, but she gave Hailey a big smile. "I've been busy."

"Sam, how is everything working out at Mark's house? Are you settled in?" asked Julie.

Sam nodded. "Everything is great. I've moved all my stuff over. But it's only been a couple of weeks so we're still adjusting."

Since she'd picked Alex up from school for fighting, she had been thinking about a woman's influence for Alex. Even though Alex was the motivation for her decision, now that she was at Mark's house, she knew it was the right decision. Sleeping with him every night and waking up to great sex was frosting on the cake.

"Hailey, how was the honeymoon? Did you love Hawaii?" asked Marlee.

Hailey blushed. "It was great. Relaxing."

"I bet." Marlee scrunched her eyes.

Uh-oh. Sam knew Marlee was going in for the kill.

"So, give us all the sexalicious details."

Hailey groaned and shook her head. "Never happening."

"Well, at least tell us if Danny appreciated the gifts we gave you?"

Marlee and Anne had picked out some very sexy outfits for Hailey to wear on her honeymoon. Outfits Sam would never wear.

"Marlee. My lips are sealed." Hailey zipped her lips.

"Spoilsport," Marlee huffed.

"But ..."

All the girls leaned in toward Hailey.

"I will say that Danny appreciated every outfit. Especially as he removed each piece. Slowly. Verrry slowly."

"Ohhh." They moaned in unison.

"And kissed me every—"

Hailey stopped what she was saying as Jake came back with their drinks. Sam wondered if he'd heard.

Oh yeah, he did.

His lips curled up into a small smile, and he winked as he passed out menus. Hailey groaned and covered her eyes.

Jake laughed, then told them what the night's specials were and promised to come back.

Sam raised her glass. "A toast to us."

The women raised their glasses. "To us."

Sam zeroed in on Claire because she was drinking water. Either she wasn't feeling well or ...

Double damn. Sam bet Claire was pregnant. Would she say anything tonight? Sam sure wouldn't be the one to squash her surprise if she didn't.

Claire clinked her glass. "Now is the best time to announce that Joe and I are having a baby."

The women squealed. They congratulated her and toasted again, this time to the new baby.

"That Joe is a sneaky one for sure." Marlee laughed.

Sam glanced at Mark's cousin. Claire looked so happy and relaxed. She'd gained the weight she'd lost during her ordeal, but on closer inspection, it looked like there was some baby weight on her.

Claire's case had been difficult, but reconnecting with her first love, Joe Harkin, was the best thing that had happened to her and Joe.

Joe had wasted no time asking Claire to marry him and apparently getting her pregnant right away. The onetime self-professed loner was no more.

"Do the guys know?" Sam asked.

"They will tonight. We wanted to wait until I was three months along before saying anything."

They were interrupted when two servers came out with their meals. It thrilled Sam that Claire was pregnant. Thrilled that Mark would be a ... what would he be? He was Claire's first cousin, so the baby would be what? His second cousin? No matter.

It was nice to see the family growing. Not just Joe and Claire but the whole KnightGuard Security family. Joe and Claire deserved all the happiness they could get.

Sam swallowed hard. What would it be like to be pregnant with Mark's child? To make their own family. How would it affect her work? Would she stay home full-time or continue working? She knew Mark would make a great father. But could she keep a baby safe considering the line of work she was in?

What would happen if Mark died or if she did? She'd never gotten over her parents dying, and then when Suzie died ... that was on her, too. She couldn't protect the ones she loved. For the women around this table and her employees, she would do everything in her power to keep them safe.

Nah, she wasn't going there. She'd been avoiding his marriage proposal for months. Not that she didn't love him; she did. Sam didn't know why it was so hard to say yes.

---

"READ THEM AND WEEP, SUCKERS," hollered Joe as he threw his cards on the table.

The guys groaned.

Joe was on a lucky streak tonight. Mark had zip in his hand and tossed his cards on the table along with Hank, Ben and Pete as Joe raked in the cash.

"Guess this is your lucky night," growled Hank. Mark mentally laughed. Hank didn't stand a chance. He had a tell that they all knew and hardly ever won. Occasionally, he got lucky, but not tonight.

"Lucky in more ways than one," said Joe. He gave them a big grin. "Claire's pregnant."

The table got quiet.

"Holy shit. I'm going to be ..." said Mark. "Damn, what

would that make me? I guess officially a second cousin, but Uncle Mark will do." Claire was his first and only cousin. She got up the courage to escape an abusive marriage and reconnected with her first love, Joe. They had to fight off her dead husband's deranged mistress, who was now in a mental facility. KnightGuard Security had stepped in, and Sam had taken the nutjob down. Stressful times for all of them. Joe was his best friend and SEAL brother, making this moment even more poignant.

"So how long before the kid is born?" asked Hank.

"The kid, as you say, will arrive in approximately six months."

"How's Claire feeling?" asked Mark. "You guys must be beyond excited."

Joe took a swig of beer and placed the bottle on the table. "Claire's feeling better. She hasn't had much morning sickness, which I'm thankful for. I would have hated to see her go through that." He gave a heavy sigh. "We're excited, but I have to admit, I'm scared shitless. I know nothing about babies or small children."

Mark understood that. "Tell me about it," he huffed. "Thank God Sam is around. Not that she knows any more than I do about kids, but she's more in tune to Alex's needs."

"Don't worry. It'll come naturally," said Pete. "Axl is an easy kid, and Jack sleeps all the time. Julie and I help each other with them."

Mark looked at Pete. The no-nonsense strapping man almost lost his then-girlfriend Julie and her son when he couldn't accept Julie's stripping so many years ago. They talked about their differences, and after they married, Julie got pregnant almost immediately. Their son, Jack, was a couple of months old.

"So when are you and Sam tying the knot?" asked Ben.

Conversation stopped. All eyes turned to him.

Letting out a heavy sigh, Mark shook his head. "Man, I'm trying, but Sam ..." He stopped. "Sam is afraid to get married for whatever reason. It has something to do with losing her parents and her friend Suzie. She blames herself. She wants to protect her heart and everyone she holds dear."

"Have you talked to her about that?" asked Hank.

"Humph. As if. She closes up whenever I ask her what the problem is."

"I am so glad that I don't have woman problems," said Hank.

"That's because you don't have a woman." Joe lightly punched him in the arm.

"True, that. But I'm not looking. I like my life just the way it is, free from stress, drama and especially commitment."

"Oh, you are going to fall hard, my friend," said Ben.

"Nope, nope, and nope." Hank shook his head. "It's never happening."

Joe stood. "Now that I cleaned you losers out and we know Hank has no love life, I'm going home to my sexy, pregnant wife who"—he glanced at his watch—"should be home right about now."

The men cleaned up the table and brought the beer bottles to the kitchen.

Mark said goodbye and closed the front door.

Sam wouldn't be back until later tonight. She had a case she was working on that required odd hours. He missed her.

He settled in front of the TV, hoping a game would be on, to take his mind away from one small woman.

Joe and Pete were lucky men. Ben was engaged to Marlee, and they would get married later this year. Hank, well, Hank just hadn't found the right woman, but he would.

He poured himself a scotch—stopped. Hell, he poured two more.

Might as well get drunk, then wonder why Sam wouldn't

commit to marriage when she obviously loved him. He was glad she was living with him now. He had more time to convince her marriage was the best thing for both of them.

# CHAPTER TWENTY

"It's so good to have you back." Sam hugged her Aunt Marcia. "How was vacation?"

Marcia smiled. "It was great. I'm mad at myself for never going on a cruise before."

Sam had never been on one herself. The thought of being on an enormous ship with hundreds of people drinking and carousing never appealed to her. But hey, lots of people loved cruising, so who was she to say otherwise?

"I hear you hired Jenna full-time and she's helping Phil," said Marcia.

"Yup. I want her to learn about the office. She's organized and smart. Phil can help train her to do some of his work."

"Terrific. I'm glad she worked out. Sometimes you don't get what you're hoping for with these temp agencies."

"True." Sam looked around Marcia's desk. All her cute personal items were placed on top, including the candy jar that drew employees to her desk like bees to honey. Marcia never had children, so there were lots of pictures of nieces and nephews, especially ones of her and Danny as kids. She wasn't a biological aunt but had been best friends with Sam's mother ever since they'd graduated from college.

Her hair was short and gray now, but her blue eyes still twinkled when she looked at Sam and Danny.

"Anything special that I need to know?" Marcia asked.

Sam shook her head. "Nope. Several of us are going over to the shelter today to give self-defense lessons. Jenna is coming with us."

"Good idea. A woman should know how to defend herself."

The front door opened, and two men walked in. "My new clients are here. I'll talk to you later. Would you send Hank in?"

Marcia nodded.

An hour later, Sam had secured the contract for security cameras around a new real-estate company.

Hank was taking point on installing the cameras.

Sam was proud that KnightGuard Security was growing so fast that she could hire new employees and branch out into the private investigation business.

She had the experience, but when she established Knight-Guard Security, she only wanted to concentrate on private security.

At three o'clock, she called out to Jenna that it was time to leave for the shelter. Jenna expressed an interest in the self-defense lessons KnightGuard Security offered the women. She'd been going for the past three weeks and was learning fast.

Hank and Luke would meet them there.

Penny had told her that several new women with a couple of kids had moved in. Sam preferred the one-on-one. It gave the women more hands-on practice.

"Ooof." Damn, she was going to be black and blue tomorrow. Jenna got up from the mat and blew out a breath.

"Jenna, you need to watch my body and anticipate my moves," said Luke. He gave her a big grin. "Or else you're going to be spending a lot of time on the mat."

She turned to him. "Oh yeah, big guy." She wagged her fingers at him. "Bring it on."

And he did. She was flat on her back on the mat again. How did she miss that last move?

"Again?"

Jenna leaned over, placed her hands on her knees and huffed. "Not just yet. You look like you need a break."

Luke cracked up. "Good one, Jenna."

She walked over to a small table and grabbed a cup of water. Who knew self-defense could be so hard? If it were up to her, she'd only concentrate on kicking a guy in the balls. Over and done.

The other women were taking it all too seriously. It wasn't as if a guy was going to randomly attack every woman he saw. Besides, what were they all doing here hiding out? They should grow some balls and take care of problems as they arose, not run away. She sighed. It was none of her business.

One factoid she learned working at KnightGuard Security was that Sam had spent a lot of time and money at the shelter over the years.

Why? As far as she could tell, none of Sam's friends had used a shelter. Why spend time and money on something you don't use?

She shrugged. It wasn't her time or money, so she didn't care. She never would have found the shelter if Sam hadn't driven. They had parked around back. Sam put in the code for the gate and told her that KnightGuard had secured the funds for the fencing. One more way they were making it safe for the residents.

It was nice to get out of the office. Working at Knight-Guard Security had its benefits, and strangely, she admired Sam. The woman owned her own business, was tenacious; she held her own and never let the alpha dogs in the company intimidate her. Sam was everything Jenna wanted to be.

There were lots of lessons to learn from Sam about running a business that she could use when it was her turn.

Jenna drank another cup of water. The lessons would go on for another hour and she had lots to learn. One never knew when self-defense lessons would come in handy.

# CHAPTER TWENTY-ONE

"Sam. Sam."

Sam dropped the groceries she was unloading and raced into the living room. Alex had been dropped off by the babysitter from her after-school activities and sounded panicked.

"What?" She stooped down and ran her hands over Alex's little body. "What's wrong, sweetie? Are you hurt?"

Alex scrunched her eyebrows. "Nooo."

"Why did you call me?"

"I wanted to tell you I have a new friend."

"New friend?" Sam waited a moment for her heart to start pumping again. Friend? Dealing with kids, especially little girls, was full of drama. "Come on into the kitchen and have a snack. You can tell me all about her."

"Him."

Him? Alex sat at the table as Sam poured her a glass of milk and handed her one of the cookies that Laura had baked and dropped off. Sam brought her coffee cup over and sat across from Alex.

"So tell me about him. What's his name?"

"Milo. He's new to the school, and he's really, really funny. And nice. He helped me with my letters."

Alex's eyes teared up. "But some of the kids don't like him and made fun of him. I hit them." Her little lips pursed up. "The teacher didn't see me."

Crap. Alex had been to the principal's office several times since school began, usually for fighting.

"Why did you hit them?"

"They were calling him limpo and gimpy."

"Why?"

"One of his legs is shorter than the other." Alex straightened her shoulders. "I won't let them call him names. I want to protect him."

"It takes a lot of courage for someone to stand up to bullies, but sometimes ..." Sam took Alex's hands in hers. "Sometimes we have to use our words, not our fists." Well, didn't she sound like a hypocrite. It wasn't advice she'd ever taken to heart.

Alex's eyes teared up. "Why do people call other people names? It's not nice."

"No, it isn't, and you're a brave little girl for sticking up for your friend. But hitting them isn't the answer. Promise me no more hitting." *How many times had her parents and grandparents said that to her?* She hadn't stopped.

"I promise." Alex interrupted her thoughts.

"What? What do you promise, sweetie?"

"I said I promise not to hit so much."

Sam scooched down and looked into Alex's innocent eyes. "Alex, it's a lot easier to hit someone than it is to change their mind. But I've learned people have to make up their own minds when they are wrong. Then the idea sticks with them. Hitting them makes them angry. Do you understand?"

Alex bit her lip, thought for a minute, and nodded. "I

understand. But if I talk to someone and they don't change their mind, can I still hit them?"

*Yes.* "No. It doesn't work like that. Will you try talking with them first from now on?"

Alex mumbled, "Okay."

Sam laughed to herself. *Bloodthirsty little beast.*

"Why don't you invite Milo over some weekend. I'd like to meet him."

"Ohhh, that would be fun." Alex clapped her hands. "He's really funny and nice."

Alex wandered off, leaving Sam at the table, wondering how her mother ever felt about her fighting. She always stuck up for the underdog. But shortly after her parents died, one little girl teased her and Danny for not having parents. She had a mommy and a daddy, Sam told the girl as she pummeled her, but they were in heaven. The girl never teased them again.

Not for the first time, she wondered whether her mother was proud of her for standing up for the bullied and weak or embarrassed because she was sent to the principal's office so often. She shook her head. It didn't matter because Sam would always stand for those weaker than her. She had to believe her mother would have been proud of that.

One of the programs that had helped her was Tae Kwon Do.

Her grandparents had enrolled her in the after-school program. Not only did it give her confidence but it channeled her excess energy and gave her self-respect and discipline.

The classes that her employees taught at the shelter usually had a couple of kids in them and were in the afternoon.

It would be good practice for Alex to go with her to the shelter as well as enroll in a Tae Kwon Do after-school class. She'd check with Mark. He had the skills to teach Alex, but it would be better to come from a teacher who had experience with kids. Two things Sam knew for sure were that you were never too young to learn self-defense and you never knew when you would need it. Although she prayed Alex would never have to protect herself.

# CHAPTER TWENTY-TWO

C olin stepped out of the tiny shower seconds before the lukewarm water turned frigid.

He had the water flow timed to the second, especially after freezing his balls off the first time it happened. He hated this dump. Soon enough, he'd be rolling in dough. Then he'd get one of those spiffy condos on the water, have someone come in to clean and whatever. The whatever got him excited.

No sense thinking about the future. Picking up a towel from the floor, he sniffed it. Ewww. Musty and sour-smelling. He shrugged. At least it was dry.

His dump didn't come with a washer and dryer. Everything had to be hand-washed as needed. And clean towels weren't a necessity.

Pulling on a pair of sweats, he debated shaving but decided not to.

It was a rainy Saturday. No work today.

The only things on his schedule were watching a game on the vintage TV in the corner, fuzzy as the picture was, and listening to the mics that he'd planted in Mark's house. How lucky was he that day—meeting Sam Knight, being able to plant the mics and getting paid to do work he loved.

He hoped to hear something useful.

He heard Stone mention to one guy at work that he was looking forward to spending time at home with Sam and the kid.

The mics wouldn't work long-term. He needed to get any information he could before the batteries died. He wouldn't get another chance to go back to Mark's house. He planned to be long gone before they ever found the mics.

Colin knew from Chrissie that the bitch who owned Salt & Sea told Sam about her problems, and he wondered whether Sam had put two and two together yet. If she hadn't, he needed to step up the harassment, not spread it out. Calling to complain about food poisoning at Salt & Sea and then damaging the cars in the parking lot was fun and done.

His scheme was to tease and torment Sam—well, her friends—before the coup de grâce. But he also needed to move forward quickly and get on with his plans. Sam's death would be the grand finale. He was going to make sure she burned in hell for putting Tony in jail and destroying his livelihood. Well, for any number of reasons.

He grabbed a cup from the sink that wasn't too stained and poured himself a cup of coffee. Damn, the sink was full again. A dishwasher didn't come with his place either. Later, he'd call Chrissie to come and clean. Loved that he could and that she hated it but came anyway.

He pulled the carton of milk out from the fridge, smelled it. Aaagh—sour. He shook his head. At least he had sugar.

He liked his coffee like he liked his women. Smooth and sweet with no back-talking.

Pulling out a chair, he sat at the rickety wooden kitchen table, turned on his phone and dialed the SIM card on the mic.

Conversations started rolling in. Oh, fun. Sam was taking the girl to a friend's house. But first, Sam was going to buy fencing equipment for the class the kid was taking. Wowsers. That was big news. *Fencing? What a waste of money*.

Mark was going to Tampa for some special materials for the next project his company was working on.

Yup. Their lives were chock full of mystery and intrigue.

Sam and her team were teaching self-defense at a nonprofit center for abused women on Thursday—now that was interesting.

Somebody named Claire was planning a party to celebrate the director's ten years at the shelter. He liked parties. Maybe he'd invite himself to the party somehow. But then again, maybe not. The hulks at KnightGuard would most likely be there, and he wasn't a fool. Besides, Sam and Mark would wonder why he was there.

He remembered that a couple of Tony's ex-girlfriends, the bitches who testified against him, lived at a shelter in Black Pointe for a while. How many shelters for abused women were in the city? One thing he knew was that the shelters didn't advertise their address.

It would be great if it was the same one Tony's exes lived in.

Could he get that lucky?

If the director had been there for that long, she surely knew those women. He knew where the shelter was located from the tracker on Sam's car.

He needed to think about how he wanted to handle the director. Perhaps a visit and a special present from him to celebrate her ten years as a lying scumbag bitch would be in order.

# CHAPTER TWENTY-THREE

Penny closed the shelter door behind her and shut her eyes—inhale and exhale, repeat. She stretched her neck to loosen the tight knots that were giving her a headache.

Today had been a traumatic day with new clients coming in. She felt sick when she had to turn away a woman with two little ones because the shelter was full. Luckily, another shelter in the next town over had room for them.

The past few days had been oppressively hot, although ominous black clouds were forming in the distance. The continual heat and humidity brought out aggressions, so it wasn't unusual to have a larger than normal intake on days like this.

Sounds of children's laughter wafted past the door. She loved hearing the little ones laugh after living in fear for so long. But their laughter caused her pain. Memories of a small boy with a bright smile caused a tear to run down her cheek. Aaagh. Not going there today. Life was good—she nodded to herself. Life was good.

Sam and Claire were coming in soon to discuss more

funding for the shelter and its programs. They were a godsend.

Sam believed in empowering women, and her generosity with time and money made life a little easier for the women and kids who gave up everything to be safe. And Claire, gosh, her coming into millions and giving it away? Score for the shelter. Claire was happy now, but Penny could tell there was pain in her past.

The building next door was for sale, and she hoped to convince them to buy it or at least help with the down payment.

It was a heartbreaking commentary on the times that more shelters were needed for abused women, although she was grateful for the space she had and sad that she needed more space.

Lydia, the nighttime intake person, had already settled in. Penny walked to her over-the-hill-but-still-running sedan. Tonight, she would watch a movie, preferably a comedy, and have pizza delivered. She pulled out her key to unlock her car.

The drive home was only twenty minutes on a good day. She pulled into her driveway and breathed a sigh of relief. Home. Just that one word made everything all right.

The fact that it was her home and not an apartment or shelter room made it even better. The tiny house wouldn't win any house and garden awards, but it was perfect for her. One of these days, she would plant a little garden in front and paint the front door. Oh, and get brand-new furniture to replace the thrift shop finds—one of these days.

A drop of rain fell on her face.

Remembering she had clothes on the line to bring in, she walked around to the back.

Darn, the basket was inside. Penny inserted the key into the back door and put the keys back in her pocket. Suddenly, she was pulled backwards by a hand that covered her mouth. An odd odor hit her. What was it? It smelled like varnish.

What was wrong with her? The hell with trying to identify odors. She needed to run from the danger. Her body was shaking. Penny whimpered. She felt dizzy and tried to pull away. She tried to scream. But the man was strong; he kept her upright, digging his fingers into her mouth.

Struggling to get out of the man's grasp, Penny tried to remember all the self-defense moves the KnightGuard Security employees had shown the women. She wasn't there for all the classes. A mistake she'd remedy if she got out of this alive.

She tried to headbutt him, but the man anticipated the move and held her tightly to his body. Penny couldn't get enough room to kick him or stomp on his insole.

The man pulled her back into the trees surrounding her house. Even if she escaped, the fence surrounding the property was too high to climb. Oh God, was he going to rape her?

Could anyone see him? Should she fight or let him have his way? Damn, what did the books say? She couldn't remember. Or was he going to kill her? Maybe she should have cut down the trees. Funny how trivial things passed in her mind.

She squirmed and tried to wiggle her way out of his grip. Branches scratched her arms and legs.

In a flash, he turned her around, holding her hands together over her head with one of his. A mask covered his face, but she saw two angry brown eyes assessing her.

"Stop fighting, bitch." Spittle flew at her face. Ugh.

She tried to kick him, but it angered him more. With his other hand, he ripped her blouse down the middle. Buttons popped everywhere, exposing her chest.

Then he swung at her stomach, connecting with her solar plexus. Dreadful memories of similar past incidents flashed through her mind. She doubled over, the breath knocked out of her, but he wasn't done. He swung his fist at her face, then repeated it once more.

"I told you to stop fighting." He let go of her hands and pulled her up by her hair. Penny gasped for air—the pain.

Penny's eye was closing.

Her cheek was on fire, she was gulping for air, and she was sure that her head was missing a clump of hair. Penny knew the man wasn't done with her. She had to do something to help herself.

Her keys! She always carried pepper spray on her key chain.

Her hand fumbled for the keys in her pocket. She touched them, but her hand was sweating and slipped off the slick cannister.

She tried again. Clasped the cylinder tighter.

The man pulled her hair harder. She tried to reach for his hands, but he was much taller than her. Tears fell down her cheek. With his other hand, he pulled down her bra and squeezed her breast hard. She screamed.

He laughed.

Finally, she clasped the pepper spray. Pulled it out quickly. Uncapped it with one hand while she tried to push his hand off her breast with the other.

She brought the canister up, praying she wouldn't spray herself, and pushed the button.

A stream of pepper spray hit the man in his face. He screamed, "Son of a bitch!" and covered his face with his hands, trying to brush the pepper spray out of his eyes. His eyes were red and raw looking, but that didn't stop him from backhanding her.

The last thing Penny remembered before she blacked out was falling to the ground.

DAMN THE BITCH.

Colin's eyes were on fire. He got in one last lick, threw the woman on the ground and then stumbled into the bushes. He didn't dare touch his eyes. Besides, they were mostly closed. But he had to get away before someone spotted him. His car was a block over—a long block over.

Colin's heart beat like a drum. He pulled off the mask and put it in his pocket. Liquid from his face dripped down his chin. Either it was his nose running like a sieve or he was drooling. Didn't matter. He was in agony.

Panic set in. Which way was his car? His body turned in circles. Finally, he sat down, sure that he sat in a thorn bush when he felt something puncture his ass, but it didn't matter. The bitch was still passed out next to him, and he kicked her in the side for good measure.

He had the good sense to know he was panicking. Deep breaths. Shit, that hurt. His lungs were on fire. He had to get out of here and call Chrissie.

After what seemed like an hour, Colin got up. The woman was still on the ground. He hoped he hadn't killed her, but he had other things to worry about. Like where his car was?

He finally remembered where he parked. He slipped out of the driveway. Cars whizzed by him. What the hell was going on with this traffic? There had been little when he parked. He knew he was staggering like a drunk, but he could hardly see. Colin prayed no cops were in the area. He didn't want to explain why he'd been pepper-sprayed.

He needed to flush his eyes with water. Did he even have water in his car?

Of course not. Why would he? He'd never expected to get that much resistance from the woman or that she carried pepper spray. He needed to get to his car now. Keeping close to the bushes on the sidewalk, he finally spotted it and reached for his keys. Spent five minutes in agony trying to open the car door. When he finally did, he eased into the passenger side. No way in hell could he drive. He pulled out his phone and stared at the numbers, which were floating and fuzzy. Finally speed-dialed Chrissie.

She didn't answer. Where the hell was the bitch?

He waited a few agonizing minutes and dialed again. She answered, and he told her to get her ass over with water and leaned back. He'd never felt such burning pain in his eyes. His lungs were still screaming for air.

Where was Chrissie?

Had it been fifteen minutes, like she said? Was she lost? Chrissie never could follow directions.

He leaned into the seat, tried to catch his breath and not touch his eyes. Why did all this shit fall on him?

A knock on the window made him jump. Chrissie opened the door.

"Holy crap. What happened to you?"

"Never mind. Did you bring the water?"

"Of course. I brought a gallon."

He got out of the car. She poured the water over his eyes. Some of the intensity of the burning went away, but his eyes were still burning.

"I need you to drive me home."

"Okay." She sniffed at him and gagged. "You need to take those clothes off. You stink."

Great. Now he had to strip on the street.

No cars were coming at the moment, so he quickly took off his shirt and pants. He rolled them into a ball and threw them into the trunk.

"Get me home. We'll get your car in the morning."

He opened the passenger door, and Chrissie got in the driver's seat.

Thankfully, it was Friday night. No way would he have

been able to go to work the next day and explain why his eyes were red and puffy.

His entire plan was beat to crap. A total disaster—well, not quite. He got in some good licks on the director.

Damn. His elation plummeted when he realized that he never got to give the bitch his message for Sam.

---

SAM AND MARK rushed into Black Pointe General Hospital. Sam had received the call that someone assaulted Penny at her home the previous night.

The waiting room was eerily quiet. The receptionist told her what room Penny was in, and Sam pressed the elevator button to the sixth floor.

"Do you want me to go in with you?" Mark asked on the way up.

*Did she?* Yes.

But she'd have to make that determination when she saw Penny.

There it was—room 602. The door was half-open.

A nurse walked by as Sam knocked on the door. "She's sedated right now. But you can go in."

Sam let out the breath she was holding and nodded to Mark.

They walked into the room, and Sam gasped. Penny looked so small lying on the hospital bed.

An IV had been inserted into her hand. She looked like a mummy. Her head was wrapped in bandages. One eye was closed, and the other was puffy and swollen. Bruises from the attacker's fingers were turning colors on her face and neck. Who knew what other injuries she had? Dried tears streaked Penny's cheeks.

Someone had savagely beaten her.

"Jesus," Mark hissed. "Who would do something like this?"

"Some asshole who's going to get a new one when I find him," said Sam.

Penny moaned and thrashed about. Sam placed her hand on Penny's arm and softly rubbed it. The motion helped calm Penny a little.

"I'm going to have whoever is free come and guard her until we know what's going on. She doesn't have any family here."

"Good idea," said Mark. "It makes me sick to my stomach to see someone, especially a woman, beaten like this. I wonder what happened."

Sam shook her head. "We won't know until she wakes up. Let's talk to the nurse."

They walked to the nurse's station to ask. No one had much information except a neighbor heard Penny moaning, came over to investigate and found her beaten and lying in the bushes.

Mark was going to call Phil and ask if there were any security cameras nearby that could identify the man.

Sam settled in a chair by Penny's bed. Mark stayed for a while and then left to get some coffee. Penny groaned and opened one eye.

"Penny, I'm so sorry. Can you tell me what happened?"

Penny closed her eye and then opened it again. "I hurt."

Sam gently rubbed her hand. "I know, hon. We're going to catch the SOB who did this to you. Did he say anything?"

"No. Just hurt me."

"Did he rape you?"

"Tried but pepper-sprayed him." Penny groaned again and closed her eye.

"Shhh. Don't talk. I'll be sitting here for a while." Sam kissed her forehead. "Sleep now."

Sam stood and stretched her body; tension was knotting her muscles and giving her a headache. Random things were happening. Was it a reflection of the times or something else?

Mark came back with a cup of coffee for her and sat next to her. He looked at Penny and sighed.

"Phil is checking cameras. Did she say anything else?" Mark asked.

"No. Penny didn't live in the best of neighborhoods, and I'm not sure what kind of security they have at her place. I'll have Hank check it out."

"Sam, do you think this violence is connected? First Laura, now Penny?"

Sam sipped her coffee. "It's so hard to know. The Riverwalk is filled with locals and tourists, and where tourists congregate, you have criminals and crime. That wasn't the first time damage was done to cars in Laura's parking lot. The last time it was kids thinking they were funny. Penny doesn't live in the best of neighborhoods, and there's a lot of crime in her area. Let's wait and see if Phil can pull anything up."

Mark gave her a small smile and reached for her hand.

Between mending fences with Mark, adjusting to having a child around, running a business, and with everything else that was happening, Sam was overwhelmed. She didn't know if these events were directed at her or just random. Either way, it was painful to watch her friends hurting.

## CHAPTER TWENTY-FOUR

I t had been a long week, and Sam was glad when Friday night came. Penny was on the mend and staying at home. Sam had whoever was free drive by and check in on her.

Time to relax and share a meal with friends or family. Mark and Sam prepped the meal, laughing and sharing a beer. Mark loved to barbecue, cook, bake, whatever, and she enjoyed eating. It was a match made in heaven. The weather was perfect for eating outdoors. The grill was sizzling. Burgers were in the fridge. All they needed were guests.

The doorbell rang as they relaxed in the living room. Hailey and Danny were expected for dinner, and the couple was usually early, so their being late without calling was unusual but not worrisome. Sam let out a sigh of relief; she hadn't wanted to call them, too much like stalking.

Sam glanced at her watch. "I'll get the door. Why don't you bring in the chips? They must be hungry."

Mark got up to bring in the snacks.

She opened the door, and Hailey stomped in, followed by a concerned-looking Danny.

"Wow. What's got your shorts in a twist?" asked Sam after she gave them hugs.

"You won't believe what happened," moaned Hailey.

Sam studied her, checking her up and down. Nothing seemed out of place.

Outside of Hailey's face being paler than normal, she was impeccably dressed as usual in slacks and a sleeveless top. Her blond hair was neatly in a ponytail—no marks, scrapes or injuries. So no one had attacked her. She hadn't fallen. Had the store been robbed? What was the problem?

"What happened?" Mark chose that moment to come out with a tray for the chips and dip, a glass of wine for Hailey, and a beer for Danny. He laid them on the coffee table.

Hailey collapsed onto the sofa. Her nostrils flared, and she was gesturing so boldly, Danny moved the refreshments away from her. It surprised Sam to see Hailey so upset since she was usually an even-tempered woman. Sam sat and patiently waited while Hailey got herself under control.

"My book group met this afternoon. We had the most engaging conversation with that new author I told you about." She looked at Sam for confirmation.

"Yes. I remember you telling me about her."

"Well," Hailey huffed. She rubbed the back of her neck. "We broke up around four o'clock after the book signing." She gave a small smile. "A very successful book signing, I might add."

Hailey reached for the glass of wine and took a big gulp. Too big a gulp. She choked on it, and Danny patted her back. When Hailey got herself under control, she said, "I was closing the shop when the author and several women who had been at the signing raced back in. Their tires had been slashed."

"Crap!"

Hailey bobbed her head. "I know, right?"

"Where did this happen?" asked Mark.

"Behind the shop," said Hailey. She reached for the glass of wine again, but her hand shook, and she pulled it back.

"Was it one tire on each car or more?"

"One. Not that it makes any difference. It happened to five cars, all parked directly by the back door where my signs are. I checked the other cars in the lot that were farther away, but they weren't damaged. I'm going to assume someone was targeting my store or me."

Sam pictured the cute bookstore that Hailey owned downtown. Her business, The BookShop, was in an alley off the main drag, surrounded by several upscale clothing stores, a coffee shop, and a bistro.

People were constantly walking up and down the alley.

Parking was on the main street or in the parking lot behind the buildings. There were five parking spaces, all marked, for each business in the back. The area was populated enough that there weren't many safety issues, unlike the more touristy areas.

Hailey exhaled and sat back on the sofa, tapping her feet. Danny put his arms around her neck and started massaging her shoulders; she gave a slight groan and relaxed into him.

"I hate to be such a downer." Tears formed in her eyes. "This has never happened before, and if it gets out that parking around my shop isn't safe, I'll lose customers."

"I'm sorry that it happened to you," said Sam. "Did you catch anything on camera?"

"Well, that's the thing," Hailey said. "The cameras only got a partial view of the area. All you can see is a single person. It looked like a man dressed all in black was moving between cars, stopping every once in a while and ducking down. Now I know why."

"I looked at the tapes when I picked Hailey up," said

Danny. "The streetlight was out, so it was difficult to see where he ran to or if he had any identifying features."

He looked at his wife. "We'll put more security cameras back there as soon as possible so you don't have to worry."

Hailey gave him a small smile, and he kissed her forehead.

"Did you call the police?" asked Mark.

"Yes," said Danny. "That's what took us so long. The police took everyone's information. We called for tow trucks and Triple A and made sure everyone would get home okay." He sighed. "Nothing like this has happened before in the area."

Sam leaned back in her chair and took a long sip of wine, mulling over what they said. Hailey's news was disturbing on a couple of levels. A slight shiver sent her Spidey sense into overdrive. The news that Hailey's customers' cars were targeted distressed her. This destruction felt too close to home.

And now that she thought about it, Laura had a similar problem at her restaurant.

However, her restaurant was in a touristy area, with many out-of-towners walking around.

The crime rate was higher there and damage to vehicles wasn't unusual, so Sam thought little about it when Laura mentioned it.

But with Laura's restaurant and Hailey's shop targeted, it was too much of a coincidence. Then Penny's attack. She hadn't connected them. But if she were a betting person, they were connected. Was this a message the stalker was sending? That he could reach her anytime through her friends? If that was the case, he was in a world of trouble because no one attacked her friends or family. But first, she had to catch him. And that was proving difficult.

She shrugged her shoulders. Nothing to be done tonight. She would relax and try not to think about these events.

Tomorrow, when she got to the office, she'd call her friend on the police force and ask if they had any more information. Then she would call the girls and tell them to watch out for any unusual activity. She'd have Hank Peterman install the security cameras for Hailey and ask Phil to look at other security cameras in the area. The police wouldn't do much more than look at Hailey's cameras, but Phil was extremely good at what he did. Maybe they'd get lucky and could glimpse someone's face.

What else was she missing? There had to be something she could do, but what?

The stalker hadn't targeted her personally, left no threatening messages or even tried to attack her. She was cautious and hadn't seen anyone overtly following her. So it made sense that someone she didn't recognize could have followed her when she met her friends at Neptune's Navel, Salt & Sea or the bookstore and she wouldn't have known. They could have followed her friends to where they worked or lived. Whoever was following her was smart—and good.

Since she had the weird feeling that someone was watching her, she'd been extra vigilant. Was it time to let the office know there was a problem? Another thing to put on her to-do list. She hated to use up company time with no concrete evidence, but those around her were getting hurt. It was time.

The stalking had to be stopped before it got out of hand and someone died.

If only she knew who to look at or where.

## CHAPTER TWENTY-FIVE

**D**anny stood in her doorway. "Knock, knock."

"Hey Danny, come on in."

"I wanted to update you on the camera installation"

"Great." Sam leaned back in her chair.

"Hank and I went to the BookShop this morning and installed them. Hailey's whole parking lot is now covered. Although security cameras back there should have been the landlord's problem, not Hailey's." Danny pulled out a chair in front of her desk and sat down.

"I agree. Any problems with the installation?" asked Sam. She'd placed the work order first thing Saturday morning, and the cameras arrived last night.

Sam wasn't allowing anyone to terrorize her friend and sister-in-law. On the one hand, she hoped the creep would come back and they could catch him. On the other hand, she didn't want Hailey to be working and worrying about her store, her customers and her safety.

Danny leaned back into the chair, folded his arms and stared at Sam. Silence.

"What?"

"Are you going to tell me what the hell is going on?" he asked.

*No.* She didn't want to. She hadn't wanted to drag her brother or the other employees into something being done to her by some unknown character. Something she thought she could handle herself, but perhaps she was fooling herself. Perhaps she was too wrapped up in herself to realize she needed help. Perhaps it was time to come clean with her friends and employees before one of them got seriously hurt or killed.

She took a deep breath and exhaled, trying to get the butterflies in her stomach to stop moving. Danny deserved an answer, but she couldn't get the words out. Her attention moved to shuffling pens around the desk. *How long could she postpone her embarrassment and admit she needed help?*

The sun coming through the blinds created a zebra effect on her desk. She noticed the dust motes dancing in the air. Considering the gloomy atmosphere in her office, they probably weren't dancing but fighting. Dust motes, pens—she was deflecting, and that wasn't like her. Where was her courage? What was wrong with her that she couldn't take the blame for this? She was being foolish, letting her ego get in the way of the safety of her and her friends.

She glanced at Danny. It didn't take a genius to know that her brother was not happy with her. His arms were crossed, and he glared at her, but he hadn't yelled, growled, or snarled. Yet his anger hovered over him like a black cloud.

Usually, she was the one who got angry.

Danny had always been the lover, preferring not to cause a scene until he had no choice. The army gave him skills that he didn't need to use very often, but when he did, watch out. If the stalking and damaging of property was to prove the point that the stalker could get to her anywhere and anytime by attacking her friends—it hurt her badly. Danny glared at her but didn't say a word.

More pen-shuffling. She couldn't look at him. The silence was deafening.

"I'm being stalked," she finally mumbled.

"Are you shitting me?" Danny slammed his fist on her desk, causing her pens to roll away. "Why haven't you said anything?"

He rubbed the back of his neck. His brows knitted together. He opened and closed his mouth like a guppy. He was furious.

Her heart beat wildly. She wasn't scared but embarrassed.

He closed, then opened his eyes and huffed, "Okay then. Why don't you start at the beginning?"

"A couple of months ago, I had this feeling someone was watching me."

Sam clearly remembered when she first put a name to her uneasiness. "I was at Moon Beach, contemplating life just before you and Hailey got married."

Danny's mouth fell open. "You've been dealing with this for two months? Alone? What the hell were you thinking?"

Sam rubbed her chest. "I guess I wasn't." She placed her elbows on the table and rested her head on her hand. "I haven't said anything because I haven't seen anyone who looked suspicious. When Laura told me about problems at the restaurant, I dismissed it as a typical stupid crime at the Riverwalk. I'm still on the fence about Penny. She lives in a dicey neighborhood. But when Hailey described the destruction in the parking lot, I suspected this stalker was targeting my friends. I didn't want to involve the company before I knew for sure."

Sam pushed her chair back and stood. "I've been a fool for

putting my friends and family in danger because I didn't want to ask for help." A flush crept across her cheeks and down her neck.

Danny came around her desk and pulled her into his arms. "Sam, you are not alone in this world. You protect everyone. You need to let those closest to you know when you need help."

"I know." Sam sighed. "I know. It's so difficult to let someone help me. I'm the one who owns a security company. The one who should be able to find a stalker. The one to protect those around me."

"Why? No one is alone in this world. We are a community of people helping each other."

He let her go and returned to his seat. "Ever since we were little, you took charge. Protecting, supporting, standing up for the bullied, always making sure everyone was safe. You've never asked anyone for help. But this time if you don't —I will."

Sam tapped her fingers on the desk and nodded. *Yes*, it was time to ask for help.

Danny interrupted her thoughts. "Does Mark know?"

She shook her head. "I haven't mentioned it yet. I was planning to talk to him tonight."

"Glad I'm not going to be part of that discussion. He's going to be pissed."

That was an understatement. Sam slumped in her chair. "I know." Pissed was probably too kind for what Mark would be. It wasn't a discussion she was looking forward to, but it had to be done. Now.

Damn, she ran a security company. They investigated, provided protection, and solved problems—that's what they were good at.

Her staff was more than competent to handle this situation. They did it every day.

But first, she had to let them know there was a problem.

Then they could develop a plan of action and find the bastard who was targeting her and her friends.

She knew it would get worse. It always did.

# CHAPTER TWENTY-SIX

They were enjoying drinks after a late dinner. Alex was in bed. Sam thought it was a perfect time to talk to Mark about the stalking and how it related to the incidents that had occurred.

They were relaxed. Or as relaxed as she was going to be. Mark was laughing at something that had happened at work. Her heart was beating like a jackhammer.

He frowned at her, then squinted his eyes. "Something on your mind, babe?"

She tried to be professional about it. Give him just the facts. Tried not to make it worse than it was. She failed. Mark's lips thinned. He sat there processing the information. Then he yelled, "Goddamn it, Sam, why didn't you tell me this before?"

She blew out a breath. "Look, I wasn't a hundred percent sure, and I didn't want to worry you."

A vein in his neck bulged and twitched. His brows knit together. His eyes narrowed. Silence. At that point, she knew she'd said the wrong thing.

"Worry me?" Mark's voice got quiet.

"Yeah?" she mumbled and hated that it sounded like a question.

Then he slammed his hands on the table. "Worry me? What the hell? Am I four years old? Do I look like I need protection? And why would you assume I wouldn't want to know that someone was stalking the woman I love and that I wouldn't want to protect you?"

"Look, Mark. I can take care of myself." Sam stood by the chair. She knew she was not handling this right. Hell, not even close to right. What a mess.

Mark stalked over and stepped into her bubble. She stepped back, something she never did, but he followed her until her back was against the wall.

He placed his hands on her shoulders.

"Sam, I know you can take care of yourself. I've seen you in action. Remember?" he said softly.

She nodded.

"I'm a SEAL, and if some slimewad thinks he's going to put his hands on you or torment your friends to get to you, it's not happening, babe."

"Mark, this is my business. You need to step back. I do this for a living."

She knew the minute his eyes got darker that it was the wrong thing to say. Crap, nothing was going the way she hoped.

He removed his hands and took a deep breath, then another. Pursed his lips. Took his time responding. "Sam. Understand this. I know you can take care of yourself. I'm so proud of you. But you tend not to ask for help. I bet you haven't told your employees yet. Have you?"

She shook her head.

That had been the most embarrassing part of the conversation. How would her employees react? They'd be mad and probably wonder why she was in charge if she didn't trust them with this information.. They would see that her actions, rather inactions, put them all in danger.

"Damn." He ran his fingers through his hair. "I love you. I'll step back and let you handle this, but remember, I may be an ex-SEAL, but I'm also a guy—a guy who wants to protect the love of his life. I'm not letting this go. I want to know what is going on. What the plan is. So deal with it. Understand?"

How could she answer that? She was the protector. She didn't need protection. Did she? But just maybe her ego was again getting in the way of things.

"Yes, I understand, and I'm sorry I haven't mentioned this before to you. I've scheduled a meeting at KnightGuard tomorrow." Sam put out her hand and rubbed his arm. "I promise I will get this under control."

"And?"

"And—" Sam sighed. "I will keep you informed."

He stared into her eyes and nodded.

The anger in his eyes had been replaced by lust.

"Good." He got up real close and hugged her. Whispered in her ear, "Now get in the bedroom and take your clothes off." Mark's voice was soft but demanding. "I need to fuck you. Now."

Sam understood his fears and his need to be close to her. She'd never want anyone hurting him, either.

She'd take this break because she knew that tomorrow, all hell was going to break loose. Her employees were going to rake her over the coals, and she couldn't blame them.

# CHAPTER TWENTY-SEVEN

Outside, the weather was as ominous as the looks her employees were giving her. They were all sitting around the long conference table in her office. Sam had asked Marcia to make sure they were not disturbed.

Sam had outlined what she knew about the stalker, which wasn't much, and when it started. She explained that she thought the incidents at Laura's restaurant, Hailey's shop and possibly Penny's attack were aimed at her and that she had no idea who was stalking her or why.

There was silence as everyone absorbed the information.

The disappointment on their faces was distressing. Her heart thumped to its own beat. She'd let her people down. The open-door policy she'd always touted was just words right now, and Sam felt a deep sadness and disappointment that she kept her personal life so close to the vest. Why had she? *Ego.* The situation had affected her friends. She didn't know who would be next. Sam was lost in thought, and she jumped when a loud rumble of thunder shook the building.

"Sam, I'm gonna say not mentioning this was a mistake,"

said Ben. "If Marlee had been targeted and I didn't know about the threat until now, I would be furious. Right now, this creep has only damaged cars. What if the next time, one of our women gets hurt or worse?"

Ben was right. She knew Ben still hadn't forgiven himself for not protecting Marlee better when he first started working at KnightGuard Security.

Of course, he had just come off a case where his girlfriend had been killed in front of him, and the failure still haunted him. Sam shivered. That had been a bad case. Marlee Burns, now Ben's fiancée, watched the CEO of her company, Robert Gilligan, kill her boss after he accused Robert of embezzling from the company. Robert's girlfriend and co-conspirator, Amber, pretended to be Marlee's friend.

Then Robert and Amber tried to kill Marlee by setting her house on fire. It had been a convoluted mess.

Sam swallowed hard. This fiasco was her mistake; she couldn't blame her employees and friends for being upset.

But at least they weren't yelling at her like Mark had when she told him what was happening.

"Got to agree with Ben here," chimed in Joe. "If two of your friends have already been targeted, Claire, Grace, or Julie could be next. Or the babies. Creeps don't care who they hurt." Joe scowled. The vein on the side of his neck twitched. He kept his voice low and modulated, but Sam knew he was furious.

"Amen to that," said Pete.

Sam looked around the table. These were her employees and friends.

She was embarrassed that she hadn't mentioned anything to them before. Danny had been kind to her yesterday. However, he had been furious that his wife was targeted and all because Sam had kept things close to the vest.

"Tell us what you think or know so far," said Veronica

Styles. Veronica was a new hire in an all-male company and was fast becoming one of the more popular employees with clients, mainly because some women were more comfortable with a female security guard. She could kick ass with the best of them. "This has got to stop before someone gets killed."

Sam spent the next few minutes telling them what she thought or knew.

"Do you think this is someone you've dealt with before or helped put in jail?" asked Hank.

"Good question. Let me think." She closed her eyes, rummaging in her mind for all the cases where someone went to jail. There weren't a lot because KnightGuard Security provided mostly protection for celebrities, politicians, or events. Although lately they were investigating fraud and missing-person cases.

"This is what I've come up with so far. Grace's stalker, Ken Williams, is still in jail. He was never well-liked, if at all, so I'm not sure anyone is taking up his cause. His girlfriend, Rachel Lang, got out of jail a year ago and moved away. Grace tells me she moved to California and has given up her political blog," said Sam.

"Robert Gilligan and Amber Logan are still in jail," said Ben.

Sam glanced over at him.

He threw up his hands. "Hey, I keep up with things. They had no problem trying to burn Marlee alive. I will be checking on them for a long time."

So who else had she a run-in with?

There was Aaron Oakman, the man who stalked and kidnapped Julie Harrington, now Julie Carson. Aaron was dead. Sam knew that for a fact since she killed Aaron when he tried to shoot her. After forcing Julie to strip and all the other horrible things Aaron did to Julie, it was all good. She would never feel guilty about killing him.

"Anyone else?" asked Joe. Claire's ex-husband was dead, but Keith's mistress, Hillary Santmeyer, was alive.

Sam tapped the table and blew out a big breath of air. "Besides Hillary, who's now in a mental institution, the only other person I had trouble with and put in jail was Tony Moranti, and that was a few years ago. I heard he died in prison about three months ago."

"Jeez, that's a name I haven't heard in a while," said Danny. He shook his head. "What a shithead. I'm glad he's dead, and I hope it was a painful death."

"Who's Tony Moranti?" asked Veronica.

*Who's Tony Moranti?* Just the blood-sucking slimeball who abused Suzie, her best friend from high school, and then killed her. The buffoon thought he'd gotten away with murder, but there were other women out there that he'd abused who were more than willing to talk if it meant putting him in jail.

Moranti was Sam's first foray into the world of investigations. After she completed her BS in criminal justice and a year of studying criminology and firearms training, she applied for her Class CC Private Investigator Intern license. Then the hard work began. She needed a licensed PI as a sponsor.

She went through half of the agencies in Black Pointe before Otis Hood took her under his wing. She'd heard it all before she started working for Hood Private Investigations— you're too short; you're too inexperienced; you're a female— our clients only want males; you're tiny; how would you take someone down?

Otis had watched her at the gym and had been impressed. They started talking.

He'd been amazed that she held her own in the self-defense department. Otis hired her and taught her everything he knew, and when he helped her bring Tony Moranti down for Suzie's murder, her life was complete.

Otis helped her set up KnightGuard Security after he retired. He passed away last year.

Sam explained who Tony was and what he did.

"Could he have someone in the area avenging his incarceration?" asked Luke.

"I don't know, but Tony's the only one I had dealings with who grew up here, maybe still has friends around. They were all a bunch of lowlifes. I wouldn't put it past any one of them. Besides, I believe he was selling drugs. That might be one avenue to explore."

She turned to Phil. "Why don't you get started on finding everything you can about Tony, who his friends were, who visited him in jail, who his girlfriends were, where he lived, etc., and when you have the information, we'll revisit him."

There wasn't much else to discuss. First, though, Sam looked at her employees, who had become friends. She owed them more than an apology, but it was a start. "I'm sorry I haven't mentioned this. I'm sorry I didn't trust you with this information, and most of all, I'm sorry some of your loved ones, my friends, have suffered. Please forgive me."

No one said a word.

"Sam, I believe I speak for all of us, especially since I've been here the longest," said Pete. "We all look up to you. However, you put the company, us and our families in danger. If this happens again, I'll be the first one out the door."

Sam closed her eyes and took a deep breath. She'd been so caught up in her feelings, she hadn't considered how her friends and employees felt—that she betrayed them by not confiding in them. Pete wasn't wrong. She felt ashamed.

"Fair enough." A flush crept along her cheeks. " I am sincerely sorry. This will never happen again. I trust all of you with my life." Her hands were sweating. Sam prayed they would accept her apology.

Pete looked around the table. She saw several barely imperceptible nods, then he looked back at Sam. "Apology accepted. But please don't cut us out again. We are all good at what we do. You're not alone here. This is a dangerous business, and we need to protect each other."

She looked around at all the faces she cared about.

They were not just her employees but her friends. They had her back, as she had theirs. It was time for a change.

She wasn't alone.

# CHAPTER TWENTY-EIGHT

R iverwalk was bustling. Not only did Sam have to park a block away, but she had to dodge a half dozen groups of people window-shopping on her way to Salt & Sea.

She and Mark were meeting Luke and Grace for lunch. Mark was coming from one of his projects in the opposite direction, so they drove separately.

It wasn't often they all had free time on the weekend.

The weather was iffy, a chance of rain, but that didn't dampen the spirits of the hordes of tourists packing the awning-covered outdoor dining areas along the Riverwalk.

Reaching the bistro, Sam walked into a calm oasis. Large palm trees separated the tables into small islands and were gently swaying in the breeze as the doors opened. Soft jazz played in the background. Tension flowed out of her body as she took a deep breath and let it out.

Her friend Laura had created a fun and funky restaurant, serving good food with a great atmosphere.

It was a far cry from the rundown speakeasy Laura bought years ago. It was also the place where she'd met Mark, who had been renovating the bistro. Sam snorted. Her big, brawny SEAL was surprised as hell when he saw her take down that thief. She'd appreciated the fact that he hadn't stepped in to take over. It was one of the many things she loved about him.

The restaurant was crowded, as it usually was on weekends. Sam spotted Grace waving to her, said hello along the way to a couple of servers she knew, and walked back to the corner booth. Laura kept this booth open for when the girls met or for special guests. Guess they were the special guests today. She was grateful that they didn't have to wait for a table.

Sam blew them a kiss and slid into the booth. "How did you get away from those adorable sons of yours?" she asked Grace.

"Adorable?" Grace rolled her eyes. "As if. Connor is driving me crazy; he keeps asking for a puppy, and Aiden goes around looking for it, saying, 'Where puppy? Where puppy?'"

"Grace, it's not that bad." Luke chuckled. "The kids are with my dad today. He's probably spoiling them like crazy. And if I know him, he is more than happy encouraging Connor to ask for a puppy."

Grace groaned.

Mark glided in beside Sam and kissed her on the cheek. "Sorry I'm late. Traffic. And what's going on down here? I've never seen so many people."

"Art Walk. It's the first year the galleries are holding it," said Luke as he leaned over to shake Mark's hand.

"Grace, I haven't seen you in a while, although I see Luke's money on poker night."

Luke snorted.

"How are you doing?" asked Mark. "You're looking beautiful."

Grace rolled her eyes, then filled him in on the kids and the piece she was working on for the newspaper.

The server came over, handed them menus, recited the day's specials, and promised to return.

Laura had an appointment today and wasn't working in the kitchen, but the kitchen was in good hands. They settled on their choices, and the server came back and took their order.

"Sam, I heard what happened to Hailey and Laura," said Grace. "Have you found anything about who's doing this?"

Sam shook her head. "I wish. We've gone over all cases where someone went to jail and is still there. Phil is looking into all their history, including Tony Moranti. He's dead, but if you remember, he's from Black Pointe, and we think he might have a friend or relative who's into revenge."

The waiter interrupted them again when their meals were ready. Their meals were plated like works of art, and Sam couldn't help thinking Laura had lucked out with her chefs and with the new employees that she'd been stressing about. Well, not so much luck because Laura was carefree in some ways but a stickler when it came to business.

Grace's eyes widened. "Oh my. I haven't heard Tony's name in years."

"Tony Moranti. Who's he?" Mark cocked his head in confusion.

Sam realized she'd never told Mark about her first case as a private investigator. It happened a few years before they got together. Sam explained to Mark and Luke who Tony Moranti was and how he ended up in jail for killing her friend Suzie.

Those had been exciting times for her. She worked with Otis Hood after college, learning the craft. Otis had helped her set up KnightGuard Security. He'd been a tough but fair mentor, she'd learned fast. She still missed his grumpy face.

"Oh, Tony was Sam's first big case when she started out," said Grace.

Luke looked interested. "You mentioned his name the

other day but I don't remember the case.. Probably it was
before I started on the police force. What happened?"

"I was at the shelter when a woman approached me asking
if I had graduated from Black Pointe High School."

She'd never forget meeting Naomi Fields at the shelter.
The external bruises and black eye Naomi had come in with
were just shadows on her face, but the internal scars might
never go away. Naomi had only been there a month, and she
even smiled occasionally.

" I told her I had and she asked what year. When I told
her the year, she wondered if I knew a Suzie Shaw," said Sam.

Naomi went on to tell her that she'd met Suzie at the
fishing camp.

"Suzie was my best friend in high school." Sam wiped a
tear rolling down her cheek. Suzie Shaw, sweet, kind, lovable
Suzie. Her life cut way too short by an animal.

"Naomi told me that Tony Moranti had killed her. I
always suspected that. Suzie had been dating Tony for a
while. He was older than her. I never said anything to her
because she was in love with him, but I thought Tony was a
two-faced liar, always smiling to your face but a bastard
behind your back. I hadn't heard that he abused women until
Naomi told me. Otherwise, I would have stepped in." Sam
shook her head and sighed. "I wish Suzie had confided
in me."

"Oh, Sam. Even if she had, the fact that she was in love
with him—you know there's nothing you could have done,"
said Grace.

"I could have beat the shit out of him." Sam banged the
table with her hand. "But you're right. Suzie would never have
forgiven me."

"If I remember correctly, Tony claimed he wasn't abusing
women," said Grace.

"Yeah, well, Naomi said he was lying, that she heard him

ask someone if he took care of the body and the guy said yes, he'd buried her where no one could find her."

"But she didn't recognize the voice or hear a name?" asked Mark.

"No," said Sam. "Naomi said it was the middle of the night and she was in another room, half-asleep."

"Why didn't she speak up when the police were investigating?" asked Luke. He shook his head. "Why am I even asking? If everyone spoke up when they witnessed a crime, we'd have no crime."

"Oh, Luke, you know how it is when you're young and afraid. Suzie had disappeared, and Naomi and her friend Diane were terrified of Tony. He was a beast. He abused them and one other woman that Naomi knew of," said Sam.

Luke took a bite of the panini he'd ordered and nodded. "They were lucky to get away from the bastard. I hate abusers."

Sam understood being young and afraid. But that didn't excuse someone from letting a beast get away with a crime. She remembered praying the women would testify. It was the only way of getting justice for Suzie and redemption for the women who looked the other way.

"I asked Naomi if the women would be willing to talk to me and the police. Naomi said she would but couldn't speak for the other two women." Sam reached for her glass of water and took a sip. It took Sam a year to track the other women down, convince one of them to testify, and get Tony convicted and then sent to jail.

"Naomi's last words to me were, 'I'll have to get out of town, as they say, because Tony will come after me.'"

"Poor Naomi. She must have been terrified, and yet she was so brave," said Grace.

The server interrupted their meal to ask if they needed anything else. They didn't, but Sam realized she'd hardly touched her meal. The salmon salad she'd ordered looked delicious. Her stomach rumbled. Time to eat.

"Did she testify against him and then leave town?" asked Mark.

Sam nodded her head. "Naomi had so much going against her when she came to the shelter. She was alone and afraid, yet she still testified. I admire how much courage that must have taken."

"Amen to that," said Luke.

Tony had cursed her up and down and swore he'd get even. He never did. Now he was dead.

Was it possible he came back from the dead to haunt her? Not him but someone close who wanted to avenge his death?

"I understand how much you cared for Suzie. Did you feel vindicated?" asked Luke.

*Vindicated?* "Yes and no. It was double-edged sword. I got justice for Suzie, but she was dead." Sam shrugged. "I don't know if that's vindication, but I never felt guilty sending Tony to jail."

"So you think someone connected to him may be your stalker?" asked Mark. "Why now?"

"I don't know, but someone connected to him makes sense. I run a security company that investigates and provides protection. We haven't had many unhappy people making threats, although it comes with the territory. What's happening now feels personal. Someone knows who my friends are and knows that hurting them hurts me."

"He had a cousin at the camp, didn't he?" asked Grace.

"Yes, but we never got his name and Tony was convicted, so ..." Sam shrugged.

"What are you doing to get more information?" asked Mark.

Sam sipped the wine she ordered. "Phil is looking into visitors Tony may have had in prison to see if any names stick out. Maybe he had a girlfriend who visited. Naomi remembered a Chrissie ... Chrissie Thorne, who was hot for Tony."

Sam stopped and took a sip of water. "Damn, I just remembered Chrissie's name. The cops never found her. I'll pass that name along to Phil. Naomi told me his girlfriend's name after the trial, but he'd already been convicted, so I didn't need it."

"Getting that information may be tough. The prison might not give Phil the names of Tony's visitors. Then you'll have to go through the Freedom of Information Act, which might take a little time," said Luke. "I know someone who might help if Phil has a problem."

"How will you be able to find out if Tony and this stalker are connected?" asked Grace. "It's been a while since Tony went to jail, and he's dead."

"I'm not sure. It's the only lead that makes sense." Sam grimaced. "I have zero to lose if we investigate and find it has nothing to do with Tony. Of course, if it isn't him, then I don't know where or who to look at."

Even as she said those words, Sam knew in her gut there was a connection to Tony—now they just had to prove it.

Even in death, the bastard was tormenting her.

# CHAPTER TWENTY-NINE

Recess was Alex's favorite time of day. She got to play with Milo, swing on the swing set and explore the schoolyard. But school was over for the day, and the schoolyard was quiet.

Sam was picking her up to bring her home. Miss Walker was waiting with her.

She had the picnic table to herself and swung her legs back and forth. It was hard to sit still because tonight Uncle Mark was taking her to the mall for pizza. Then he promised to bring her to Build-a-Bear so she could get Sammiedoodles a new outfit.

She never brought Sammiedoodles to school because that mean ol' Kaitlyn would take her and throw her on the ground.

Sammiedoodles was her first-ever bear, and she never wanted her to get dirty. Mama never had extra money for dolls or stuffed animals.

Mama—she missed her a lot. A tear slid down her cheek.

Uncle Mark was nice, and so was Sam. She had new

friends and clothes that fit. Uncle Mark told her stories of Mama when she was little, and she loved hearing them.

There was no one on the playground. All the after-school kids were having fun in the gym while she sat out here bored.

When would Sam get here? A white car pulled up. Yeah! Finally. Sam was here. Alex got off the picnic table and started running toward the car. The passenger door opened.

"Alex, wait," shouted Miss Walker.

Alex turned and waved to Miss Walker.

"It's okay. Sam's here."

Alex got to the car and was going to hop in, but something was wrong. Where was her car seat? She should be getting in the back. Sam knew that. She opened her mouth to remind Sam, but to her surprise, the woman wasn't Sam.

"Hey, Alex, Sam asked me to pick you up and buy you ice cream. Jump in."

Alex hesitated. Her hand was on the edge of the door.

She didn't know this person.

Her voice was harsh, mean-sounding. The woman had on big sunglasses and a hat. She smiled, but it wasn't a nice smile —Stranger Danger.

"I said get in the car, bitch," the woman hissed. Now she looked mean. Alex turned to head back to Miss Walker, but the woman grabbed her arm.

Miss Walker was screaming at Alex to stop.

Alex knew something was wrong. She wasn't getting in the car, but the woman was hurting her and not letting go.

She only had a couple of self-defense moves, and they slipped her mind. Not knowing what else to do, she bit the woman's arm —hard. Latched on until she tasted blood in her mouth. Then jumped back when the woman screamed and let go of her.

The woman cried, "Bitch!" then took off with the door still open and flapping around.

Miss Walker reached her, patted her down and then scooched down.

"Alex, honey, are you all right?"

Alex gulped. "That woman called me a bad name and wanted to take me."

"I know, honey. I know. You are very brave."

"I bited her."

Miss Walker gave her a little smile. "That was very smart of you, Alex. Now let's call Sam and Uncle Mark and tell them what's going on."

"Am I in trouble?"

"No, sweetie, you're not."

They walked back to the school. Miss Walker had her sit on the bench outside Principal Hart's office.

Today was the first time she sat outside the principal's office without being bad. Or had she been? Her stomach started doing flip-flops.

Maybe Sam had sent the woman and she bited her. Alex groaned.

She was in trouble again.

SAM RACED toward the principal's office.

She'd been running late and tried to call Anne to ask her to bring Alex inside until she got there, but Anne's phone was busy. Then, when Anne called her about Alex almost being abducted, she was already in the parking lot. Bile formed in the back of her throat. She opened the car door and upchucked, wiped her mouth, waited for her stomach to settle and her heart to stop thumping.

The corridor to the principal's office was longer than Sam remembered. Her feet felt like they had cement blocks on them. Her chest tightened, and her lungs were constricting, even though she was gulping air.

It was so quiet in the hallway. But Sam heard kids laughing in the distance, probably the after-school kids playing in the gym. The air was heavy with scents of melted cheese and pizza that mingled with the acid roiling in her gut.

The office door was open, and she saw Alex sitting on a wooden bench. She had on her favorite pink sparkly top and the little white skirt decorated with hearts that they bought the last time they were at the mall. Her little sneakers twinkled as she swung her legs back and forth. The contrast between the tiny, scared girl sitting in the chair and the happy outfit made Sam want to cry. Little kids shouldn't have to deal with this shit.

What had the person done to Alex? Had they hurt her? She was going to kill whoever tried to hurt Alex.

Anne was sitting next to her, holding Alex's hand, and got up when she spotted Sam.

She was ready to grill Alex, but Anne put her hand up and gave her the look—*notch it down.*

Anne was right. No sense making more of this with Alex than necessary. Sam slowed down and gulped fresh air, hoping to calm her racing heart. She'd called Mark on the way over, and he would be there in a couple of minutes.

Bending down to face Alex, she gave her a small smile. "Hey, sweetie, heard you had an interesting experience. Are you okay?"

God, she wanted to scream, but not scaring Alex was more important.

"You're not mad at me, are you?" Alex's eyes teared up, and her little lip trembled.

*Mad? Why would she even think that?* Sam gathered her into her arms.

"Never." She sat down, pulled Alex onto her lap and

clasped her arms around her. "Can you tell me what happened?"

"I was sitting on the picnic table waiting for you. Miss Walker was watching me. I saw your car pull up, and I ran over. But a strange woman was inside and said that you asked her to pick me up because you were busy."

*Oh, God.* Sam took a deep breath.

"Okay, then what happened? What made you not get in the car?"

"She didn't have my car seat, and when the woman smiled, she looked mean." Alex looked at her with wide forest-green eyes. "You wouldn't send a mean woman to pick me up, would you?"

"No, honey, I wouldn't. Besides, I would always tell you if someone else was picking you up. Then what happened?"

"She grabbed my arm, and I bited her, then she called me a naughty word," said Alex. "Remember the bad word you told me not to use?"

Sam nodded. She and Mark had a discussion with Alex about repeating certain words after several incidents at school.

"Then she let go of me. Then Miss Walker pulled me back, and the woman drove away." Alex bit her lip. "She didn't close the car door."

"Sam, I am so sorry. I shouldn't have been on the phone. This is my fault." Anne bent her head and wiped at a tear.

"Anne, this is not your fault. You were watching her." Sam looked at Anne. All the color had drained from Anne's face, and Sam shuddered. "Who knew someone would try to kidnap Alex?"

Footsteps thundered down the hall.

"Alex. Sam." Mark was racing down the hall, his eyes darting around, looking for danger.

He slid to a stop and sat down next to Alex and Sam.

After inhaling and exhaling deeply, he lifted Alex from Sam's arms and placed her on his lap. "Hey, sweet pea. Heard you fought off a monster today."

Alex giggled. "No, I bited her."

He looked over Alex's head toward Sam. She knew he'd want details, but this wasn't the place. She shook her head.

"Why don't we go home, have some ice cream, and you can tell me all about it," said Mark.

"'Kay."

Mark stood with Alex still in his arms. Anne touched his shoulder. "I'm so sorry."

"Anne, we'll talk later," said Mark.

Anger simmered in his brown eyes. Sam knew he wasn't angry at Anne but at the situation, but now wasn't the time for niceties. They would talk to Anne later.

Anne nodded and sat on the bench. A tear streamed down her cheek. Sam patted her arm, told her she'd call later, and followed Mark out.

Alex was talking a mile a minute about ... what?

Sam wasn't listening. She was sorting through what had happened.

A woman tried to kidnap Alex. A woman! Here, she thought her stalker was a man, but was it possible she was wrong? Who could it be?

Her team had already gone over the women that they had encountered. Who else knew Alex was living with Mark? Outside of their friends and family, no one she'd dealt with.

Hillary Santmeyer was in a mental facility for the foresee-able future. Rachel moved to the west coast, and Amber was still in jail. Did they have friends or relatives who would seek revenge? She didn't think so. It would be unusual for most people who weren't involved in crime to take revenge.

So who or what was she missing?

# CHAPTER THIRTY

Mark was checking up on the built-ins for the new office for Mr. Roy when he got Sam's call. Colin was a master craftsman, and it showed. Mr. Roy had chosen teak for the credenza and bookshelves, and it looked outstanding in the large room.

The elation he'd felt for the new office was shredded when Sam told him that someone tried to kidnap Alex.

He couldn't remember driving, parking or walking into the school. Happy pictures of families, hung on the hallway walls, passed by in a blur as he raced to the office.

Seeing Sam, Anne and Alex quietly talking calmed him a little. Thank God Alex was okay and calm. Him—not so much.

After he talked to Anne and saw for himself that Alex was all right, the three of them left.

Alex held both their hands, happily chattering as they walked to the parking lot. He was still hyperventilating. The SEALs had taught him how to shallow breathe, and it worked on assignment. Who knew family drama could throw that off?

Mark strapped Alex into her car seat and got behind the wheel of his truck. He hung his head, willing his heart to stop thumping. It didn't work, so he inhaled and exhaled deeply. Neither did that help, but he couldn't sit in the school parking lot forever.

Sam indicated she would follow him to his house.

She was probably wondering why it was taking so long for him to get moving. He turned his truck on and headed home.

The pipsqueak in his back seat was everything to him. She reminded him of his sister every day, especially in her mannerisms, her optimism, and her joy for life. If he lost Alex, he would lose a piece of his heart—a huge piece.

The almost-abduction didn't scare Alex, which he was thankful for.

She talked nonstop all the way home. He now knew everything about Milo, her favorite person in the world, and Kaitlyn, who wasn't. He knew what Alex ate for lunch today, what she ate yesterday, and what she was going to eat tomorrow. What her favorite color was and what she was going to wear to school tomorrow.

His head was spinning. Who knew little girls talked so much? Usually, the babysitter picked up Alex and stayed with her until he or Sam got home. Is this what she went through every day? She deserved a raise.

Finally, Alex took a deep breath and stopped talking as they pulled into his driveway. Sam was right behind him and parked beside his truck. Alex unhooked her car seat, jumped out of the truck, ran over to Sam.

"Sam is that what you do all day?" Alex widened her eyes.

Sam stooped to pick Alex up. Alex's little face was even with hers. Sam's eyebrows pulled together in a frown. "What do you mean, sweetie?"

"Do you chase bad guys? Do you kill them?" Alex put her

little hands on each side of Sam's cheeks and stared into her eyes. "Have you killed a lot of bad guys?"

Where the hell had she picked that up from? Sam never talked about her business in front of Alex. But they say little pitchers have big ears, so he guessed that saying was true.

"Ah. Ah." Sam looked at Mark in panic. He gave her a smirk. Coward that he was, he sure wasn't participating in that conversation.

"No. I don't chase bad guys. If they get in my way, I deal with them. While my employees carry guns for protection, we try not to kill anyone."

Alex seemed okay with that explanation.

"Uncle Mark?"

"What, Alex?"

Alex pursed her little lips. "Can I have a gun for protection?"

Then she added, "All my friends have them."

Mark stopped mid-stride.

*A gun?*

*What the fuck?*

Alex was only five years old. Where the hell did she get that from? *And all her friends had guns?*

He thought he heard a snicker from Sam. But when he looked over at her, her face was blank, although her shoulders were shaking. He gave her a dirty look.

"Alex, honey, we'll talk more in the house, but you are not getting a gun. First, you're too young to have a gun. Second, guns hurt people, and third, I'm sure your friends don't have guns."

"Oh. Okay." Alex looked up and shrugged. "Next time, I'll bite harder."

Mark shook his head and growled. "There won't be a next time."

There would never be a next time.

Mark wondered if he should home-school Alex—no, that wouldn't work. He had a company to run, and keeping Alex in the house forever wasn't practical—was it? No.

He and Sam needed to come up with a working plan to keep her safe.

They walked into the house. Sam put Alex down and took her backpack into her room.

"Anyone for milk and cookies?" Sam asked when she stepped into the kitchen.

Alex raised her hand and shouted. "Yes. Me. Me."

"Mark?"

"I'll have—never mind. I'll get it myself." Mark walked over to the bar and poured himself a Scotch. "Sam, do you want a drink?"

Sam came in with Alex's treat. "Nah, I'm good."

After Alex ate her cookies and drank her milk, he and Sam discussed with her what to do in an emergency.

Mark thought they had gotten through to her and that she understood about strangers and danger. When she asked if she could go play in her room, he said yes.

He settled back into the sofa and looked over at Sam. "I'm betting this has to do with your stalker."

Sam sighed and nodded. "God, I've never been so scared in my life when Anne called."

"Tell me about it."

"Oh dear, I've got to talk to Anne later." Sam lowered her head. Her stomach clenched. *What a clusterfuck.* "She was beside herself that this happened."

"Wasn't she outside with Alex?"

*She'd better have been.* But Anne was extremely responsible. This could have happened to anyone.

"Yes, she was close by but on the phone. She yelled for Alex to stop when she saw her running toward the car, but

Alex kept going. It's your call, but I think Alex needs to be punished for not listening. What do you think?"

Alex needed to learn to listen. Maybe he could insist she not leave the house for a year. Two?

"Yes. She planned to have a playdate with Milo this week. A fitting punishment might be to cancel it." It pained him to say that. Punishing little girls or any female was not something they learned as SEALs or believed as a man. But his responsibility was keeping her safe. She needed to be more careful.

Sam nodded. "Good idea. Then it's over and done. She'll be unhappy for a couple of days but hopefully will remember not to run off willy-nilly."

"Okay then." Mark finished his drink in one gulp and slammed the glass on the table.

Sam winced.

"I'm at a loss here as to who would do this? Someone who knows you? Me? Any ideas?"

Silence. Sam was deep in thought. She let out a heavy sigh.

"I'm sure this has something to do with my stalker. Here I thought it was a man, but maybe it's a woman. I don't know how she knew about Alex and where she went to school." Sam shook her head and sighed again. "Phil is digging into everyone's past that we've dealt with. He's checking visitation lists at the prison where Tony was and his friends. If there's something there, he'll find it."

She threw up her hands. "I don't know what else to do. Knowing a woman tried to kidnap Alex has thrown a wrench into everything I believed." She stared at Mark. "I promise you I will resolve this. And nothing or nobody is going to hurt that little girl."

Mark got up and started pacing.

Sam knew how important Alex was to him.

He needed to be careful about what he said to her. This wasn't Sam's fault. He was positive it had nothing to do with him. It was her stalker. But he wasn't sitting down and letting Alex or Sam get hurt. It was time to get more involved.

Mark stopped pacing and sat down. "I know this is your area of expertise, but I can't sit back and let anything happen to Alex."

Leaning forward, he ran his fingers through his hair and blew out a breath of air. "She's all I have of my sister. Damn, Amanda trusted me to take care of Alex. I can't, won't let anything happen to her."

"Mark. Look at me."

He looked over at the woman who held his heart.

"I will never let anything happen to Alex."

Mark gave her a small smile. "I trust you to do that. But it almost happened. This isn't only about you anymore. It's affecting everyone around you."

"You're not telling me anything I don't know," she snapped. Sam tapped the fingers of one hand on her arm. "This is so frustrating. Phil is on this, and I'll step it up at work. Plus, I'll have one employee stay with Alex after school as added protection."

"Good. We also need to talk to Anne to see if she can add anything. Would it be best if we both go or only one of us?" asked Mark.

"I'll go. In fact, I'll call her when I leave. Best to get this done ASAP. I don't want Anne to feel guilty. I've warned my friends to be on the lookout for strange men. Although I never thought it could be a woman. Anne did what she was supposed to do, and I know she contacted the principal and police. They'll stop by later to talk to Alex." Sam picked up the plate and glass and walked towards the kitchen.

Mark was thankful he didn't have to deal with another female tonight. Anne was a good person and extremely responsible. Sam was close to Anne and would smooth things over. She was doing all she could to find who was stalking her. But there had to be something she was missing. He hated going behind Sam's back, but almost losing Alex put him on edge. He was going to talk to Joe Harkin, former SEAL buddy and his best friend, to get his perspective.

SEALs were good at making plans. A, B or Z, they came up with plans on the fly. Was there something he was missing? Something he saw or heard? Could it be someone who wanted to get back at him?

A CAR HORN HONKED, and Sam jerked.

Darn, that was the second time today that she was lost in thought. She needed to keep her head in the game. On the way over to Anne's condo, she'd called the office and spoken with Phil. He had nothing to share with her yet.

She blew out a deep breath. What the hell was going on? Why couldn't she get a handle on this problem? It was as if the stalker was a ghost and following her around.

Anne's condo was the next block over, and Sam turned left into the parking lot. Her footsteps were heavy as she walked to Anne's door, then rang the bell.

The door opened. Anne's eyes were red from crying, but she gave Sam a small smile and stepped aside.

"Sam, I am so sorr—"

"Don't apologize. This isn't your fault." Sam reached out to hug her friend. It wasn't her fault. Anne was a conscientious teacher and friend. Down deep, Sam knew Anne would do anything to protect her students and friends. If anything, this was her fault. She should have had someone from KnightGuard Security watching Alex.

"Let's sit down, and you tell me what happened. What you saw or thought you saw."

Anne sat across from Sam, wringing her hands. "I don't know much. I saw Alex on the swing set, and then she got off and sat on the picnic table. My phone rang, and the next thing I see is Alex skipping to the car and the car door opening. I hung up the phone and screamed at her to stop as I was running toward her. She wasn't even thirty feet from me.'

"Why did she go toward the car?"

"It looked like yours."

"What do you mean?"

"It was a white SUV just like yours."

Oh, dear lord. What was going on? Someone staged this to look like her car. She would have Phil check for cars like hers especially at the rental agencies, although she wouldn't be holding out for any definitive answers. There were too many white SUVs in Florida.

Anne settled back and fiddled with the fringe on one pillow. "Also, the phone call was weird."

"Weird? How so?"

"It was the wrong number."

Sam tapped her fingers on the armrest. White SUV that looked like hers. Wrong number at the same time someone was trying to abduct Alex. Coincidence? Hell, no. A master strategist planned this. She would have Phil pull footage from around the school for several blocks and see where the SUV headed.

"Is Mark angry with me?" Anne asked in a small voice. She shuddered. "I wouldn't blame him if he was."

"Anne, nobody is angry with you. We're so glad you were there. Otherwise ..." Sam winced. "Otherwise, things would have been a lot worse."

"I talked to the principal," said Anne. "The school has been putting off installing security fencing around the building. It's time for them to do it and to put better pickup policies in place."

"Couldn't agree more." Sam stood. "Listen, I want to get to the office and talk to Phil. Then get home. Mark is worried, and I want to keep him updated."

"Let me know what you find out."

"I will." Sam hugged Anne. "Please don't obsess about this. We will get to the bottom of it."

She got into her car and knocked her head on the steering wheel.

The list of what Phil had to do was getting longer.

Her list of who was trying to hurt her was getting longer and more personal, but she had no suspects.

She had no control over anything, and it was frightening.

# CHAPTER THIRTY-ONE

Sam was in the office early the next day because Phil wanted to show her what he'd pulled up. It was quiet now, but in a couple of hours, the office would be humming. She wanted this time alone with Phil. He'd been fooling around with footage since she asked him to last night.

It wasn't the first time, she wondered how she lucked out getting Phil to work for her. He'd been offered high-paying jobs from a couple of much larger companies and turned them down. She couldn't afford to give him the salary or perks they could offer. He was in a small office basically by himself, although Jenna shared it with him for the time being. At some point, after Jenna spent time learning what the other office staff did, she would have her own cubicle.

She'd asked Phil once why he worked for KnightGuard Security. His answer was noncommittal, but the gist of it was that he was good friends with Pete. He had served time in the military with him and trusted Pete to be working for the best company around. He also loved the freedom he had to do what he loved. Phil had a free hand in the IT department. It worked for her, and she was grateful for his work.

"So this is what I pulled up," said Phil. Today, he wore one of his beanies. This one said, "Back me up."

She could only shake her head. Sam had no idea where he was getting them from, but they were usually interesting.

"Okay. What am I looking at?" Sam pulled a chair over and watched a white SUV similar to hers hauling ass until it stopped a block away and the driver shut the passenger door. They followed the SUV for a few blocks and watched it turn into a parking garage.

"Great. We can access the cameras there and get a license plate."

"Well, no," said Phil. "Watch." He fiddled with the tapes. "This is an hour later."

They watched the SUV drive out of the garage. "Is it the same person driving?

"I don't think so. It looks like a man," said Phil.

"Who is it?" Sam was disappointed. She'd hoped this would be easy.

"I don't know. It was as if someone was there waiting for the car."

"Do we have a license plate number?"

"Smeared with mud."

"Were you able to track it after it left the garage?" Sam rubbed the back of her neck. A headache of epic proportions was forming. So many questions left unanswered. She was obsessing about this unidentified woman and who she was working with. Or was the woman working alone? Why were Sam and her friends targeted?

Why couldn't this be easy? Just identify the creep, catch him or her and send them to jail.

Phil shook his head. "I tracked it for a few blocks, then nothing on camera feeds."

"Where did the woman go after she got out?"

"The garage is connected to a department store. The

woman took the elevator down a flight and walked into the entrance. I bet the guy also walked into the store and then waited in the garage. It's a busy place, people constantly coming and going."

"So we lost her."

"Yep." Phil twirled in his chair. "I'm sorry, but I couldn't find her walking out."

"And we don't know where the man came from."

He shook his head. "Nope."

"So basically, we have nothing."

"Yep."

"Well, aren't you a Chatty Cathy."

"I'm sorry, Sam. There's only so much I can do. I can pull feed from the cameras if they're positioned right. If the woman had on an identifiable outfit, we could follow her. But we're out of luck. The store is huge with four exits. If she changed outfits or blended into with a crowd of people going in or out of the store, there is no way to recognize her."

Sam gave him a small smile and sighed. "Sorry. I'm not complaining. It's frustrating. I'm not blaming you or your magic fingers. What about the phone call Anne received? That wrong number?"

"Nada. It was from a burner phone," said Phil.

"So we have nothing." Sam couldn't hide the disappointment in her voice. They were no closer to identifying the woman and still had no idea who the man was.

"Well, not exactly. I did hunt down Chrissie Thorne. She's from Georgia. She's moved several times, had a name change to McMasters, then changed it back, but I don't have a current address on her. I'll keep checking though."

"McMasters. She's the girlfriend who visited Tony in jail."

"Yup. But that's all I could find on her."

Great. Well, that solved one mystery. Chrissie Thorne and Chrissie McMasters were one and the same. Chrissie was involved with Tony. But they were no closer to identifying the woman who tried to kidnap Alex and still had no idea if a man was involved. The only thing for sure that Sam knew was one, possibly two people were terrorizing her friends and family, and she didn't know when they would strike next.

# CHAPTER THIRTY-TWO

Chrissie was in agony. But she had to go to work.

She'd already taken yesterday afternoon off with the excuse she had a doctor's appointment. Today she could have used that appointment. Who knew little kids could bite so hard?

She prayed the damn thing wouldn't get infected. She stared at the wound and the perfect little teeth marks, and Chrissie hoped the kid didn't have any transmittable diseases. Did she need a tetanus shot? Chrissie couldn't remember the last time she had one. She knew the shot lasted for ten years. Hmmm, ten years ago, she was eighteen. Her mother made sure she was up to date on shots, so perhaps she was okay. If not, dying would serve her right for getting involved with Colin and little kids.

The internet was filled with great advice on what to do if bitten by a human. Hard to believe so many people were bitten by another person. What was wrong with society? It boggled her mind. Didn't change the fact that there was intense pain around the bite area or that the skin there was reddening.

She grabbed the salt water and poured it over the wound.

The small scream came from her. Holy crap! That burned. Colin helped yesterday as best he could, but it didn't seem to bother him that she was hurt. He was only concerned that she didn't get the kid. Tough shit.

Chrissie slapped another bandage on it and looked in her closet. All her tops were short-sleeved or sleeveless. Great. It was hot, but she could hold a sweater over her arm. Perhaps no one would notice the bandage. She pulled on a top that matched her skirt and buttoned the last of the front buttons as she looked in the mirror. Her arm was pounding from the exertion. Chrissie took a deep breath, all the while telling herself to suck it up.

The drive to KnightGuard Security was an adventure. Well, not so much an adventure as torture she was experiencing. Every turn she made pulled at the wound, creating more pain.

Finally, she got to KnightGuard Security's parking lot and walked into the office. Said hello to Marcia. Tried not to grimace as the old lady went on and on about nothing.

The feeling that she forgot something nagged at her. She had her purse. The sweater covered the wound. What was she missing? She looked into Marcia's eyes as she was talking. Oh, shit! She forgot to put in the brown contact lenses. Were they in her purse? In her pain, had she forgotten to pack them?

Chrissie excused herself and ran to the ladies' room. She stared into the mirror at the gray eyes she'd inherited from her mother. She reached into her purse and felt for the plastic contact lens case. Not there. Damn, damn, damn.

Did she leave the case at home? Chrissie opened the purse wide, sorted through makeup, wallet, and other shit. All unimportant right now. Her stomach clenched. This couldn't be happening. She rummaged through her purse again and finally spotted the case deep in the other pocket. Whew! Footsteps outside the ladies' room door had Chrissie jumping into a stall. A woman entered, washed her hands and left. Chrissie opened the door and quickly put the lenses in.

She got to Phil's office and pulled out her chair. The pain exhausted her. She looked at her desk. Had the invoices multiplied since last night? Sam had her learning all aspects of the office, but she never imagined there were so many little parts to the security business.

Phil was at his desk. He was always there. If she didn't know better, she'd have thought he lived there. He sat at his computer, spying on the world and doing who knew what else —he loved it.

Grunts from the exercise room interrupted her thoughts.

"Good morning," said Phil. She stared at the beanie on his head that said, "I can turn you on." Where the heck did he get those? He had several beanies he wore, all with oddly sexual innuendos. He gave her a big grin when she shook her head.

"Morning." Chrissie sat at her desk, tucked her purse in the drawer. Yelped when she looked up into Phil's concerned face only inches from her own.

"Jeez, you're bleeding," said Phil, his brow wrinkled. "What happened?"

Chrissie looked at her arm.

Yup. Little pockets of blood had seeped through the bandage. It was slipping off, exposing the wound. Crap.

"It's nothing. I had an accident."

He leaned over to inspect it.

"Jeez, it looks like an animal bit you." He bent over closer and touched the bandage.

"Yeah, I had a run in with my neighbor's dog. She won. I

lost." She pulled her arm away. Her stomach was fluttering. Why wouldn't Phil just leave her alone?

"That sucks. Have you had a tetanus shot?"

"All up to date."

Phil squinted his eyes. "I'm happy to help rebandage it. I have some first-aid experience."

She picked up her purse, stood, pasted on a smile and said, "I'll take care of it. No worries."

Phil shrugged.

Looking into the mirror in the ladies' room, Chrissie could only shake her head. How did she ever get into this mess? Why did she ever get involved with Colin?

Playing along with Colin started off fun. He was a distraction and good fuck. His ego, however, always got in his way. He thought he was in charge because she never questioned him. He wasn't a bad man—just stupid.

If Colin knew that Tony had confided in her about the drug business, Colin would have gotten rid of her a long time ago.

In fact, Tony blamed Colin for his being in jail. If Colin had done what he'd been told, they never would have found that woman's body. But nooo—Colin was an idiot and lazy. He couldn't even bury somebody in the woods so they'd never be found.

Being in jail meant Tony had to depend on someone to help him. He had Roberto, but he also had her.

The one thing she and Colin agreed on was that Sam Knight had to be taken down.

It would have been easier for her to develop the business herself. It was small now but would continue to grow. But stupid her just had to stay with Colin and involve other people to help him achieve his goal. Serve her right. No one was getting hurt except for her—figuratively and physically. Damn Colin and his need for revenge.

Hopefully, Phil and the others wouldn't put two and two together and realize how she got the bite. Hopefully, the little beast wouldn't remember which arm she bit.

But hope was for idiots and innocents. She was neither and needed to be more careful.

# CHAPTER THIRTY-THREE

Colin slammed his phone down on the scarred table, not caring that it bounced once and landed on the floor. Not caring whether he broke the face. Not caring that he put yet another dent in the shabby scratched table. And not caring that he would most likely have to give up part of his security deposit to cover damages.

He'd worked out every small detail, and all Chrissie had to do was follow the plan. Well, she got part of it right except the vital part—kidnapping the little girl. Not that he enjoyed kidnapping kids or would have harmed the little girl, but he knew it would scare Mark and Sam. He'd planned to keep the kid at the cabin for a day and then release her.

Everything was planned with precision: from renting an SUV that looked like Sam's to knowing what time the girl got out of school and where she waited. Then waiting for the perfect time when the teacher would get the call that would distract her. Colin hoped Chrissie had tossed the burner phone she'd used. He needed to remember to ask her. He couldn't have any more plans go to hell.

Chrissie had pulled through with phone numbers. The

stupid women had exchanged phone numbers with her that one time at the restaurant when Sam Knight introduced her to her friends. Then she and Colin practiced the timing until Chrissie threatened to cut his balls off if she had to do it one more time.

The plan was perfect.

Chrissie had asked for time off for a doctor's appointment, and no one questioned where she was going or if she would be back that day. As far as he knew, they loved her at KnightGuard Security. Sam even offered her a full-time position.

He couldn't get away from work to help her because he hadn't quite finished a carpentry project, and Mark was checking up with him every day since the owner of the building was eager to move in.

It helped to have friends in low places. One of his friends rented the car as a favor for one he had done in prison for the guy's brother. They couldn't tie the rental to him. He'd bought Chrissie a burner phone so she could call the teacher. The plan had been perfect.

Until it wasn't.

Who knew a little kid could bite so hard? Chrissie sure wasn't expecting it. The kid chomped onto her forearm like a bulldog and wouldn't let go until Chrissie pushed her away.

The bite was still red, raw, and bleeding when he got home and found Chrissie there. The skin was broken, and tiny teeth marks marred the injury. They cleaned it up as best they could and slapped a bandage on it. Chrissie complained about the pain, and Colin told her to work through it. She told him to stuff it.

He took a long swallow of beer, wiped his mouth with his hand.

His plan was coming together, although not without minor glitches. Sam's girlfriends were on the lookout now, so he wouldn't harass them anymore. KnightGuard Security had placed extra security cameras at the bistro and bookshop. Smart. The next time, he might not be so lucky.

He expected the kid would be under twenty-four-hour protection from now on, so another kidnapping try was out.

Sam's final days were coming, but he wanted one more big bang. One that would hurt Sam a lot more than punctured tires and scratches on cars. Something that she couldn't imagine.

What could he do that would hurt her without physically hurting her? He chugged another swallow of beer. Who meant a lot to her? He smiled to himself.

Oh, of course. It was Mark, hands down.

Olly oxen free—you're it.

# CHAPTER THIRTY-FOUR

I t was raining the proverbial cats and dogs.

Mark stomped out of the first floor of the new four-story lawyers' office he was building, which was now behind by three weeks.

Stone Construction barely started working on the building before it rained for the past two weeks. Not just a drizzle of rain, it was a heavy downpour—a monsoon—with a sprinkling of thunder and lightning just to keep everyone on their toes.

The tradespeople were lined up and the materials delivered. But the materials were floating in water, and he needed to deal with covering them better. Mark was fed up with the rain and everything else, including his relationship with Sam.

He pushed, and she pulled. Back and forth, back and forth they went. Why wouldn't she just say yes to marriage? Sam knew he wanted more from their relationship. He wanted to get married.

Marriage didn't solve problems. He knew that. But it made the commitment between two people stronger. She was already living in his house, and it thrilled him to wake up next to her each morning. But call him a caveman—he wanted everyone to know Sam was literally and figuratively his.

He hoped Sam knew he would always be there for her. But that silly piece of paper told the world that they were together, that they made the commitment. If anything happened to him, she would get the house and his insurance, and there would be no problem with guardianship of Alex.

His parents were happily married. Sam's parents had been, too. It was an institution he believed in.

Bah, enough negative thinking for a day.

The guys were coming over for poker tonight. He could get drunk and hopefully win back some of the money he lost the last time they played.

Since it was still early, he could relax a little before they got there.

His truck was parked close to the building.

He pulled the hood of his jacket over his head, ran out, clicked the truck door open and stepped into a pothole, almost losing his balance. Damn, not only were his clothes soaked, but now his work boots and socks were, too.

Perfect. Well, the good news was he had time to dry off and change before the guys came.

The bad news was that he needed to get the pothole filled in before someone got hurt.

Nothing to be done about the pothole today, but as soon as the rain let up, he would have it taken care of.

The cab of his truck was steamy, the windows fogged, and he couldn't see anything. He wiped the rain from his forehead, turned on the defogger and relaxed in the seat. The windows would take a few minutes to clear up. He didn't have to sniff himself to know he smelled like a wet dog. Plus, he was getting chilled. A change of clothes would be nice right now.

A red light on the dash caught his attention. Hmmm, the

brake light. Guess it was time to get them replaced. He would handle that tomorrow.

After pulling out of the lot and barely avoiding another pothole, Mark sighed in disgust. If the rain didn't stop, the whole parking lot would be a giant pothole. He would waste more valuable time filling it in.

Traffic was heavy, considering the wet weather.

Mark thought about tonight.

Did he need anything else for poker? Chips, nuts, beer, and whiskey? Nope. He had those.

Maybe some chicken wings would be an excellent addition. He knew the perfect store that made the best wings. Best of all, the store was on his way home. His clothes and shoes were soaked; another stop couldn't make things worse.

The new joint was off the main highway. After driving a few miles down the road, he entered the highway and merged into traffic. Wingz & More was at the next exit.

The exit was coming up. He put on his blinker and applied the brakes to slow down. His foot went straight to the floor. Damn. Mark tried pumping the brakes. Nothing.

Cars were in front and behind him. Were the brake lights working? He hoped so. A car honked behind him.

The exit was coming up fast, and the road was on a decline. The truck was gaining speed, heading straight for the minivan in front of him. He pumped the brakes again, praying—nothing. Now he was on the minivan's tail. The rear window was sporting a stick figure decal of Mom, Dad, three little kids, two dogs, and a cat. Great. He honked his horn, once, twice. The driver ignored him.

Time for a defensive move, one he didn't want to make. But he also didn't want to rear-end someone.

Looking left, he noticed the road overlooked and merged into a major thoroughfare. That wouldn't work. He wasn't into killing himself today or anyone else.

On the right-hand side, the road merged into a single lane with a stand of live oaks and bushes off to the side. There was a break in traffic. He aimed for the woods, staying on a grass path until it disappeared. He pulled the emergency brake and thankfully the truck stopped suddenly but crashed into the bushes. The motion caused his head to bounce off the steering wheel. Stunned, he could only sit there. Everything hurt—probably nothing more than abrasions. Mark hoped nothing else was damaged. Thankfully, the bushes and incline stopped the truck, but not so hard as to deploy the airbags.

A loud cracking noise caused him to look out. There was a huge thump. One of the smaller live oaks crashed down on the roof, breaking the windshield, spreading pieces of glass on the seat and in his scalp. Blood oozed from cuts on his head. He struggled to unhook his seat belt. His hand was on the door handle, then he heard a big whoosh. Another falling tree was the last thing Mark saw before he lost consciousness.

---

COLIN LAUGHED. He'd been following Mark for miles. Because of the heavy rain, there was no way Mark could identify his truck. He was several cars behind Mark on the highway. He watched Mark get off the ramp, realize the brakes were shot and that he wouldn't be stopping easily. Driving slowly past Mark's grand exit through the bushes and into the trees, he was just in time to see a second tree fall on Mark's truck.

*Not so bright now, are you?* It had been a bold move, cutting the brake line.

It was worth getting up early on his day off and following Mark to the work site. He'd parked his truck a block over so Mark wouldn't see it.

While Mark checked the building, he'd slid under his truck and cut the brake line.

It would either cause a big accident or an annoyance, but he wanted Sam to know that he hadn't forgotten Mark. Too bad it was raining and muddy. His clothes were drying on his body and smelling foul—small price to pay for the satisfaction of knowing the hurt on Sam Knight's face.

The kidnapping of the niece had been a bust. But he'd targeted and scared a couple of Sam's girlfriends and now he got the big fella—perfect.

He couldn't imagine how a smart woman like Sam Knight hadn't caught on yet to who was tormenting her. He couldn't make it any easier, could he?

Chrissie had heard they were looking into connections and would keep him posted.

She said they were especially interested in Tony and his visitors. He wasn't worried. He never visited Tony in jail. Of course, he didn't have to. He'd been in the same jail and talked to him there. Chrissie had visited Tony a few times under her married name, McMasters, but she'd changed it back a few years ago and hadn't visited Tony since.

All the high school friends Tony knew had dispersed by the time he'd gone to jail. The good news was that the cops didn't get Tony him on drug charges—just the murder.

The dealers hired by Tony were still in the business, especially that two-timing bastard Roberto, but they had Colin locked out. He was working for peanuts while they were getting the big bucks. If it wasn't for his best friend, Dwight, and a couple of other men, he wouldn't have any business at all. But that was going to change.

His plan, after killing Sam Knight, was to get Roberto to deal with him, or he'd deal him out.

Well, he'd deal him out anyhow, but Roberto didn't have to know that. He'd been screwed enough.

Back to real time now. It was time to rachet up the harassment, do something a lot bolder, more impactful. Hmmm ...

Tomorrow he'd get together with Chrissie to plan how to speed the game up and end it once and for all.

Sam had offered her a permanent position, which had surprised him. But then again, Chrissie was a fast learner. She could get another job when they moved—or not. The drug trade provided lots of money. The sex was good, but he could get that from any of the women who hung around him. Chrissie could help him if she were still around and agreeable.

The one thing he knew was that he didn't need a woman to complete him.

# CHAPTER THIRTY-FIVE

Sam never laid on her horn as much as she did on the drive to the hospital after getting the call from Joe that Mark had been injured and was in the ER.

What was it about rain that had people doing stupid things on the road? Like "let's drive with our flashers on so nobody knows if I'm in trouble or just an idiot"?

It was common sense to pull over to the side of the road into the breakdown lane to let all the cars move into traffic and avoid hitting you.

By the time she got to the hospital, she needed a drink —or two.

Black Pointe General Hospital—Déjà vu.

Sam got out of her car, pulled her rain hood up, and ran into the emergency room. The doors swished open, and a volunteer at the desk greeted her. A security guard sat in the back, watching who entered.

Not that long ago, she was rushing here to be with Penny.

Then before that, checking on Grace, after someone had kidnapped her. Grace had escaped, but not without raw, bloody burns on her wrists from the ties the bastard used on her. Her feet had been battered and bloodied from running through the woods barefoot.

Sam hoped never to come here again, especially for someone she knew. But if wishes were horses, pigs would fly.

"Mark Stone."

The volunteer asked for identification, then she looked up the room number and gave it to Sam. Her heart thumped loudly in her chest, covering the sounds of soft crying, screeching ambulance sirens, low voices rumbling, and phones ringing.

She glanced around the packed waiting room and at the vacant eyes of people sitting on rigid plastic chairs, praying for miracles. The smell of fear, sickness, and disinfectant assaulted her nose. She swiped at the sweat forming on her brow. She forced herself not to run toward the doors where she'd find Mark.

Joe said he would meet her here.

Apparently, he called Mark just as the ambulance unloaded him. A nurse answered Mark's phone, hoping it was a relative or friend, told Joe what happened, and then he'd called Sam.

She sprinted down the hallway past drawn curtains, machines and people making ungodly noises, and doctors and nurses going about their business.

Mark was in the last bay.

When Sam opened the curtain, a nurse was checking his vitals. His eyes were closed. Dried blood covered his head and hands. Bruises were forming on his face.

Her hands trembled as she reached over to touch his arm—an arm that was cold to the touch. She swallowed hard.

Mark hadn't moved. She clasped his hand. She needed to hold on tight.

"Is ..." Her voice quivered and caught in her throat.

Please, God, make him be okay. She swallowed hard. "Is he okay?"

The nurse glanced over at her. Put a finger up. She was taking his pulse. When she finished, she patted his arm.

"And you are?"

"His fiancée." Sure wasn't taking chances with not getting in to see him. Although stretching the truth a little, she wasn't lying. She would be his fiancée someday.

"The accident knocked him out. He has some glass fragments in his head. The doctor has ordered a CT scan and lab tests. He might have a concussion, but it doesn't look like there are any life-threatening injuries."

"Why is he unconscious?"

"The EMTs said a tree hit the roof of his car after the accident and probably knocked him out."

"Wait," said Sam. "Are you saying he had an accident and then got hit by a tree?"

"That's what I heard. You can check with the police for more details."

Several nurses came in and connected Mark to an IV, then an EKG for monitoring his heart, and closed the curtain. Sam was alone with her thoughts, but hearing the strong *beep, beep, beep* of Mark's heartbeat relaxed her.

The curtain opened, and she looked up to see worried looks on Joe and Ben's faces. "How is he?" asked Joe.

Sam closed her eyes and tried to stand. Her weak knees forced her down. She gulped back a moan, but a single tear dripped down her cheek.

Joe knelt in front of her. "Sam, it's gonna be all right. Mark's a strong guy."

But would that be enough?

She prayed it would—but things had a way of going to shit sometimes.

"What does the doctor say?" asked Ben.

"I haven't spoken to the doctor yet. The nurse said they're taking tests. It doesn't look like there were any internal injuries. But they're going to do a CT scan because they think he has a concussion."

"What happened?" asked Joe.

He pulled a chair over, turned it around, and sat down.

"I don't know everything, just that he had an accident, and then a tree fell on the car. I need to speak with the police and get more details."

Ben walked over to the bed. He let out a deep breath. "Sam, I know you have a friend on the force. But I still have friends there. Let me ask around. That way you can stay with Mark."

"Thanks. I appreciate that."

Ben left, and Sam settled back in the hard chair. Joe in the other chair.

Joe wasn't a talker, which she was thankful for.

Mark had been his best friend since the SEALs, and seeing Mark lay there had to be hard on him, too. The irony of it was that they had gone on many missions together without too many injuries, and yet an accident back home put Mark in the hospital.

Mark looked peaceful. She hoped he wasn't hurting. There were so many questions that she wanted answered. Like what happened? Mark was conscientious about vehicle maintenance and a careful driver. Did the heavy rainfall have something to do with the accident? Was another driver careless?

And damn, there was Alex. Sam didn't want to leave Mark. She called the sitter and asked her to pick Alex up and stay with her until Sam could figure out what to do.

Her phone started ringing. Sam spent the next half hour answering questions from friends asking what they could do. "Pray" was all she asked.

Joe was fielding other calls. Finally, silence. She let out a deep breath.

"This sucks."

"Yeah," said Joe.

It was getting late, and Joe left, promising to be back soon. Sam rested her head on the bed. It would be a long night. Sam's mind drifted to how she met Mark.

*The thief was thin, too thin, but what he lacked in weight, he made up for in upper body strength. He'd pushed Laura to the ground and grabbed Sam as they came out of Salt & Sea and pressed her against the brick wall.*

*His foul-smelling breath made her want to vomit, but she had to concentrate on the thief. He brought his arm up and across her throat, cutting off her air while he was reaching for her purse.*

*Sam guessed he expected two women would be no match for him. Wrong!*

*In a smooth move, Sam had one-two punched him in the face with a palm strike, pulled out of his hold, then kneed him in the groin. The attacker screamed and bent over in agony.*

*She went in for the kill, punching his face until he was on the ground. Then she got his hands behind his back. She had zip-ties in her purse and asked Laura to get them.*

*A dark-haired man came running over as Sam was straddling the jackass. Laura was still hitting the thief with her purse. Sam yelled at him to call the police.*

*He called, then leaned against the wall and watched her tie the asshole up. Didn't volunteer to help. He stayed with them until the police showed up. Didn't say a word until the police left.*

*Then he smirked and said, "Good work." She tsked and let it go, never expecting to see the guy again.*

But it could have easily gone the other way if Laura hadn't stepped in to play Cupid.

*The next day, she got a call from Mark asking if she wanted to get coffee. No, thank you. Sam had a business to run. She didn't have time to date.*

*He called every week for a month. Laura finally asked her what was going on. She told Sam that Mark was asking about her. Although it was none of her business, she thought that they were perfect for each other.*

*Sam only shook her head. Not happening.*

*Laura was tenacious. They were having lunch one day at the bistro when Laura got up to supposedly check on the cook. Mark slipped into the booth. The traitor waved from the kitchen and smirked.*

*She and Mark had a great conversation and discovered both were building their respective businesses, had little time for dating and had mutual friends.*

Turned out one of her employees, Joe Harkin, had served in the SEALs with Mark—small world.

It took about six months for them to realize they had a real connection. Three years later, they were still together, and she'd never looked back. Mark was it for her, and if anything happened to him, she didn't know what she would do.

It was dark when Sam woke up and looked around. It was a new room. She remembered following the gurney late last night. She stood up and stretched, hoping Mark would open his eyes.

The insistent beeping of machines hadn't kept her up. Sam hoped she hadn't missed Mark waking up or needing something.

His eyes were still closed. Now was a good time to use the restroom and get a cup of coffee. Her mouth felt like a cotton ball.

She walked past a waiting room and saw a familiar crowd. Their friends were there talking quietly.

"Hey." Grace got up and waddled over, put her arms

around Sam and hugged her. "How's Mark doing? Is he awake yet?"

Sam sighed. "I just woke up, and he's still asleep." She looked around the room. " How long have you been here, and where are the kids?"

"Luke is with the kids. He thought it was more important that I be here for you. We've been here most of the night, although I'm going to leave soon. Marlee will be here for you."

Pete walked over. "Is he moving at all?"

She shook her head. "I don't know anything yet. I was going to get a cup of coffee."

"Why don't you go sit with Mark, and I'll bring you a cup," said Pete. Joe nodded in agreement.

Sam closed her eyes. This was what she needed—comfort and support from her friends. The anxiety she'd been fighting eased. She'd felt a little alone sitting with Mark, not wanting to ask for help, but her friends came through. Why was she always surprised? They always came through, just like she did for them.

The restroom was on the way back to Mark's room. Sam washed her hands, looked into the mirror and didn't recognize herself. She looked like a racoon. Her eyes were lined with dark circles, and what the heck was going on with her hair?

She couldn't do anything about the dark circles. But she ran her fingers through her hair, then splashed some water on her face. Feeling somewhat human again, she stepped into Mark's room, sat in the plush chair and picked up his hand. Felt the callouses from work, the warmth in his fingers. A tear dripped down her cheek.

"Don't you dare die on me. We have so much more living to do."

"Am I dying?" asked a weak voice.

Sam yelped.

Mark opened one eye and squeezed her hand.

*He's okay.* She let out a huge breath. "Shit, you scared me, and no, you're not dying."

He gave her a cheeky grin. "Good to know. What happened? How did I get here?"

"You had an accident, and then two trees fell on the truck. They brought you in last night. Nothing's broken, but you were unconscious when they brought you in."

Mark was silent for a minute. "I remember my brakes failing and steering the car off the highway into the woods, but that's all. I didn't hurt anyone, did I?"

"No, you were lucky."

He shook his head. "I can't believe my brakes failed. The brake light came on, and I was going to bring the truck to the shop the next day."

Joe and Claire popped their heads in. "Great, you're awake," said Claire.

Joe walked over and clapped Mark on the shoulder. "If you wanted a vacation, you could have just taken one."

They all laughed, which broke the tension.

The doctor knocked on the door and strolled in. "Good. You're awake." He looked around at the small group. "If you all could leave the room, I'd like to check my patient."

Mark grabbed Sam's hand. "She stays."

The doctor shrugged. "Fine by me."

Joe and Claire left after informing Sam that they would tell the others the good news.

The doctor looked at the chart and listened to Mark's heartbeat.

He had Mark follow his finger back and forth. "Headache?" he asked.

"A little."

"How about blurry vision or nausea?"

"No."

"You have a slight concussion. There's no reason for you to stay here any longer, as long as you have someone at home to keep watch."

"He does," said Sam.

"I'll sign the order to release you. If you feel worse, have blurry vision or vomit, you need to come back."

"Understood," said Mark.

Mark's clothes were in the small closet, and Sam helped him dress. It felt good to be doing something positive. She couldn't wait to get Mark home, where she could smother him in kisses.

He sat on the bed waiting for the nurse to come with a wheelchair. Their friends stopped in to say hello and left.

"Where's my truck, do you know?"

"They towed it to George's garage. I'll call him later," said Sam.

"Good. I would love to know how bad my brakes were. I thought I had them replaced a short time ago. I'm so thankful I didn't hit anyone."

She would call George when they got home. The failing brakes were a mystery, but she trusted George to be thorough.

Sam wondered what happened and prayed this wasn't part of her stalker's plan.

## CHAPTER THIRTY-SIX

T wo days later Mark was feeling sore but much better. They had gone to the crash site and saw where Mark had stopped and the two trees that had fallen on his truck. Several other trees lay on their sides and must have been loosened by the torrential downfall. He was lucky to be alive.

While they waited to hear back from George about the brakes, there was one more person Sam had to find who might have some answers.

It took Sam about a week to find Naomi Fields. Sam sweet-talked Penny into giving her Naomi's information. She always knew that Penny was the perfect person to run the shelter. It was hard to get any information from her about clients. However, she and Sam had a good working relationship, and it helped that Naomi knew and trusted Sam.

Sam was surprised to find out Naomi moved to St. Petersburg. She always thought Naomi would move as far away from Florida as possible. But it was a lucky break for her. She could see Naomi in person. It was easier to talk in person. Sam asked Penny not let Naomi know that she was coming.

She didn't want to take the chance that Naomi would say no to her visiting.

It was early morning when Sam left for St. Pete. The purplish sky was ablaze with salmon streaks, puffs of pink, and the huge yellow orb sitting on the horizon; it was a vision she never tired of. Florida had always been her home except for the few years she lived in D.C., when she went to college.

Naomi had been helpful in solving Suzie's murder. Sam hoped she could shed some added information on that weekend. There were questions she wanted answered that she hadn't thought to ask at the time.

The drive from Black Pointe to St. Pete took about three and a half hours. It wasn't a drive she was looking forward to, and she would head back later unless it got too late to drive home. Naomi had given Penny the name of the store where she worked. Not all the women who left the shelter gave their new addresses. They felt safer being anonymous.

Hours later, the sky was a vivid blue with white puffy clouds. She passed several conservation areas, which Florida had in abundance; a variety of lakes; a few historic little towns; and miles of nothing until the scenery changed to congested developments and strip malls as she got closer to Tampa Bay.

She'd been enjoying the scenery and sky, but all the while she was adjusting the rearview mirror, checking to make sure no one was following her. She couldn't be too careful.

As Sam arrived in St. Pete, her stomach rumbled. It took a while to find a parking space. As soon as she parked her car, she found a water-view restaurant, spied a corner table, and sat with her back to the wall. A sizzling platter of fish tacos was served to the couple at the next table and looked delicious. That's what she ordered with an iced tea. Waiting for her meal, she glanced around the rustic open-air restaurant. The owners had painted the walls a soothing green. The wooden floors were dark. A few booths and chairs and tables were scattered around the restaurant's center. The owner carried the nautical theme around the walls with oars and stuffed fish.

Pulling up Naomi's information, Sam noticed her work-place was close to the restaurant. The atmosphere was peaceful, and her mind wandered back to when she first met Naomi at the shelter. Naomi's body had been beaten and bruised, but the abuse hadn't crushed her spirit. The courage she'd shown when she volunteered to testify against Tony Moranti still amazed Sam. Not only that, but Naomi convinced another woman to come forward, and their recollections put Tony Moranti in jail for murdering Suzie.

Getting a bottled water to go, Sam followed the directions to the art gallery off the Boardwalk where Naomi worked. It was a cute shop surrounded by a small marina and other interesting shops. Avoiding crowds of people shopping, she opened the gallery door, the bell announcing her arrival.

The crafts were unusual. Sam wished she had more time to browse, but business first. She walked over to the register, where a young woman was ringing up a customer. She waited until the woman was finished with the transaction to ask about Naomi.

"Naomi is in the back. I'll get her."

A few minutes later, Naomi and the cashier walked out of the back room. Naomi stopped and stared, her mouth open. Her face turned white, like she'd seen a ghost. Sam supposed in a way she had. They hadn't been in contact for over ten years.

"Oh hell, no."

Well, that wasn't the reception she expected, even though Penny warned her that Naomi might not want to see her.

Naomi's eyes ping-ponged around the store—what was she afraid of? Sam hadn't brought anyone with her.

"Naomi, please just hear ..."

Naomi grabbed Sam's arm and pulled her into the office. "You should have called and saved yourself a trip," she hissed.

Sam clenched her jaw, took a minute to answer. "I'm sorry, but I really need to ask you a couple of questions." She put her hand on her heart. "I promise I wouldn't have bothered you if it wasn't important."

Naomi stared at Sam for a minute, then sighed. "Fine, but I fear you're bringing trouble to my door."

"I was careful. No one followed me. Only two people know I'm here, and neither will say anything."

Naomi shook her head. "You don't know that. I'll give you a few minutes. Then you have to leave and forget you know where I work."

"I promise." Sam looked around the small office. "Is there somewhere we can talk, or could we meet up later?"

"I don't want to talk here. The Java Bean is around the corner and has great coffee and a fabulous view of the water."

"Sounds good."

"Let me get my purse, and we'll leave."

A half hour later, Sam had little more than she came with. Maybe a couple of suggestions she could explore but nothing substantial. Naomi had rehashed events at the fishing camp when she testified, but there was so much more that Naomi hadn't paid attention to. Like where the cabin was located.

"It was somewhere on Cypress Lake. My friend always drove, and it was usually dark, so I'm not sure where it was exactly located."

Cypress Lake was huge and in the middle of a forest with lots of fishing camps tucked into it. Sam had been there several times because Luke's friend Seth Bowman owned a camp there. Hmmm, she hadn't spoken to Seth in a while. Maybe he could shed some more information.

"After the trial, you remembered a Chrissie Thorne who would come up occasionally."

Naomi was silent for a minute. "Right. Chrissie was with Tony a lot. I think she lived out of state and her mother was friends with the uncle who owned the camp. It wasn't Tony's uncle but his cousin's uncle through marriage or something like that." Naomi shook her head. "It's been so long. I don't remember anything else."

"Do you remember what she looked like?"

"She was pretty. Long, streaked black hair, gray eyes. It was always her eyes that made her stand out."

Gray eyes? Streaked black hair? The only new person Sam knew who had black hair, not including the workers at Mark's company, was Jenna. Jenna's black hair wasn't streaked or long, but she was pretty and had brown eyes. She'd throw her name out anyhow.

"Do you recognize the name Jenna Payton?"

Naomi thought for a moment and shook her head. "Doesn't ring a bell."

Finally, Naomi got up. "I have to get back to work. It's enough that Tony promised to get even, and I've lived in fear since then. I've kept my head down. I'm making a good life for myself, and I don't want it ruined."

"Well, Tony's dead."

"Good riddance. But still ..."

Sam interrupted her. "I'm sorry if I've caused you angst. Look, I've already forgotten where you live. From the bottom of my heart, thank you."

"Don't thank me. Just don't come back." Naomi spun away and walked back to her office.

All righty then. The trip home was long. Sam was upset that Naomi still feared for her life, but she'd been careful driving here, checking for anyone following her.

If it hadn't been for Naomi's testimony, Tony would never

have been convicted and sent to jail. She'd testified that she heard Tony slapping and arguing with Suzie earlier in the day. It had been late at night when she heard Tony asking someone if they had taken care of the body, although Naomi didn't know who Tony was speaking to. But they mentioned a car trunk and "buried far away."

Whoever Tony had asked to bury Suzie's body wasn't too bright and was lazy. He buried her off a path used regularly by hikers with dogs, and one ambitious dog dug up part of the tarp. Between the DNA in Tony's trunk and on the tarp, plus the women's testimony, Tony's prosecution was a slam dunk.

Naomi offered little more than Sam already knew.

When Sam got back to the office, Phil could research the information she got. Hopefully, it was enough so they could narrow down who was targeting her and her friends.

# CHAPTER THIRTY-SEVEN

I t wasn't hard to follow Naomi home.

Women were so stupid. No wonder they needed a man to guide them. Naomi never checked her surroundings. Never looked left or right. Never saw Colin following her.

Promptly at 5 p.m., she'd left the shop and walked a block to her beat-up two-door red hatchback.

Colin couldn't believe that someone had a vehicle in worse shape than his junker, but there you go. It felt good to sit in the air-conditioned truck after the sitting in the brutal heat, even though the AC blew mostly warm air.

He'd been in St. Pete for a while and had a few hours to kill before Naomi left work.

Colin had time to explore the Boardwalk. It had lots of shops to look in, if you were into collecting real art or tchotchkes, but he wasn't into seashells made into ashtrays, door hangers, or wind chimes. He didn't have the big bucks to buy authentic art, not that he would waste his money on art, authentic or not.

He grabbed a cup of overpriced coffee, found a bench,

and people-watched for a while. The sun beat down merci-
lessly and made his head itch under the wig he was wearing.
He didn't dare scratch or move the stupid wig around. The
one thing he didn't want was to have Naomi identify him and
spoil his fun with Sam Knight. He was saving that revelation
until the end.

Naomi had changed very little from when she and her
friends were coming up to party at his uncle's fishing camp.
Still good-looking in that trampy way. Short skirt, V-neck
top, long black hair, but she was using less makeup.

Naomi and her girlfriends would show up in their bikinis
or tiny shorts and halter tops, just asking for it. They'd flirt
with all the guys. They always wanted to hook up with Tony
even though he was rough with them. He'd choose one of
them and give them cash and drugs. Or they'd come to party,
smoke weed, get drunk, and find someone to fuck and not
necessarily in that order. Then they'd take one of the cabin's
three bedrooms or find a spot in the woods and get their
jollies.

Chrissie would come up occasionally. She had been Colin's
first crush, but she'd always been with Tony. Even after she
married that shit-for-brains Julian McMasters.

That had been her one mistake. She married Julian to
get Tony jealous. It didn't work. Tony still fucked her. In
fact, it excited Tony knowing that he was fucking with
Julian. Julian was a wannabe drug dealer but was always so
strung out on drugs that he never knew Chrissie and Tony
were hooking up. No one cried when he died, least of all
Chrissie.

On the weekends that Chrissie couldn't make it down,
Naomi or Diane was Tony's second choice, especially after
Suzie died.

They had good times until the girls decided they didn't
like the occasional slap to put them in their place. Then they

all forgot the good times and testified that Tony had abused them and beat them—lies.

He had no idea where Diane, the other woman who testified, was living. Someday he might find out and pay her a visit. But today—Naomi was his.

She was finally going to learn what it meant to testify against his cousin.

It was just luck that Chrissie was walking back to Phil's office when she overheard Sam telling Phil that she finally found out where Naomi Fields was living. She wasn't privy to those conversations.

When Chrissie told him that, he felt a lightness in his chest that he would finally get justice for Tony. The tracker was still on Sam's car, but he wouldn't have known who Sam was visiting if Chrissie hadn't mentioned it.

Sam planned on visiting Naomi today at Art Creations in St. Pete. Who would have thunk that Naomi would still be living in Florida? After the trial, she'd disappeared. He and Tony tried for months to find her. They figured she had gotten as far away from Black Pointe as possible. They should have known she wouldn't.

If he'd suspected that Naomi was this close, he would have visited her earlier. Tony would have loved hearing he'd taken care of her.

It was as if the stars aligned. He had Naomi's address, and he had the day off. Work was slowing down, not that he cared. In a short time, he would disappear and then build up Tony's—rather, his—drug trade.

All he had to do today was drive to St. Pete and wait.

He watched Sam enter the store, then saw the two women come out and walk around the corner. For kicks, he entered the store and looked around. Nothing in there interested him, just Naomi.

The women talked for a half hour, and then Sam left.

He didn't.

He followed Naomi to a poorer section of town.

She lived in a converted motel—one of those two-story jobs with stairs at either end of the upper floor. At some point, someone had painted the outside a lime green, but the paint faded and was peeling, reminding Colin of a lime with a sunburn. They tried to spruce it up by painting the front doors assorted colors. As if that would make a difference. It only made the place look more pathetic.

Colin watched as Naomi parked her car and opened the door to one of the first-floor apartments. Good. First-floor apartments made everything easier—a quick in and out. He glanced around for cameras and found one facing the street. Stupid. There should be more.

He'd give her a minute to put her things down, and then he'd come a-calling.

Tapping his fingers on the steering wheel, it was a long minute.

Finally. Time to party. He got out of the car and knocked on her door.

"Just a minute."

He heard footsteps, didn't see a shadow by the peephole. Did Naomi even check before she opened the door? Guess she thought she was safe after all this time. *Surprise!* Stoolies were never safe, and that was a lesson she would learn the hard way.

Naomi opened the door a crack, the cheap chain still on and peeked out. Finally, he looked at the woman who'd ruined Tony's and his life.

"Can I help you?" She cocked her head. Didn't show any sign that she recognized him for a second under the disguise. Guess he was forgettable, but what he planned for her wouldn't be.

Then her eyes widened. She finally recognized him. She

knew what he was there for. Naomi started hyperventilating before taking a deep breath and slamming the door in his face.

*Oh no, bitch. It isn't going to be that easy.* He looked around. No one was in the parking lot. He stepped back and kicked the door open. Naomi had just reached for her phone. He slapped it out of her hand and gave her a one-two punch to the gut.

Naomi crumpled over and was moaning on the floor trying to crawl away from him. Colin reached down and grabbed her hair while crushing her phone with his foot. No one was going to interrupt him.

Party time!

Naomi was about to find out payback was a bitch.

# CHAPTER THIRTY-EIGHT

"Sam knows it's about Tony," said Chrissie as she covered herself with a threadbare blanket. The apartment Colin rented was missing many niceties. Hell, not just the extras but the necessities of life. It was dark, dank, and dirty. Depressing, just like Colin.

Unfortunately, weekly booty calls from Colin were just one more thing she had to endure. She needed to keep him happy for a while. No sense in having him get suspicious about her ultimate goals. He wasn't part of them. When she got control of the drug business, the only booty calls she'd have would be ones she called.

But Colin's apartment—ugh. He was a pig. Dirty clothes everywhere, dishes in the sink, used utensils sitting on the counter. And when had he ever washed a dish? The lazy bastard called her to clean the damn apartment. Soon, she wouldn't have to worry about things like that.

"How do you know that? Did the bitch say something to you?" Colin was in the bathroom shaving and stopped mid-stroke to ask.

"She had me call all the security guards into a meeting the

other day. I had my earphones on so I could listen to their conversation."

Colin wasn't the only smart one. He'd given her a tracker for Sam's car, and she knew he put mics in Mark's house. She had the foresight to put a mic in Sam's office. Sam's loft above KnightGuard Security's office would have been an excellent place for a mic too, but she didn't have access to it.

But in looking ahead, it would be wise of her to remove the mic from Sam's office ASAP. Sam was bound to start looking for mics and find it. She'd be suspect since she was the only new person in the office. She'd remove it first chance she got.

"She asked IT to look into visitors that Tony had."

"Stupid bitch. She'll never find my name on the list. I never visited him." Colin laughed. "Didn't have to since I was in the joint with him part of the time."

Colin finished shaving and toweled off the remains of the shaving cream from his face. A piece of tissue was pasted on a spot where he cut himself. He wrapped a towel around his waist and walked into the room, the steam from the shower following him like a ghost. "After I got out, I sent Dwight to visit and report back to me."

"Why Dwight?" She thought only Roberto had visited Tony.

"I had him go because he works for me and I didn't want anyone to know I was visiting Tony just in case." He sneered at her. "And I'm glad now. They'll never connect me to Tony."

Hmmm. She would need to get rid of Dwight too. He was about as bright as Colin and built like a sumo wrestler. How had Colin kept this fact to himself for so long? What else wasn't he telling her?

Phil might recognize her picture if he got the records from the prison. However, her ID had her married name on it. Nobody knew who Chrissie McMasters was nor Chrissie

Thorne. Not only that but she changed her name back to her maiden name years ago after she stopped visiting Tony. Getting the job at KnightGuard Security had been a cinch because of the fine work Rusty did on her driver's license and background. Having a cousin who was the best at making up fake documents and history was a blessing. The irony was that Jenna Payton was her mother's maiden name. But mom was dead, and Chrissie McMasters didn't exist.

Well, she would have to keep her wits about her.

Tony died a few months ago and was in prison for ten years, so he had a lot of visitors.

"We'll worry about that when the time comes. I'll keep my ears open in the office in case our IT guy, Phil, finds out more."

Colin got a sly gleam in his eye. "Maybe you should share a little of that sweet pussy with him. Make him forget whatever he finds."

No surprise there. She'd been thinking the same thing. That is, until she got promoted. Phil wasn't a black or white kind of guy. He hacked for fun. But morally, he was straight as an arrow. He flirted, but she suspected that was all he did. She wouldn't be seducing him easily, if at all.

Although it wouldn't have been a hardship. Phil was a hunk, had dimples, which she loved, was smart, and was particularly good at his job.

Phil was more intense than she'd imagined. The flirting man was gone, and a focused, hyper-secure Phil had emerged. He'd written out an entire plan of action for her, hour by hour.

While it would be nice to gain some computer skills, she wouldn't be needing them in the business she was going into. Selling drugs was not something you put on a spreadsheet on the computer and maintained. That was a good way of incriminating yourself if the police ever showed up, and she wasn't that stupid. She hoped Phil wasn't so good that he would put two and two together. It would ruin all her plans.

"I took care of the bitch who testified against Tony."

"What did you do?" asked Chrissie. Not that she cared.

"Not much. Let's just say, that one won't be doing any talking for a while. Besides, I told her if she did talk to anyone else, I'd find her and kill her."

"Good." Chrissie had little sympathy for the women who testified. She could imagine what Colin did. He could get vicious when he felt like it.

"It's time to ratchet up the surprises. I'm tired of playing games and living in this crappy apartment. I need to get the drug operation up and running."

Colin walked over to the bed, ripped the blanket from her body, threw the towel wrapped around his waist on the floor, and spread her legs.

"Next stop, baby, is a nice apartment, lots of money and an even better car. Then power. All the power a kingpin deserves. Those suckers that took over Tony's drug trade are history."

He started pounding into her again. Chrissie groaned like Colin expected her to, but her mind was far away. Colin was so stupid. He would never get to be in charge. Her plans to take over were in place.

Colin didn't know it, but he was the one who would be history.

# CHAPTER THIRTY-NINE

The office was quiet Tuesday morning.

Sam was still bothered by Naomi's reaction when they met.

It wasn't so much her reaction but the fear in Naomi's eyes. However, there wasn't much she could do about that. After all this time, she hoped Naomi had found some peace. Tony had done a job on Naomi, and it made Sam sick.

She was concerned that Naomi thought she would bring danger to her, but only Penny and Phil knew where Naomi was living.

"Luke, grab your jacket. We're going to visit Seth Bowman."

"Oh, goody. A field trip." Luke closed his computer and shadowed Sam to her car. "He should be out at the fishing camp this time of year."

"I know. I called yesterday. Seth said he'd be there all week."

Taking advantage of the downtime, she figured it was a good time to visit Seth Bowman. He, Luke, and Ben were good friends, and she'd met Seth, who owned the cabin where

Ben discovered his now fiancée, Marlee Burns, hiding out from her murderous CEO when Ben was on vacation there.

They got into Sam's SUV and headed west. The thirty-mile lake was a good hour's drive from Black Pointe.

"It's looking cloudy," said Luke.

Black clouds loomed in the distance, but that was nothing new. Every day for the past week, black clouds had covered the sky.

*"Cloudy with a Chance of Meatballs."*

"Whaaat?"

Shit!

Had she said that out loud?

Sam glanced over at Luke. He smirked at her. Yup. Her badass reputation was going south for sure.

"Well, I guess I know what you and Mark were doing last night. Hot date? Although I might have chosen something racier to watch."

"Stuff it."

"Yes, ma'am."

She glanced at Luke again. He wasn't smiling, but his shoulders were shaking.

Damn, she would never live this down. "For your information, we watched the movie with Alex." Then, after Alex went down for the night, she and Mark went to bed and got to the good stuff. Something Luke didn't need to know, and she wasn't sharing.

"Good to know. So tell me, when you and Mark met, was it love at first sight?"

Good God. Luke was on a roll. What was going on?

"What are we having, a kumbaya moment?" asked Sam.

"If you want."

"Stuff it."

"Is that all you can say? Besides, Mark's already shared that information. You know I love a good love story."

Sam sighed. Mark was the extrovert in the family. She knew he'd shared some relationship information but not the personal stuff.

"He loves you, you know."

"I know. Now can we sit here and be quiet?"

"Sure." Luke nodded and stared out the window. "So what do you want to talk to Seth about."

*Two seconds*. It took Luke all of two seconds to get back into his Chatty Cathy mode. Sam groaned. It was going to be a long trip.

"Hmmm." Sam fiddled with the radio, which was playing static. She needed calming music—now.

Luke cleared his throat. She hadn't answered him.

"I got some additional information from Naomi Fields, one of Tony's victims. She'd been at the cabin with Suzie and another woman."

"What would you hope to accomplish by finding the cabin after all these years?"

Good question. Sam gazed at the scenery whizzing by. The abrupt change still amazed her. Big city one minute interspersed with mobile homes and little rundown cracker houses the next, and in between were huge conservation areas, small towns, and lots of cattle ranches.

"I'm not sure. I'd like to get the owner's name and have Phil check it out. Besides, it might give us a clue as to who the cousin is. The police never got that information, and the women couldn't remember exactly where the cabin was because a friend had driven them up at night. The cops never found the friend. They canvassed the general area, but there are hundreds of houses, cabins, shacks, and RV parks around the lake. A lot of owners weren't there. The cops couldn't cover it all. I want to ask Seth if he has any suggestions on where to find it."

"Lake's huge."

"I know. I'm hoping with the additional information Naomi gave me that Seth might recognize the camp."

"Ah. Don't get your hopes up."

"I'm not, but I won't give up. I'm sure whoever is stalking me is clever and connected to Suzie's case."

"So tell me about Suzie. I know you told us about putting Moranti in jail, but I don't remember much about the case. It happened a year before I started on the force."

"Suzie was the sweetest person ever. Her death devastated me."

"Where did they find her body?"

"Well, they found her body off a path somewhere around Cypress Lake."

Oh, Suzie, sweet Suzie. The emptiness in her chest came back with a vengeance.

"Suzie and her family moved to Black Pointe when I was a freshman in high school. Grace had moved up north by then, and I was missing her so much. Suzie walked into class that first day with the biggest smile on her face that I'd ever seen and a hello for everyone. She was so upbeat and bright, you'd never have known that she came from a crappy family. Everyone wanted to be her friend, but for some obscure reason, she chose me to be her best friend."

"Wonders never cease."

"What?" Sam wasn't sure she heard Luke.

"Nothing." He cleared his throat. "She sounds nice."

"Yeah, she was. She had this model's figure that all the girls envied." Sam chuckled. "She ate like a horse and never gained weight. She claimed she had a fast metabolism."

"How did you become friends?"

"We became close friends after our first lunch together when we realized we both lost our mothers when we were young," said Sam. "However, Suzie's mother was alive but a drunk and absent from her life. Her dad worked all the time, so he had no time for her. She didn't have siblings or relatives living close by. She was a lost soul in that respect. We spent a lot of time at my house, and my grandmother doted on her. Suzie needed the love and stability that my grandparents provided."

Suzie made Sam laugh, and Sam envied how kind Suzie was to everyone.

Suzie was sunshine to Sam's darkness.

She admired Sam's sense of justice and standing up for others. Suzie reminded her of Grace. *Use your words, Sam.* She was a loyal friend, even though Sam got into a lot of trouble. A tear slipped out of her eye, and she discreetly wiped it away.

"Sweet."

"Yeah." Sam let out a frustrated breath. "I found out that she was pregnant when she was killed. I don't know if she knew or not. She never mentioned it to me."

All Suzie ever wanted in life was to be loved, get married, and have lots of children. She would have been a great mom.

"That's sad," said Luke.

Sam lost it when she found out a few years later that Suzie had been murdered and the police never found her murderer. She went on a verbal rampage for days until her mentor, Otis Hood, sat her down. He told her if she wanted justice, she needed to stop talking and get moving.

"That bastard Tony Moranti beat her and killed her, and I wonder if he even knew she was pregnant. He just tossed her body away like a piece of garbage."

Silence.

"It was a good thing he died in jail," said Luke. "I hate abusers in all forms. Watching Grace embrace her pregnancies has been my greatest joy."

Sam nodded. Yeah, all was good with Luke and Grace after their rocky start. Luke was the detective who investigated a murder that they accused Grace of. He didn't trust her and almost ruined their relationship. However, two kids later with a third on the way, the only fault Sam could see—if it even was a fault—was that Luke was overly vigilant. Making Grace rest all the time, cooking and watching the kids when he could. The resting part drove Grace crazy, but Sam suspected she secretly loved it.

"Turn right here." Luke pointed to another dirt road.

"I hear your brother Liam is out of the service. Where is he now?"

"At my grandpa's farm in Haywood Lake. He's met a woman who wants to open a center for returning vets and to train service dogs."

"Wow. Great project. What's Liam going to do? Help run it?"

Luke sighed. "I don't know. He's having some issues that he won't talk about. I know the quiet time there is good for him. Whether quiet time is what he needs, only time will tell."

"Well, if he ever wants to come work for KnightGuard, I'm sure we can fit him in somewhere until he's comfortable."

"Thanks. I appreciate that. It's a wait-and-see situation, though."

Sam followed the winding road until they saw the sign for Seth's fishing camp.

"I never asked, but where does Seth live when he's not at the fishing camp?"

"He has several rental properties around here and a house outside of Black Pointe. Busy guy."

"It seems."

The fishing camp was off to their right, and Sam turned in the driveway and parked at a little store. The aging sign stated they sold fishing licenses, bait, whatever else anglers needed, plus groceries. Seth had done a nice job painting the old clapboards but keeping a nostalgic feeling.

Seth walked out the door just as they parked. Luke was out of the car first, shook hands with Seth and leaned in, slapped his back and stepped back.

Sam approached Seth, who went to shake her hand but said "Screw it," leaned in and hugged her.

"Hey, Seth. It's been too long," she said. He was a foot taller than her, and she was hugging his chest. Awkward.

"It has been. I was surprised to hear from you." Seth looked around the camp. "Everything seems calm out here. Come on back to my office and tell me what you need."

They followed him into a cabin next to the store with an office sign on it.

Ben and Marlee had stayed in one of the larger cabins when she was on the run from her murderous CEO. This cabin was on a smaller scale.

The rustic cabin had paneled walls covered with fish of all sizes. However, all Sam could concentrate on were their eyes. Bulging dull blue, green, yellow, red, and black eyes stared at her. Yuck. She'd never fished, had no desire to fish, no desire to sit out in the hot sun for hours and catch nothing or to clean whatever she caught.

"Geez, how many stuffed fish do you have?" asked Sam.

"Lots. But they're not stuffed. They're molded of plastic. Basically, they make a mold around the fish with plaster. When it's dry, they open the mold and take out the fish. Then cover the mold with fiberglass resin. When that's dry, they peel it out, put the two sides together, paint it and add glass eyes."

"Good to know." Sam added those factoids to her mental drawer of useless information. Seth was way too excited about dead fish.

Seth pulled out a chair from behind his desk and sat

down, motioning for them to take the seats in front. Even sitting down, he was tall. Sam bet if she walked over, they would be eye to eye. *What was she thinking?* They came here for help, and she was comparing their heights. She needed a vacation for sure.

Seth steepled his hands and asked how he could help.

"Years ago, people used to come up here and party at one of the camps. The woman I spoke to couldn't remember where it was located, but she remembered bits and pieces, and I hoped something would ring a bell with you."

"Well, you're placing a lot of faith in my ability to finger a specific property." Seth gave her one of his signature grins.

"Hey, if anyone would know, it would be you."

Seth tilted his head to the left, and he tapped his fingers on his desk. "The lake is huge. It has over one hundred lake-front properties and at least double that with cabins in the woods." He blew out a deep breath. "Give me what you got, and maybe something will jump out at me."

"Okay. What Naomi remembered was that the cabin was an old-style cracker type, with a screened-in front porch. It was close to the lake. She said there were no houses around it, but they passed a small store and RV park on their way up. She wasn't sure how far away the store was from the cabin. The only unusual feature in the cabin was the woodwork in the kitchen. Tony's uncle was a woodworker."

"Hmmm. There are so many cabins here and a few general stores. Many of the general stores have gone out of business. There are a lot of old-timers here. Let me ask around, and I'll get back to you."

"Great. The sooner, the better."

"Is there a reason you need the information?"

Sam thought about what she could tell Seth.

Would it be a reflection of her investigative skills if she

told him that someone was stalking her and that Knight-Guard Security had no idea who?

Oh, who was she kidding? They needed to catch the stalker now. Pride be damned.

"Yeah. I've picked up a stalker. One who is harassing my friends, and I'm sure I'm next on the sicko's list. We just don't know who it is or why, but I feel it's connected to Tony Moranti."

Sam told Seth about what was happening in Black Pointe.

Seth's eyes widened. "Shit."

They were ready to leave, and Seth walked them to the car. "I heard about Mark's accident. Do you think that's connected?"

"Yes. That's why I need any additional information that you can get."

"I'll get on that today and call if I hear anything."

They said goodbye. The clouds still hung in the sky like a black coffin, but the rain never came, and they were on their way back to the office.

"What I don't understand is how this stalker knows your friends and where you're going," said Luke.

Neither did she, and it was frustrating. Something nagged at her subconscious.

Fisheyes. Fisheyes? Eyes!

"Someone has eyes and mics on me."

That had to be it. She was an idiot. Mentally slapping her head. She was too close to this investigation, and the saying "can't see the forest for the trees" flashed through her mind. "Remember when we found the cameras and mics at Grace's condo?"

When Luke and Sam had gone to Grace's condo, they found apps on her computer and hidden cameras and mics.

"Yeah. That was a good call," said Luke.

"When we get back, we're checking my loft, the office and my car."

Sam didn't think anyone had been up in her loft since she rarely had anyone over and her employees had no reason to ever go up there. It could be a new client or maybe one of the many vendors they had in the office.

All she knew was that the sooner they got a handle on the stalker, the safer everyone would be, including her. Especially her.

# CHAPTER FORTY

I t was black and hidden under the front bumper like a squashed insect.

"Damn." Sam clenched her hands into a fist. A fist she wanted to pummel into the face of whoever put the tracker on her car. Luke had found it when they got back to KnightGuard.

"This is the almost perfect ending to a shitty week," she hissed.

"I wonder who put it there? It all makes sense now how this asshole knew where you were going," said Luke.

Sam pulled out a baggie. "Put it in here. My friend at the station owes me a favor. I'll ask him to check for any identifiable prints and run them."

Luke placed the device in the baggie. "If your guy can't, I still have close friends on the force I can ask. Also, we need to check the office and your loft. Phil and Ben are still here. I'll get them to help."

"We're growing so fast, it might be a good idea to check for bugs weekly," said Luke.

Sam sighed. One more thing to think about. "You're right,

and I think it's time to put a fence with an electric gate around the building."

Luke nodded his agreement.

She was thankful there wasn't too much area to cover. Nobody outside of her employees went to the back offices, especially where IT was located. Phil was conscientious about locking up when he wasn't around, but they still checked.

Her heart ached with sadness that this was what her life was reduced to—an unknown enemy spying on her and hurting her friends and family, and she couldn't do anything about it.

Three exhausting hours later, they came up empty on hidden cameras and mics.

Sam was in her office, sitting at the conference table that usually brought her happiness, and put her head between her hands.

At least when they had searched Grace's condo a couple of years ago, they'd found hidden mics and cameras. She didn't know what to make of the fact that nothing was at KnightGuard.

A tracker on her car wouldn't tell someone who her friends were, just her location. Exhaling a long breath, she leaned back in her chair. Her life and career were heading into an abyss that she wasn't sure she could get out of. How had everything become so confusing? Why was the answer evading her?

There was something they were missing. What?

How was this stalker so clever? He or she had been hunting her for weeks now, and she was nowhere closer to finding out who it was. Mark would be home late, and Sam desperately wanted to hold him. Have him comfort her. The situation was getting her down.

"Crap!"

She had a moment of clarity. Mark's house was where they'd find what they were looking for.

That's where they would hide the cameras and mics since she was hardly in her loft anymore. She was living full-time at Mark's house. How stupid was she? This was Private Eye 101, and she failed.

No wonder they didn't hide mics at the office. Mark's house was perfect and the perfect place to get all their personal information. Sam shook her head. Since Alex's arrival and her friends being targeted, she'd been distracted. Add in her complicated relationship with Mark, the new employees, and a multitude of other problems, and thinking clearly apparently was off the table.

---

IT DIDN'T TAKE LONG to find the mics at Mark's house. One was installed in the kitchen underneath the table. The table where they ate meals and laughed. Where they discussed what was going in their lives. Where they felt safe. The other was in the bathroom.

Sam rubbed her chest and shuddered. Her worst fears had come true. She'd brought evil to their house, and it was up to her to destroy it before this jerk destroyed everything and everyone she loved.

"Sam."

"Yeah?"

"We need to get Mark in on this. Find out who's been to the house," said Luke.

"I know."

She bowed her head and inhaled. Held the breath. Exhaled. Her hands were clammy, and she wiped them on her pants. She didn't want to talk to Mark to tell him that she endangered his niece even more than the attempted kidnap-

246 LILA FERRARI

ping. The niece he loved with all his heart and soul. The only precious thing he had left of his sister. She also caused his accident by her carelessness.

Yeah, that was going to go over big.

"He should be home in an hour. Thankfully, Alex is with the babysitter. I'll call Joyce and ask her if she can bring Alex home later. Why don't you guys go home? There's nothing else you can do here."

Luke, Ben, and Phil said goodbye, and Sam sank onto the leather sofa. The glass of wine she poured sat on the table, and Sam wondered if a glass would be enough to erase the pain—probably not. A case of wine wouldn't either.

Part of her felt better that the KnightGuard Security office and her loft didn't have any devices, but Mark's house? She could only shake her head. The breakfast muffin she'd eaten so long ago sat like lead in her belly, and she worried about how Mark was going to react. Sam wanted to hide, stick her head in the sand and not show her face ever.

But that wasn't her. She needed to be strong and take the fight to whoever was after her.

The alarm beeped, and Mark walked in. He stood in the open doorway and stared at Sam. She gave him a weak "Hi," and before she could say anything else, he'd closed the door and rushed over to her.

He sat next to Sam and pulled her into his arms. He kissed the top of her head.

"I'm so sorry," she whispered.

"Nothing to be sorry about. But to be sure, why don't you tell me what you're sorry about."

Sam explained how they found the mics. Mark didn't say a word. He just sat there, no emotion on his face.

"I've brought danger to our home," whispered Sam.

"It could have happened to anyone."

Sam shook her head vehemently. She was sweating

profusely; the stress was ratcheting up. Was Mark listening to her? She brought danger to their door. Why wasn't he mad? *Why is it so hot in here?* Sam's body felt like she was in a giant sauna.

Could she confess what was in her heart? Could she trust him to understand? Taking a deep breath and exhaling, she took a chance.

"I'm afraid." She could hear his heart thumping steadily in his chest, unlike hers.

"Sam, you never have to be afraid. Look at me." He released his arms and placed both hands on the side of her face and looked deep into her eyes. "We are in this together. Good or bad. You are not alone."

She sighed. "Realistically, I know that. But I can't help feeling I could have done more. I never wanted you or Alex to get hurt."

"Humph. As if someone could hurt me. I'm a SEAL. Remember?" He smiled at her. "Uncle Sam made sure I have all the skills I need to protect my country and family."

"I know, but ..."

Mark kissed her forehead. "No buts. We're in this together."

He kissed her cheeks. "Whoever this asshole is, he is not going to win."

He kissed her mouth. His tongue insistent that she open for him. Then he plunged in. A desperate kiss that made her feel all tingly. Then guilty because this was serious. She pushed away from him.

"No distracting me, buster. We need to figure out who's been in the house and go from there."

Mark smirked. "I'll distract you later. Okay, then, let's make a list. It's been a couple of months, and so many people have been in the house. Would you get me a beer? I have to think about who's been here."

Sam brought back a beer for each of them and settled in a chair. No sitting on the sofa with Mark. They'd never get anything done.

He picked up a pad and pen, then rubbed the back of his neck and sighed. "I hate this."

"I know," said Sam.

"We need to go back a couple of months, since that was when you felt someone was watching you. I think we should include events also. Something might stand out."

"Agree."

They sat in silence for a few minutes. "I sensed this was a problem just before Danny and Hailey's wedding. Let's start there and go forward."

Mark nodded. "First, there was the problem at Laura's restaurant."

"Right, she had the problem with cars in her parking lot. Thankfully, insurance took care of most of the expense."

"Then, I hired two new employees, Mia and Colin. I checked their references carefully. There were no red flags. I also hired some laborers, checked their references too."

"Okay, Jenna started. Naomi said Tony's girlfriend Chrissie had long, streaked black hair and gray eyes. I did ask Naomi if Jenna's name rang a bell even though she has short black hair and brown eyes. It didn't. The agency screens all their hires, plus Phil double-checks. No red flags."

Mark drew a timetable and added names and events.

"Oh, then we went to Amanda's funeral, and Alex came to live here." Mark frowned. "It seems like yesterday, doesn't it?"

"Yes, but with the sadness came joy. Alex is special," said Sam.

Mark smiled. "Yes, she is."

They sat in silence for a minute.

"Marcia came back from vacation, and I hired Jenna full-time." It was a good move for the company. Jenna's skills were wasted welcoming people. Sam had high hopes for her, and she fit right into the company .

"Colin Woods came to the house to build the bookshelves."

"Oh, right. He did a great job. They look terrific, and Alex loves sitting on the bench to read."

Mark added the names to the table and looked over at her. "Yeah, he's a master craftsman. My clients love the work he's done."

Sam grimaced. "I don't know whether to include Penny being assaulted or not. What do you think?"

"Might as well add it." He wrote Penny's name down. "I've had poker here. But I trust those guys with my life."

"Then Hailey had that issue at the store, and that was when I put everything together," said Sam.

"Right. I've had Travis and Micah and two of Micah's cousins over to build the swing set in the backyard. They were here all day, in and out of the house. I'll get their names and check them out," said Mark. "Oh, I can't forget Mia was here with the paperwork for the grant to build a center in Haywood Lake."

Haywood Lake? Sam hadn't heard about this, but she remembered Luke telling her that his brother was living there. "That's where Liam McBride is living, right?"

"Yes."

"What are you building?"

"I served on the teams with Ted Maddox. His sister is opening a center for veterans who suffer from PTSD and wants them to train shelter dogs to become companions. The cabins will be for anyone who doesn't have access to shelter. Ted is going to take over the running of the center. He already runs several support groups here in Black Pointe."

Sam's stomach fluttered. Mark couldn't keep the excitement from his voice. This was a huge undertaking, and she had no idea he was contemplating this. "Wow, that must make you feel good."

He nodded his head. "It does. I've always wanted to get to the point in my career that I could give back. I particularly like the idea of helping vets who have given so much for their country."

"Is Liam going to help him?"

"I don't know yet. Liam has his own problems to work out, although Ted's sister Joy and he are in a relationship."

Sam thought about Liam. She'd met him a while ago and thought he might make a good addition to the KnightGuard Security team if he was looking for work. Although whatever issues he had needed to be worked out first. Thoughts for another day. Back to the issue at hand.

"Keep me posted on that."

Mark nodded.

"All righty then. Let's see. We are up to Alex's almost-abduction."

"God, I will never forget that. And that was a woman who was driving. The SUV was a rental, and we never figured out who rented one of hundreds of white SUVs." Sam stood and paced. She rubbed her forehead. A tension headache of epic proportions was forming. "I just don't know how all this fits together."

Mark patted the seat next to him. "Pacing isn't going to help."

Sam sat next to him and hugged a pillow. As if the pillow would give her comfort. KnightGuard Security had never had so many puzzle parts. Her brain hurt.

"It's frustrating for sure. We're up to your accident. Phil did see a man crawl underneath your car that day but we couldn't identify him."

"Right. I still want to kill the bastard."

"So that's where we are. We don't have much, and I don't

see anyone standing out. You'll check on Travis, Micah and the cousins?"

Mark nodded his agreement.

"Okay, I'll give this list to Phil and see if he can make any sense of it. Find the missing puzzle piece. My brain is fried. We need to focus on the new people in our lives at Stone Construction and KnightGuard."

"Agree. And if Phil doesn't find anything?" asked Mark.

Sam shook her head. "Then I don't know." She was forgetting something or someone. But the why or who was eluding her.

"Sam, you look puzzled. Is something bothering you?" asked Mark.

She rubbed the back of her neck. Being so distracted wasn't like her. Whoever the stalker or stalkers were was upsetting her normal train of thought. This was more than just business; it was her friends and family who were being hurt.

"I'm missing something. Something important. Damn, I'm so off my game." She threw up her arms. "What is wrong with me?"

Mark walked over, pulled her onto his lap with her back to his chest and rubbed her shoulders.

"Ow."

"Jeez, you're tighter than a drum. After this is over, you need to get a massage." He rubbed some more. "In fact, if you go into the bedroom, take off your clothes, I'll give you one right now."

"Humpf. If I do that, nothing else will get done." Sam hung her head. What was she missing?

Maybe a trip to the bedroom was a good idea. She started to get up. Trip. *Trip!*.

"Crap, I forgot about my visit to see Naomi. We had an awkward conversation since she didn't want me there." She sighed. "But I better call Naomi and make sure she's being cautious."

Sam added that to the list of things she didn't want to do. But this mess was on her, so she'd suck it up and do what was right.

# CHAPTER FORTY-ONE

S am had tried Naomi's phone several more times—no answer.

Naomi must really be upset with Sam for contacting her. Sam searched through her contacts for Naomi's work number. If the woman wouldn't call her back, she'd call the store. If Naomi wouldn't take her call there, then another trip to St. Pete was in order. Naomi could be in danger, and she'd let this go on long enough.

Sam got up early Sunday morning and hoped the store was open. She dialed the number, and it rang eight times. Sam almost hung up. She heard a click and a breathless voice said, "This is Art Creations. How may I help you?"

"Yes, I'm looking for Naomi Fields."

"I'm sorry. She's not here."

"Will she be in later?"

Silence.

"No, she's taken a leave of absence."

*A leave of absence?* Oh, this didn't bode well. Had Naomi left St. Pete, or was it something else?

"Do you know if she's at home?"

Silence. Sam resisted the temptation to yell at the clerk, but she needed information.

"Please, I'm a friend of hers, and I haven't been able to reach her," said Sam.

"Uh, Naomi had an accident, and she's in the hospital."

*Hospital?* The phone trembled in her hands. This wasn't good—not at all.

"Can you tell me what happened?"

"Look, I'm not supposed to say anything about our employees. She's at Tampa Bay Hospital, and that's all I know."

"You've helped enough. Thank you." Sam hung up and slammed the phone down on the kitchen table. She closed her eyes and willed her heart to stop thumping out *warning, warning.*

"Sam?"

Sam opened her mouth to tell Mark what happened, but the words stuck in throat. She looked into Mark's worried eyes and shook her head. "Life sucks right now and I ... I feel lost. I just want to stick my head in the sand and pray everything goes away."

Mark stared at her for a moment, pulled out a chair and sat down. He took her hand in his. "Then forget everything and sell the business. I'll take care of you. You won't have to worry about anything."

*Forget? Sell?*

Sam gasped and pulled her hand from his. "What the hell? I'm not doing that. You should know me better than that."

Mark smiled at her. "There's my girl. Sam, you've never wallowed in self-pity. You had a moment. Now let it go. Tell me what happened and what you're going to do about it."

Mark was right. Hiding wasn't her. She always valued courage. She would step up to the plate and resolve this issue. "Naomi isn't at work. She's in the hospital."

"Oh, my God. What happened?"

"The clerk at Naomi's work told me she had an accident. I'm going with my gut here and thinking that it was no accident and someone got to her through me."

Jumbled thoughts pervaded Sam's mind.

First, she needed to call Danny and Pete and have them take over the day-to-day until she had a better handle on Naomi's situation. Mark had the babysitter Joyce on call, so Alex wouldn't be a problem. Then she would head for St. Pete and put out yet another fire and hopefully make it right for Naomi. She had one other call to make.

———

"You don't think this is overkill, do you?" asked Veronica.

"I'd rather it be too much than not enough," said Sam. She had no more information about Naomi.

The hospital wouldn't give her any updates except that Naomi was still there, and Sam wanted to be prepared. If Naomi was hurt because of her, she'd fix it. Mark had volunteered to come with her. It was a kind gesture, but it might upset Naomi to see a man. So many ifs.

"Tell me more about Naomi. Testifying took a lot of courage."

That was one thing she liked about Veronica: her empathy. Sure, the guys had it to a certain extent. They were all about protecting the weak and innocent, which was great. Sometimes women especially, needed someone to sympathize with them and hold their hand, not just solve their problems. Veronica had a hard life, had pulled herself up from the pit and made a life for herself, not unlike Naomi. Veronica would understand.

Sam and Veronica spent the time driving to St. Pete

talking about Naomi, Suzie and what they might need to do depending upon circumstances.

Finally, Sam saw the modern, five-story cinder-block hospital and followed the signs to the parking garage. They parked, walked into the hospital and lied. Told the attendant they were Naomi's sisters. Sam was taking no chance they wouldn't get in to see Naomi. At least this time, they weren't in the emergency room with sick people.

They followed the directions to the fourth floor.

A nurse was just leaving Naomi's room when they got there.

"How is she?" asked Sam.

"Well, she's resting right now, but she's got a long haul ahead of her to get well."

"What will need to be done?"

"She has a broken arm, broken ribs. She's gonna need some facial reconstruction, someone to help her at home and therapy." The nurse nodded. "A lot of therapy."

Sam listened to what the nurse said. Her feet were walking into the room while her mind screamed *run, run,* but she wouldn't run. That wasn't her.

Veronica placed her hand on her shoulder. "We'll get through this."

Swallowing the lump in her throat, Sam wiped her sweaty hands on her pants. "I know we will."

Naomi lay on the bed with her eyes closed, connected to machines, tubes and covered in bandages. The room was stuffy, with an antiseptic smell that clogged Sam's nose.

"Naomi?" Sam whispered.

Naomi moaned and opened her one eye that wasn't bandaged. Stared at Sam for a minute.

"Get out."

Well, this was going exactly how she predicted.

"No. I got you into this, and I'm going to fix it."

"You've done enough."

Sam pulled out a chair and sat by Naomi's side. "You're right. But hear me out. I had no idea a tracker was on my car and the man followed you here. I'm so sorry you got hurt."

Naomi turned her face away from Sam. "I don't care. Because of you, I've lost everything. My home, my job, everything I've worked hard for."

Her body started shaking. Tears fell from Naomi's eye, but no sound came out. Sam wanted to cry for her; she had to make this right.

"Naomi, you are a strong, courageous woman. You will get everything back you've lost, I promise."

"Humph. I won't be able to work for months. I don't have health insurance. I won't be able to drive my car." She snorted. "I won't have money for the insurance anyhow."

"Would you let me help you? Please," asked Sam. "I want to make this right for you."

Veronica interrupted just then. "Sam, I'm going to get some coffee while you explain to Naomi what you have in mind."

She left, and Sam studied Naomi. She yawned several times. She was getting tired, so Sam needed to present her plan quickly.

"Veronica came with me today. She's going to stay here until you get out of the hospital, making sure you have what you need and you're safe."

"Safe," Naomi whispered.

Of course, Naomi would want to feel safe, and Sam could provide that safety.

"Yes. Safe. She is ex-military, proficient in hand-to-hand combat and an all-around badass. I trust her with my life, and you can too."

Naomi sighed.

"She has authority to pay all your medical bills and

anything else you need. When you're released, I'd love for you to come to Black Pointe and ..."

"Noooo."

Sam put her hand up. "Hear me out. I have a loft in the KnightGuard Security building. KnightGuard Security is staffed twenty-four seven, so you'll always be safe. We'll get a nurse to help you full-time and a therapist when you're ready. I know a great plastic surgeon who will help. You can stay there as long as you want." Sam bit her lower lip. "What do you say?"

"That's too much."

"Ah, no, it isn't. It's the least I can do to help a situation that I caused."

Veronica came back with two cups of coffee. She handed one to Sam and looked at Naomi. "I guess you and I will be roomies for a while." Naomi nodded.

"I'm looking forward to it." Veronica smiled, pulled a chair close and rubbed Naomi's hand. "Everything will turn out okay, promise."

"Do you remember anything about the attack? Do you know who it was?" asked Sam.

Naomi thought about it for a moment. "He was wearing a wig, I think. But his eyes. I recognized his eyes. Cold. It made me think it was Tony's cousin. His eyes were always cold, and he liked to hit. I don't remember his name though."

Her voice got weak and low..

"Okay, are we good going forward?" asked Sam.

Naomi nodded.

Sam turned to Veronica. "I've rented you a car. Keep me updated on progress. Anything you or Naomi need, get it. No need to pass it by me. Any other problems, Marcia will handle on our end."

Veronica stood. "No problem. Miss Naomi and I will be besties by the time we get up to Black Pointe."

Sam hugged Veronica and placed a kiss on Naomi's forehead. The drive back to Black Pointe would give her plenty of time to sort out all the emotions she was feeling. At least she accomplished what she set out to do, help Naomi recover and feel safe.

# CHAPTER FORTY-TWO

I t was the first official "Bring Your Kid to Work Day." The kids at the shelter had been eager to see where Sam and her employees worked. Since it wasn't a school day, today was perfect.

Besides, Alex had been bugging her for weeks to see where she worked. Oh, she'd seen Sam's loft, but that was before Sam came to live with Mark. Alex met some of the guys when they went to the shelter. Sam tried to explain to her that there wasn't anything special about the office and her employees practiced the same self-defense as they showed in the shelter, but Alex claimed it wasn't the same thing.

So here they were. A demonstration of self-defense was on the schedule, then lunch would be delivered. They'd planned a scavenger hunt for the kids in the office. Prizes would be awarded. T-shirts were ordered. Goody bags for all were being put together. The moms would be able to relax with coffee and treats. The culmination of the day would be a movie in the exercise room. All the KnightGuard employees who weren't involved in a case would be there. Most of them had met the kids at the shelter and bonded with them. Sam had hired a small bus to bring them over from the shelter. Everyone was excited.

"Sam, look." Alex sat at Marcia's desk and was helping her decorate and fill the goody bags. She held up one party bag she'd drawn a dinosaur on.

Sam smiled at her. Watching Marcia and Alex work together was so cute. Marcia might not have had kids, but she'd taken care of a lot of nieces and nephews and was a pro at what would be popular with the kids.

"Aunt Marcia and I have one more to make. When is everyone coming? Can I show them around?" Alex said with enthusiasm that was contagious.

The door opened. Six moms and ten kids ages five to twelve stood in the doorway. Their eyes went wide and mouths opened. Overwhelmed was what Sam called it.

"I'm the conductor. Follow me," Alex shouted. And just like that, everyone was excited as Alex led the women and kids through the office.

---

"AND THIS IS where Mr. Ben works." Chrissie had taken off her headphones and was going to the ladies' room when she heard a high-pitched, familiar voice.

She peeked out of the office and saw a small red-haired girl leading around the kids from the shelter. Damn, damn, damn. She'd forgotten it was "Bring Your Kid to Work Day." She'd forgotten that the little monster who bit her would be here.

The kid hadn't seen her yet. Would she even recognize her? Chrissie had on a hat and sunglasses when she tried to kidnap her, but kids were pretty observant. The wound had healed, but there was a scar, and it still looked nasty.

The group was getting closer. Ben was talking to the kids.

She could hear the childish voice pointing out desks and computers. They were heading for the exercise room and then Phil's office.

She needed to get out of here fast.

"I don't feel well."

Phil looked over at her. "Do you need to leave?"

"Yeah. I'm sorry."

"No problem. Feel better."

Chrissie packed up her things. Peered around the door to the main office. The little leader and her group were getting closer. She wouldn't be able to make the front door without passing them. *Ladies' room! Quick.*

She hastily snuck out of the office as Alex was going on and on about something. The ladies' room was a couple of doors down, then it would be a quick one-two to the front door. She could do this.

Opening the ladies' room door, Chrissie looked around. No one was in here. Good. Listening at the door, she heard the voices getting farther away. Now was her time.

Before she could sneak out, the door hit her in the face. Got her right in the nose. Who the hell opened a door like that? She peered out. No one was there. Looked down. Oh, sweet lord, Alex was there. Staring at her. Hopping up and down.

Then the kid ran into a stall. Now was a good time to get out of here. Chrissie opened the door, walked quickly down the corridor and out. Got to her car and took several quick breaths. That was close.

---

ALEX DISAPPEARED, and Sam went looking for her, hoping she wasn't lost. It was Alex's first time walking around the office.

Where was she? She saw the kids standing around. The moms were talking with Phil. But no Alex.

"She went to the ladies' room," said Penny. "Gosh, she's adorable and so bubbly. We're getting a new perspective on the office. The kids are loving this. It's great for them to have a frame of reference, rather than just having your staff tell them they work at KnightGuard Security."

Penny looked good. It had been a few weeks since her attack, and her bruises and cuts had healed and disappeared. Sam wondered how Penny was handling the attack internally and if she was seeing a therapist. That's what took time. Penny never discussed her personal life, but Sam thought there had been abuse and tragedy in it.

Sam laughed. "This was a great idea, and I think we should do this again."

Penny agreed and walked off to catch up with the moms and kids. Sam passed Phil's office. When she got to the ladies' room, she called in to Alex.

A few minutes later, Alex came out, looked around.

"Where's the lady?"

"What lady?"

"The lady in the bathroom. She looked fam—"

They were interrupted when one little girl came running up and pulled on Alex's arm. "Come on, Alex. They're going to show us some karate."

"Yeah!"

And just like that, Alex was off. Sam walked toward the exercise room and wondered what Alex was going to say.

The guys were already showing the kids some moves, and she sat down to watch, totally forgetting everything but happily watching everyone pull their T-shirts on. *Stay the course* was the motto they'd come up with, and she liked it. *Courage* was on the other side.

Sam knew how strong and resilient the moms and kids

were. What she hoped for was that the little families would feel more comfortable with what KnightGuard Security was trying to do and feel more at ease asking for help.

The grants for housing and food were never supposed to be a handout but a hand up, and Sam hoped that was one of the things the moms got out of this today.

But then she remembered something Alex was trying to tell her before she ran off. Sam spotted Alex with Pete and walked over.

"Pete, can you give us a few minutes?"

"Sure thing." Pete moved to help one of the other kids.

Sam bent down. "Alex, honey. When you came out of the ladies' room before, you said a lady looked ... and never finished. What did you mean?"

Alex looked up at the ceiling and licked her lips. Silence. "Oh, the lady coming out of the bathroom was the lady who tried to kidnap me. The one I bited. Remember?"

Sam's heart stopped. It couldn't be true that a spy was working at her company. They vetted everyone. She kissed Alex on the forehead and raced out to Phil's office.

---

"JENNA PAYTON DOESN'T EXIST AS FAR as I can tell. The background and license are real good for a perfunctory pass-through," said Phil. "My initial search went a little deeper and didn't catch any problems. I'm going to come up with a better system for temporary workers. I don't think we should use that temp agency again."

Sam swallowed hard. The bitter taste in her mouth wouldn't go away. Her life had so many ups and downs, she couldn't keep track of everything that was happening. Not only had she put the man she loved in danger, but she also put his niece in danger, her friends in danger and brought danger to her company and employees.

"I ..." She couldn't go on.

Phil's brows drew together. He moved close to Sam and took her hand. "Sam, this isn't your fault."

"Isn't it?"

"No. It's a series of unfortunate incidents with seasoned crooks and deceivers."

"Ah, Phil? That's my business."

He sighed. "Yes, but things happen. The lesson to be learned is not to be so trusting."

Sam got up from the chair. "That bitch is not getting away with this. Give me her address." She stomped out of the office and spotted Joe.

"Joe, come with me. We're going hunting."

Joe gave her a puzzled look, shrugged and followed her out.

"Where are we going?"

"Jenna Payton's apartment."

"Jenna?"

"Yup. Turns out she was the one who tried to kidnap Alex and who knew my friends and family and where I was going."

"Son of a bitch. Why?"

"Don't know, don't care."

It took them a half hour to get to Jenna's apartment. The neighborhood wasn't great but not the worst in Black Pointe. The four-story brick building was shabby but not run-down. It looked like someone was trying to spruce the place up with some landscaping. The windows definitely needed to be replaced but were clean.

"Okay, she's on the third floor. Let's see if her car is here."

They walked around back. No cars. It looked like nobody was home, which would make their visit easier. But Sam was disappointed she couldn't deal with Jenna.

"Do you have your tools with you?" asked Sam.

He nodded and reached into his back pocket.

The steel back door looked like it had a standard lock on it. Sam wasn't playing any games with landlords, tenants or Jenna. They were getting into her apartment today.

It took Joe about thirty seconds to open the door and get them in. Sam closed it, and they walked up to the third floor. There were four apartments on each floor. Jenna rented 4B.

"Here we are."

Joe opened that door easily. They walked into a furnished apartment that was empty of personal effects.

"This makes shabby chic look good," said Sam. She looked around the one-bedroom apartment. A tiny kitchen with just the basics: sink, refrigerator, and stove. A wooden table with two chairs. A sofa, side chair and coffee table. All had seen better days but were clean. They walked into the small bedroom that contained a double bed with a side table and lamp. Linens were on the bed, and Sam shuddered at the thought of sleeping on those bed linens. Who knew who had slept on them, even if they'd been washed? A small bathroom completed the apartment.

"Okay, it doesn't look like she left anything."

"Don't care. We are pulling up every cushion, opening every cabinet and checking under the bed. She had to forget something."

"Works for me." Joe started in the bedroom, tearing the linens off the bed and lifting the mattress.

Sam opened every kitchen cabinet door—all four of them. Nothing. She checked the fridge and freezer, inside the stove and microwave—nothing. She walked into the bathroom. Pulled off the toilet top. Nothing hidden inside. Nothing in the shower. No loose tiles. Nothing.

Joe came out empty-handed from the bedroom. He

checked under the kitchen table and chairs. "I guess we're down to the living room."

Sam checked under the chair and sofa cushions. Nothing.

"What a waste of time," said Sam. "I hoped to find a snippet of something that would tell me something, but it looks like we came up empty."

"Shit happens," said Joe.

Sam sighed. "Thank you, Mr. Positive."

Joe smirked.

"Well, let's go. Nothing else to see here."

Sam was about to close the door. "Wait, I didn't check under the sofa, did you?"

"No."

Sam got flat on the floor, looked underneath the sofa. "Nothing but dust bunnies. Damn."

"Here, let me move it away from the wall."

Sam got up from the floor, and Joe pushed the sofa to the middle of the floor.

A folded piece of newsprint was squished in the corner. Joe picked up and unfolded it. "Well, well, well, what do we have here?"

"What is it?"

"A newspaper article describing Tony Moranti's trial."

"Holy crap. Why would she have that? Who was she to Tony?"

Joe shook his head. "Doesn't say. It just describes the trial."

"Well, it's something. Let's get back to the office. I want to talk to Phil and have him dig some more. The clue is right in front of us. We just have to connect it."

# CHAPTER FORTY-THREE

Sam waved goodbye to Penny and gently closed the back door to the shelter, making sure the locks clicked. This was her last meeting of the day, and then she was going home, early for once.

She'd also promised to make dinner.

Having a little one at home meant dinnertime was earlier than she was used to. Sam mentally went over what was in the fridge. Perhaps they'd do takeout. She'd call Mark on her way home. Now that Alex was there, she was constantly rubbing her belly, complaining of being hungry. Who knew kids were hungry all the time? Sam smiled.

Alex was an adorable little peanut but an absolute terror to people who were mean to her friends—a sheer powerhouse of passion. Sam wondered how her own laid-back mother ever got anything done when Sam was a child, although her mother never complained.

Sam walked out into a dense blanket of humidity and wiped her brow. The air was heavy with moisture, and thunder rumbled in the distance. Flashes of lightning lit up the sky. The weather forecasters predicted a big storm was coming, and it looked like they were right for a change.

The grant meeting that she and Claire had attended had gone well. Claire's generosity would provide needed money for updating the shelter's premises, as well as providing needed cash for more programs to help women get jobs.

It was karma that Claire's abusive, dead husband never changed his will. After selling off all his property and closing bank accounts, Claire was a wealthy woman. She'd set up a trust with the money she received, and the grants provided services for the women in the shelter. Not for the first time, Sam thought Keith Willis would turn in his grave watching his money help abused women leave their abusers and get on with their lives. She was glad the bastard was dead.

At the meeting, Claire had suggested a fundraiser to encourage others in the community to volunteer or contribute to the shelter. Penny thought it was a perfect idea. Laura had already volunteered her restaurant as the venue.

Penny had also requested money to reimburse Knight-Guard Security for its help in the weekly self-defense lessons they offered to their clients.

No matter how much Sam protested that she didn't need the money and her employees were happy to help, Penny and Claire insisted she take it. Ha! The joke would be on them. She'd take the money, but she knew the employees who volunteered didn't want money for providing protection lessons. They were happy to help. Come holiday time, though, she would make sure that they got big bonuses to compensate them for their time. Then any extra cash would help fund apartments, clothes, and food for the women and their children who were just trying to get on their feet. It was the least she could do.

Her car was parked close to the back door, and Sam unlocked it as she walked down the stairs.

She hoped Phil found some connection from the scrap of paper that Joe found but something was tugging at her mind as she got into her SUV. Aargh.

Sam shook her head; nothing was coming to her. After inserting the key into the ignition, she let out a huge sigh. She and Claire had a lot to do to make the fundraiser a success.

Claire! That was it. Claire's car was still here, and she'd left the office a good half hour ago.

# CHAPTER FORTY-FOUR

Sam shut off her SUV and walked towards Claire's car, which was parked several cars over from hers. She was almost there when she noticed both the driver and passenger doors were open, and she raced over to check it out. Oh, crap. Claire was slouched over in the front seat on the passenger side.

Something was wrong. Was Claire having a miscarriage? Sam's heart pounded in her chest. The contents of her stomach roiled. *Please, God, don't let this happen.* Claire and Joe deserved so much happiness after all they'd been through.

Sam placed her hand on the headrest and bent down. "Claire, honey, are you all right?"

Claire's head was hanging down. When she twisted her head to look at Sam, it was with tears in her eyes. There was something odd about her. It took Sam a second to realize Claire's mouth and hands were duct taped. Her eyes were frantic. She was mumbling and squirming around. *What the hell?*

Sam reached behind for her gun and came up empty.

Damn. She never carried it to the shelter. Too many kids around.

Then her body jolted.

She fell into Claire's lap, her body incapacitated and cramping. Then the pain started—excruciating pain. She heard a scream. Was it Claire's mumbled scream or her screaming? Didn't matter. She couldn't move. It felt like someone was hitting her with a baseball bat. She couldn't catch her breath. Her teeth rattled in her mouth. Pain was her only thought.

A hand clamped down on her head and pulled her arms behind her back and duct-taped them—then she felt a jab in her neck.

The last thing she heard was a maniacal laugh before falling into a void of darkness.

## CHAPTER FORTY-FIVE

Colin threw the duffle bag with the last of his clothes onto the front seat of his truck. He had finished the job with Mark and wanted to finish his business with Sam.

One made him sad. The other excited him.

Sam and her friend were sitting tight at the camp.

When Chrissie informed him that Sam was meeting at the shelter today, he moved his plans up.

He'd hidden in Chrissie's car. She had the code to the shelter's fenced-in parking lot where Sam usually parked.

Chrissie parked close to the dumpster while he got out of the car. Hiding like a rat behind a dumpster wasn't first on his list of fun things to do, but what the hell.

As his daddy would say, "Suck it up, son. Ain't nothing easy in life." So what if he sat in unidentifiable mashed shit or that a thorny bush poked him in the cheek? At least the weather was still calm, although rain was coming. The occasional rumble of thunder didn't bother him, but the humidity settled over his body like a wet blanket. Nothing was dampening his plan though.

He waited for Sam's meeting to end, maybe in an hour or less. He planned on sneaking up behind Sam when she got to her car, Tasering her to incapacitate her, and then jabbing her with propofol. He couldn't have her fighting back—he thought she'd win. She would not spoil his plan.

When he'd heard the shelter's back door open, he popped his head up and spotted Sam's friend Claire walking out. Colin thought he'd hit the jackpot. What better way to get Sam Knight in his clutches than to kidnap Claire? Sam wouldn't try anything if she thought her friend might get hurt.

It was easy to pull a gun on Claire, force her into the passenger seat, then duct-tape her. Before he slapped the tape over her mouth, Claire begged him not to hurt her. *Sorry, darling, that ship has sailed.* He loved the panic on her face. Seeing scared women never got old.

It was essential to get Sam in a position where she couldn't hurt him. And it worked!

The women were tied up. He snorted. *Tied up!*

Now all he had to do was drop the women off at the cabin and exchange the car for his truck.

He'd already parked his truck ten miles from the camp on an unused dirt road. He'd drop the bitches at camp, making sure he tied them so they couldn't escape, drive Claire's car to his truck, come back with the gasoline and voilà. Easy-peasy.

Chrissie, however, was another problem. His friend Dwight informed him she'd been working the business behind his back—that bitch. Dwight found out after a drunken night with one of their contacts. After all that Colin had done for her, she betrayed him, just like his mother. You couldn't trust women. He'd take care of her at the same time he took care of Sam.

Later tonight, after Sam had time to think about the error of her ways, he'd go back and make sure the women were awake. He wanted Sam Knight to know what betrayal felt like. He wanted to feel their fear and hear their screams when he lit up the cabin.

Tomorrow, he promised to meet Dwight and celebrate. They needed to make plans for expanding the operation.

He wondered if KnightGuard Security and Mark would ever piece together his role in harassing them or eliminating Sam Knight. On the one hand, he hoped they would. On the other, maybe not. Mark would kill him for sure if he found him.

After all, he'd kept two steps ahead of them, proving once again he was smarter than the average bear.

# CHAPTER FORTY-SIX

Chrissie chuckled as she drove to the motel she was staying in tonight.

How fortuitous was it that she had the code to the shelter's security fence? Fortunately, when Sam punched it in, Chrissie had paid attention. Did Colin ever consider how smart she was? She shrugged. Probably not..

By the time the sun set, Sam Knight and her friend would be dead.. How fitting was that? The end of day. The end of life. Tomorrow would be a fresh start.

Colin didn't trust her. Somehow, information that should have remained confidential was leaked to him. She wondered if Roberto had gotten to Colin and mentioned her, or had Dwight? Colin could never control his emotions, and for the past couple of days, he'd been acting squirrelly.

But for now, Colin was taking care of business, which meant she wouldn't have to. The plan to kidnap Sam and kill her was a sound idea. She hated Sam for convincing those women to testify against Tony. Hated that Sam became a successful businesswoman while Tony languished in prison.

And yet she admired Sam's tenaciousness. Chrissie shook her head. She was not thinking about Sam anymore.

She'd concentrate on the vision of Colin sitting behind a dumpster, breathing in all sorts of sucky fumes and sitting on who knew what. It was hilarious. If a dumpster were an analogy of his life, it would be fitting. He deserved to sit in shit.

KnightGuard had no idea she wasn't who they thought she was or that she was helping Colin. They had no idea that Colin was behind all the unfortunate circumstances that had occurred. They still had no idea that Sam Knight was going to meet her maker before morning.

Chrissie fiddled with the radio and found her favorite station.

It was a lovely day, and she felt free. She belted out words to songs as she drove to the cabin; no one was around to complain that she had no ear for music.

When she saw the kid, she'd left the office and drove right to the dump she'd been renting, packed everything she brought with her and put it in her car. For sure, Sam would come a-calling, and she didn't want to be there.

When this job was done, she'd move back to the backwater town in Georgia she came from. A town where everyone kept to themselves. She'd move the drug business there. The town was so poor and everyone was related somehow. No one would turn her in, and when the big payoff from the business came in, she would buy a huge house with a pool.

Chrissie reminded herself to leave out the gun with the bullets; she would need it later.

Colin would do most of the hard work, and she'd swoop in for the cleanup.

# CHAPTER FORTY-SEVEN

S am was late. She promised to be home early, and Mark had plans for them to spend a little personal time together before Alex got home from school.

Mark figured she'd been held up at her meeting at the shelter. He was so proud of the commitment she and Claire made to help the shelter and the women and kids who lived there.

He turned on the TV, hoping for a game to distract him. He found one that had been recorded and settled in. The door opened and he looked up, hoping it was Sam.

"Hi, Uncle Mark. I'm home."

"I see that, sweet pea."

Alex giggled. She placed her little backpack next to the door and ran over and jumped on his lap.

"How was school?"

Sometimes Mark wished he never asked. Alex spent the next half hour telling him what she did at recess, what she had for lunch, who she played with and what she learned. Although he loved hearing about the fun things she did, he wished Sam had made it back early so they could have had some fun time.

An hour later, the phone rang.

"Have you heard from Sam?"

"Hello to you too," Mark said. Joe wasn't much of a talker, but a "Hello, how are you" would've been nice.

"Don't have time for this shit. Have you heard from Sam?" asked Joe.

Mark looked at his watch. It was four o'clock. He remembered she hadn't called to tell him she'd been held up, which was surprising. However, if Sam got caught up in a problem, she sometimes forgot. He wasn't worried—yet.

"No. What's going on?"

"Claire isn't home. They had a meeting at the shelter, and Claire was going to come right home."

"Maybe they were held up or left together for some reason. Have you tried calling her?"

"Do you think I'm an idiot? Of course, I did. She's not answering."

That was odd. Claire was pregnant and knew Joe worried about her. She wouldn't not answer her phone.

"Let me try Sam's phone, and I'll call you back."

Mark let Sam's phone ring and ring until the recorder turned on.

He left a message.

Little hands rubbed his face, and he looked at Alex, her brow furrowed.

"Is Sam okay?"

"Yeah, sweet pea. Let me make this phone call, okay?"

He called the office. Steve answered.

"Is Sam there?"

"Not that I know of. But let me look in her office just in case she snuck by me."

Mark waited a few minutes. Steve came back on and told

him she wasn't in her office and that her SUV wasn't in the lot.

Damn. Where could she be? It wasn't like her to say she'd come home early and not. At least not without calling. And where was Claire? Were they together?

He called the shelter. Penny answered. He asked about them, and she told him that Claire and Sam left a couple of hours ago. She put him hold on so she could check in the parking lot.

A minute later, Penny came back on the phone, her voice high-pitched. "Sam's car is here but Claire's isn't."

They hung up. Maybe Sam and Claire had another appointment and forgot to call. No. They wouldn't forget.

Panic. No, he would not panic.

KnightGuard needed to get on this ASAP.

The phone rang again. He hoped it wasn't Joe because he didn't know what to say to him. He couldn't imagine what was going through Joe's mind with his wife pregnant. Mark groaned. Of course, he could. If Sam were pregnant, he would be going out of his mind with worry.

"Mark." Penny's voice cracked. "I just walked outside and found both their phones smashed on the ground. I'm afraid something bad has happened to them."

What the hell?

The back lot had a coded gate entry, and only a few people had it.

He called Joe.

"We have a problem."

# CHAPTER FORTY-EIGHT

"I'm calling Danny and the crew. Meet me at the office," said Joe.

Mark couldn't lose Sam. Whatever happened to Claire and Sam was serious. Sam wouldn't leave if her friend was in trouble. He knew she could take care of herself.

Mark was halfway out the door when he remembered Alex. Shit. He couldn't bring her to the office. He also didn't know how long he'd be there. He sighed. His heart was roaring like a waterfall.

Joyce! Joyce could come over and stay with Alex. She often volunteered to stay over if they were out of town. But they hadn't needed her so far.

Mark waited as Joyce's phone rang and rang. If she wasn't home, he didn't have a backup. "Hello."

"Joyce, thank God. Listen, I have an emergency meeting. Can you come over here and stay with Alex?"

Silence. *Please. Please.*

"Sure, I'll be there in fifteen minutes. Should I pack an overnight bag?"

He hoped not. "That's a good idea. Thanks."

Fifteen minutes later, Joyce showed up. She told him she could stay overnight if necessary and not to worry about Alex.

Mark raced to KnightGuard Security. All the lights were on, and the parking lot was full. *Shit. Shit. Shit.*

He found a spot farther away from the front door.. Steve pressed the buzzer to let him in, and he followed voices to Sam's office.

"Pull up a chair," said Danny. "We're just waiting on Phil to pull up the cameras around the shelter."

Mark sat next to Hank and Joe. Yeah, he was a big, bad ex-SEAL, but right now, he wanted to vomit. His woman was in trouble.

He looked over at Joe and saw a similar expression on his face.

Joe's lips were tightly pressed together, and his eyes were shooting daggers. Whoever had hurt their women would be in a world of hurt when they found them.

"Okay, boys and girls," said Phil as he walked in with his laptop. He placed it on the table and aimed it at the Smart-board on the wall. "Here's what I've found so far."

They watched Claire come out of the shelter, look around, and get in her car. Moments later, she was dragged out at gunpoint by a man. The joker had been hiding on the other side of the car. A collective moan went around the table.

"Oh, sweetheart, I'm so sorry I wasn't there," whispered Joe.

The asswipe forced her into the passenger seat. He pushed her down in the seat, and Joe growled. They watched as the man pulled out a roll of duct tape and leaned in the door.

"Goddamn. That motherfucker is dead," yelled Joe.

"Let's try to keep calm and let Phil finish," said Danny. "I know we're all upset right now."

Phil sped up the tape. They watched Sam step out the back door, get in her SUV, then get out. She had a confused look on her face as she walked over to Claire's car. She bent down to look at Claire. It looked like she was reaching for her gun. The gun she never brought to the shelter because of the kids.

Mark's heart just about stopped when he saw the man come behind Sam and Taser her. Then the man pulled out a syringe and jabbed Sam in the neck. She fell into the seat, and the man pulled her unconscious body out and duct-taped her and roughly threw her in the back seat. The whole thing hadn't taken more than a few minutes.

Mark closed his eyes.

"Go back a couple of hours," said Danny.

There was nothing to see for a good hour. Then they watched a red compact drive up and punch in the code.

"Isn't that Jenna's car?" asked Hank.

They rewound the tape. "Shit, yeah," said Phil. "But Jenna doesn't exist. I don't know her real name, but she has to be in on this. I'll look at that later to see what the connection is. Let's just see where this goes."

They watched the gate open, and the car pulled close to the dumpster. The joker got out and sauntered behind the dumpster like he owned the place. He had on a one-piece brown uniform and a cap with a visor, but they couldn't see his face. The man walked behind the dumpster and disappeared. Fucking coward. Mark knew he'd sneak out when the women left.

"He looks so familiar," said Mark. "I wish we could see his face. Can you get any closer?"

"I'll try." Phil adjusted the picture. They couldn't see his face because of the hat. Mark didn't recognize a nose or ear.

But the man turned. They could see a small tattoo on the man's neck. It was a black teardrop tattoo with the initials TM in the center.

"TM, Tony Moranti. I wonder if he's the cousin?" asked Danny.

Then the man turned to face them.

"Motherfucker. That's Colin Woods," growled Mark. Why hadn't he noticed the tattoo before?

"Who's he?" asked Hank.

"Just the motherfucking guy I'm going to kill."

"He's the carpenter that works for you, isn't he?" asked Danny.

Mark nodded.

The bastard had been in his house. Had built the bookshelves and window seat for Alex. HE HAD BEEN IN HIS HOUSE.

The pain of betrayal and fear coursed through Mark's body, and he punched the table.

"Hey, Mark, I know you're mad and frustrated, but please don't take it out on the table. Sam will kill you if you damage it. She loves this table," said Danny.

Mark gritted his teeth. His face felt like cement, but he nodded and got up to pace. He was pissed—way beyond pissed—and scared. This whole time, Sam had been concerned for him and Alex. When he got her back, he was forbidding her from ever leaving the house again. He'd tie her down if he had to.

Oh, who was he kidding? When Sam came back, he'd kiss her delectable body until she begged him to stop, then he'd make love to her until she screamed for him to stop, then he'd send her to work. KnightGuard Security was Sam.

Okay. So, they had a name but not the reason Woods was abducting them, and what was Jenna, or whatever her name was, to him? Where was Colin heading with the women? It had been hours; he could be anywhere in Florida or another state.

"Claire's car has GPS. We can track her." Joe pulled out his phone, punched in his code and found the app.

"It shows Claire's car is located ten miles from Cypress Lake." Joe threw his phone down. "Damn it all to hell. That doesn't help. We still don't know where they are."

He cracked his knuckles and in a very calm, even voice said, "When we find the fucker, he's mine."

It was silent around the table.

Mark seconded what everyone was thinking. He'd gone toe to toe with Joe, and he pitied any man who wasn't a SEAL to be on the other end of Joe's wrath. However, Joe would be out of luck because if he found the asswipe first, he'd be wiping the ground with him.

"Great. Where do we go next? Cypress Lake is huge. We have no idea where the cabin is located or where to start," said Hank.

"Phil, have you checked owners' names for everyone around the lake?" asked Danny.

"Yeah, but that doesn't tell us who the uncle was. I checked the license registration on Wood's truck. It was issued to him at an old address. He moved out months ago."

Mark was confused. He'd checked Colin's resume carefully, he thought. No red flags, but perhaps Phil could use his magic fingers and dig deeper.

"Phil, I'm sending you Woods's resume. Can you double-check it for me? We're missing something, and I don't know what."

"Sure. But later. We already know it's Woods." Phil rubbed his hands across his eyes. "I'm not sure what else to look for."

"Luke? Hey, Luke." Steve poked his head in.

"What?" asked Luke.

"I have Seth Bowman on the line. He's been trying to reach Sam or you."

Luke frantically checked his pockets. "Damn, my phone is charging on my desk. I'll pick up in here."

All eyes were on Luke as he picked up the phone. "Yes. Yes. Holy shit. No. Yes, I'll tell them." Luke hung up the phone and faced the group.

"What did he say?"

"One of his older employees just got back from vacation. Apparently he knew the owner. One of his sons used to party with Tony. The son didn't know much about Colin. Thought they were cousins. He remembered Chrissie, who dated Tony. He couldn't remember where the cabin was located, but the owner is Troy Summers."

## CHAPTER FORTY-NINE

S am tried to open her eyes, but it felt like cement blocks were holding her lids shut. She took a deep breath and forced them open. Now that she could focus, she tried to bring her hands up to rub her eyes but realized her hands were taped behind her back, and she was sitting in a chair with her feet tied. Her whole body ached. Her throat hurt—no moisture in it to swallow. It felt as dry as the desert. Tension swirled around in her gut. She forced herself to relax.

She looked around and didn't recognize the small cabin, although it reminded her a little of one of Seth's cabins. So she was at a fishing camp? But whose?

In front of her were a small, faded sofa, a coffee table, and two armchairs. A glass of brown liquid was on the table. To her left was a kitchen table with two chairs and beautiful wooden kitchen cabinets. Beautiful? What the hell? That made little sense.

A small hallway past the kitchen presumably led to the bedrooms and a bath. She sniffed. It smelled old, funky, and

of fear. Where were the kidnappers? Would they have left her
and Claire alone? None of this made any sense.

Why had they been kidnapped? And by whom? Where
were they?

The better question was how were they going to get out
of here? Would the guys even know where to look for them?
Fishing camps dotted the riverbanks by the hundreds, and for
all she knew, they could be in Georgia right now. Who were
the kidnappers? Claire was pregnant, and they were both
tied up.

Mark and Joe must be frantic. KnightGuard Security
should be on this by now, but would they know where to
start? Hopefully, they would begin at the shelter. Hidden
cameras covered back and front in case some idiot abuser
thought just because the group who lived there was made up
of women, they were defenseless. Penny would have the tapes.
But did anyone even know she and Claire were kidnapped
from there? GPS on Claire's car would help if she had it.

"You're awake. Good."

Claire's voice interrupted her black thoughts.

She glanced over.

"My God, Claire. Are you all right?" Sam's voice croaked.

Claire nodded.

"Where are we? How long have you been sitting there?
Do you know who kidnapped us?"

"Whoa, Sam. One question at a time. I don't know where
we are. I think it took at least an hour to get here. You were
out the whole time. I've been sitting here for what seems like
hours. I don't know who kidnapped us. It was a man, and he
said he'd be back soon. Since you were out of it, I guess he
didn't think I was a threat."

Sam hung her head and shook it. "Damn. This is all my
fault. I knew someone was gunning for me." She had no idea

who it was, but it was a man who Tasered her and then pricked her neck with something. That much she remembered.

She looked over at Claire. "How did you get the duct tape off your mouth?"

"It must have been loose. It fell off a while ago. The man ripped yours off when we got here. Something about hearing you scream."

Well, that was weird, but Sam was glad she could talk to Claire. "I'm so sorry that you're caught up in this mess," said Sam.

Claire tsked. "Moot point now. We've got to come up with a plan."

No fooling. But what kind of plan? Sam couldn't risk Claire losing the baby. No telling how long it would take for Mark and Joe to get here with reinforcements. Sam looked around the small cabin. The kitchen wasn't far away. Claire's legs weren't tied to the chair like hers were.

"Can you try to stand and walk over to the kitchen and see if there is a knife?"

"I can try." Claire pushed up with her legs, and the chair came up a couple of inches. She grunted once, and the chair landed back on its legs.

"Damn," said Claire. She pushed up again, got a little higher and sat back down. "I'm sorry."

"Claire, take your time. You can do this. I know you can," said Sam. Having Claire get up was turning into a problem, and they were running out of time. She had to think of a Plan B or else.

"One more time for luck," said Claire. With an umph she managed to bend her body and duck-walked into the small kitchen, the chair sticking off her back like an obscene backpack.

Sam could hear drawers opening and closing. "Anything?" Please, please let Claire find something they could use.

"Damn, I can't see, but I don't feel anything in the drawers."

More thumping of chair legs on the floor. More slamming of drawers. "Ouch! I think I've found a knife."

Thank God. If Claire hadn't found something, it would take Sam a long time to get out of these ties. Time they didn't have. Claire scuttled back and sat in front of her.

"What now?" Claire asked.

"Scoot behind me and give me the knife. Get as close as you can. I'm going to cut your ties. Then you'll cut mine."

Claire positioned her chair behind Sam. *Please don't let me hurt her.* It hurt to grasp the knife, but pain was the least of their worries. Sam felt for the ties and started cutting.

"Ouch."

"Sorry," said Sam. Working backward was more difficult than she'd imagined.

"It's okay."

"Damn."

"What's wrong?" asked Claire.

"I hear a car coming down the road."

"Hurry."

Sam sawed faster. Felt Claire's hands break free.

"I'm free."

Relief washed through Sam's body. At least one of them was free. But Claire needed to get out of the cabin—now.

"Listen to me closely, Claire. Get out now. Run like heck down the road, hide if you see any cars you don't recognize, and try to get help."

Claire had loosened her ties and come around in front of Sam. "No. I'm not leaving you." Claire swallowed hard. She had dark circles under her eyes and was tearing up. A bruise on her cheek was still raw and red. Bastards. Sam would deal with whoever did that next.

Friends didn't leave friends, but Sam could handle this alone if she didn't have to worry about Claire. Even if she couldn't, at least Claire would be safe.

Footsteps were getting closer, crunching on the path. Someone was whistling, putting an innocent spin on what Sam knew was a grave situation.

"Claire, I need to take care of this. I can't if I'm worried about you. Go. Now." She put more force into the statement.

Claire hesitated, then gave her one last devastating look and quickly opened the back door, quietly closing it just as a man walked in with a bag and a jerry can.

Colin!

Why him? Would he even tell her?

"Good. You're awake." He looked at the other chair. "I see your friend escaped. No matter. You're the one I want."

The smile he gave her made her skin crawl. The situation wasn't looking good, but then again, this type of situation never did. *Think!*

Colin walked back outside for whatever reason. Didn't matter. She frantically sawed through the tape around her wrists, cutting her skin, the blood making everything slippery. She finally cut through it and started on her ankles. They weren't tied as tightly.

She heard Colin humming as he came back. She stopped sawing at her foot ties and put the knife behind her back. If Colin thought this was going to be easy, shame on him.

Another car drove up. What was this? Old home week? A door slammed. Someone was walking down the path. Were they part of this or just a visitor?

It was a woman. As she got closer, Sam saw it was Jenna. What was she doing here?

Jenna walked in the open door and stared at Sam and then Colin.

Jenna smirked at her. Wait! Jenna had brown eyes. This woman had gray eyes. And black hair.

"Jenna? Or should I call you Chrissie Thorne?"

The look Chrissie gave Sam told her everything she needed to know.

She was in deep shit.

# CHAPTER FIFTY

Claire escaped out the back door just as a man entered through the front door. Who was he? No time to worry now. She had to find help.

Bushes and trees surrounded the small cabin. Claire wondered which way to go. She peeked around a corner; the driveway was right there. She headed in the opposite direction.

Claire's heart was pounding. She had to get help. The sun spotlighted a small opening in the trees. She ran toward it. Stood in the middle, noticed the sun was behind her. East. Think. Think.

South. She needed to go south.

Claire ran through thorn bushes that tore at her skin. Heard weird animal noises in the brush but didn't stop. Her heart was thumping in fear. She wiped at the sweat pouring down her face. A stitch in her side had her wondering if she'd hurt the baby. She prayed she hadn't. This was a nightmare, and she was in the middle of it.

She ran for what seemed forever. Claire was gulping for air, cut, bleeding and still weak from being tied up, but there was no time to worry about herself. There had to be a road or a cabin with a phone or Sam was out of luck. She had to save Sam.

Crashing through a stand of bushes, Claire stopped short. She wasn't expecting to come across a road—a paved road— so soon. Cars sounded close. Were they friend or foe? Claire hid in the bushes.

Cars were traveling at a fast speed. Where were they going? Dare she step out and stop them? What if it was someone else who wanted to hurt Sam?

The sound of tires on pavement came closer. She peered out. A black truck was barreling down the road. It looked like Mark in the driver's seat. *Please let it be Mark.*

She stepped out. But she was too late.

The truck had passed her.

Oh lord, she was going to get Sam killed. A sob escaped. Her heart pounded dully in her chest. She failed.

What was that sound? Another car was coming.

She jumped back in the bushes, just in case.

Another truck. It looked like …

Joe! Oh, thank God. It was Joe. Claire stepped out and frantically waved. The truck passed her. She stood in the middle of the road and wanted to lie down and cry.

Then she heard the tires screech to a stop. Joe opened the door and raced over to her.

His face was pale. He closed and opened his eyes.

"Oh my God, Claire." He patted her body and hugged her tight. "Are you all right?"

Tears fell from her eyes. She nodded. Took a deep breath and said, "Sam needs help."

"I know, sweetheart. The guys are behind me. I'll call Mark and tell him. But you're carrying our baby. We're going to the hospital."

"No, Joe. I have to know Sam is all right."

He gently rubbed the bruise on her cheek. His nostrils flared, but he didn't say anything.

"I'm okay," Claire said.

"I'm not," Joe said in a soft voice. "He's a dead man."

He examined Claire from head to toe; his blue eyes narrowed and darkened as he took in her bloodied wrists and bruises, his lips a thin line. "Get in the truck."

"But ..."

"No buts, Claire. Get in the truck. Now."

Claire opened her mouth to protest, but the pain in Joe's eyes undid her. She hoped Joe was right and that Sam could take care of herself.

Joe opened the passenger door and helped her in. He called Mark and told him what was going on. Cars passed them with other KnightGuard Security personnel. She heard sirens in the far distance. Claire said a little prayer that they got to Sam in time.

Otherwise, she'd never forgive herself for leaving.

# CHAPTER FIFTY-ONE

Colin and Jenna? Chrissie? Whatever. What the hell was going on, Sam wondered.

"Ah, I see our captive is awake." Chrissie smirked.

She looked at the other chair. "I thought you said you had two women."

Colin looked at her sheepishly. "The other got away."

Chrissie sighed. "That's a problem. It's no wonder Tony didn't trust you to do things right." Chrissie sneered at Sam. "Well, we'll just have to deal with her."

It was all falling into place. Colin must be Tony's cousin, and so Jenna/Chrissie was Tony's girlfriend.

The blow came out of nowhere, knocking Chrissie to the ground.

"Shut up, bitch. You're just a whore."

Chrissie sat up slowly, wiped the blood from her mouth.

"Get yourself up and keep your mouth shut. Stand here and watch Knight. I'm going to spread the gasoline around the cabin."

Chrissie stood up, taking deep breaths to try and calm herself. But if her flaring nostrils and the vein throbbing in her neck were any indication of Chrissie calming herself, Sam thought they were all in trouble.

The situation was rapidly disintegrating. There were two of them and one of her. Sam only had a small knife and her wits. Fortunately, neither one of them was playing with a full deck if they thought she wasn't a threat.

Colin went outside with the gasoline can.

"Why?" asked Sam.

"Why?" Chrissie sneered. "Because you put my lover in jail. Ruined the drug business. I've let Colin take the lead on this, but he's an idiot."

Chrissie stood up and walked toward Sam.

"Tony trusted Colin to bury that bitch, and he did a half-assed job. Tony was never going to bring Colin into the drug business. He's too stupid. It's up to me now." Chrissie glared at Sam. "You should never have stuck your nose in Tony's business or put him in jail."

The smell of gasoline turned Sam's stomach. Different scenarios passed through her mind, but this one? She'd never imagined this one.

Colin came back in and wiped his hands on his pants. Looked at Chrissie. Looked at Sam. Rubbed his chin and sighed.

He stepped toward Chrissie as he reached for the gun behind his back.

Uh-oh. This didn't look good for Chrissie's future.

In a swift movement, Chrissie whipped out a gun.

Shot Colin.

The surprise on his face was priceless. He dropped his gun and fell to the ground at Sam's feet.

Chrissie turned to Sam and laughed. "One down, one to

go. I could shoot you, but I like the idea of you burning alive while you think about my pain."

Crap. Her chest tightened like a vice. She thought of Mark and Alex and her friends, the life she made for herself. She so didn't want to die, especially by fire.

Chrissie walked outside with a matchbook. Sam leaned forward and sawed away on the ties even harder. The ties broke just as Chrissie stood in the doorway. Sam kept her feet together, her hands holding the knife behind her. Chrissie never noticed she'd cut the ties. Tendrils of smoke irritated Sam's nose. It was just a matter of time before the cabin would burst into flames. She had to work fast.

Chrissie turned and walked toward her car. "No one is ever going to find you."

*That's what you think, bitch.* Sam jumped up, knife in hand. Her arms were screaming from the pain of being tied behind her for so long, but no time to think about that.

Black, heavy smoke filled the cabin. Her eyes burned. She coughed and ran outside.

Chrissie had her hand on the door handle of her car. When she saw Sam, she screamed. "What does it take to kill you?"

She reached for her gun, aimed for Sam. She thought it would be an easy shot, but Sam was fast.

Sam knocked the gun from her hand and plunged the knife into Chrissie's arm as she tackled Chrissie to the ground.

Chrissie screamed. Sam elbowed her throat. Chrissie's eyes bulged. She squirmed but managed to get out of Sam's hold, then headbutt Sam.

*Damn, that hurt.* Sam saw stars, stood, and stumbled back. Chrissie took advantage of her mistake. She pulled the knife from her arm and, in a smooth move, slashed Sam's side.

Pain cramped Sam's moves. "Aargh." This was not good.

The fire was consuming the cabin. The heat burned the side of her face. Smoke darkened their sight. They were both hacking.

Sam's side was in agony. Blood dripped to the ground. She moved toward Chrissie.

Chrissie punched her in her wounded side.

Sam screamed and bent over. Gulped in as much air as she could.

Enough already. She was not dying today.

Sam pulled every bit of energy from her core. She round-kicked Chrissie. When Chrissie went down, Sam sat on her and repeatedly punched her in the head. Chrissie screamed and tried to protect her head with her hands.

Chrissie turned her body and threw Sam off. She jumped up; fists ready. *What the hell. Is Chrissie Wonder Woman?* The woman had twenty pounds and inches on her. The self-defense lessons Chrissie learned were coming in handy. Damn, Sam knew Chrissie was a fast learner.

"Bitch." She came at Sam. Picked up the knife Sam had dropped.

It was now or never. Taking a deep breath, Sam pushed herself to get up. The wound in her side almost incapacitated her, but her life was on the line.

She grabbed Chrissie's arm. Chrissie punched her with her other arm. Sam held onto her to arm tighter and twisted it, finally breaking Chrissie's hold on the knife. The knife fell to the ground.

Sam leaned in and punched Chrissie in the ear, following with a punch to the jaw. Chrissie fell to the ground and was out.

The cabin was ablaze, sparks falling all around her, cinders sizzling on her skin. Smoke filled the air. Sam was tired—so tired.

Mark ran toward her, his mouth open. She couldn't hear what he was screaming.

He reached for her just before darkness set in.

"About time. Call the pol—"

# CHAPTER FIFTY-TWO

I t had been a month since Colin kidnapped Sam and
Claire.

Claire and the baby were fine. Joe was making sure
of that.

Sam wasn't sure Joe was happy about Claire leaving the
house, but he hadn't said anything to her. Although Sam
thought she'd seen Joe skulking behind some bushes one day
when she and Claire were out. None of her business. Sam was
just happy they were okay.

She hadn't fully recovered yet. The knife Chrissie had
sliced her with hadn't penetrated very deep, but she still
needed to be careful.

Alex clung to her whenever she was in the house. They'd
had the talk—the one where no one was leaving her and Alex
would always be protected. However, if it made the little girl
feel better to cling, Sam was all right with that.

Work was going well. She was back to working full days
after taking some time off to heal. Danny had stepped up to
the plate and taken on more responsibilities.

And Mark ... Mark hadn't said much. He wasn't angry, just contemplative.

Sam was worried about him. He'd been anxious and attentive during her hospital stay and hadn't left her side. He took time off from work to help her when she was released. He'd called her every day at work just because. He hovered over her when they were home. She suspected he asked the guys at work to keep an eye out, although no one confessed to doing that.

However, he hadn't asked her to marry him again. Sam wondered if caring for Alex and worrying about her was getting to him.

So here she was—again—sitting on the dunes of Moon Beach, contemplating her life.

It was hot and humid. The beach was packed with bathers wearing suits of every color of the rainbow. Kids screamed joyfully. Umbrellas popped up like colorful mushrooms. A storm had passed, and the waves were plentiful and robust, washing everything on their way back to the sea, cleansing the shore.

A peace came over her. She threw her negative thoughts to the wind and let the calming crash of waves surround her.

A shadow caused her to look up.

"Hey."

Mark! How did he know she was here? Sam took in the whole package. His black hair was a little longer, and it looked like he had run his fingers through it. His beard had grown out a little. He'd lost a little weight not eating when she was in the hospital but was putting it back on.

"Hey yourself. What are you doing here?"

"Just making sure you're okay." He shrugged. "I knew you'd come here to think."

Sam smiled. Somehow Mark managed to find her wherever she was. Was he stalking her? Probably. It was out of concern, and secretly she loved it.

She patted the blanket. "Sit."

Mark sat and placed his arm around her shoulder. She sniffed; he smelled of coconut sunscreen and pure man.

"It sure is beautiful here," he said as he looked around.

"Yes, it is."

"Are you okay?"

"Yes. More than okay, especially since you're here."

They spent a few minutes in comfortable silence, watching people walk by.

"Anything new with the case?" he asked.

For sure, this would be a case she'd never forget.

Waking up in the hospital had been the most frightened she'd ever been. Having her friends visit had helped, and Mark never left her side.

Colin Woods was dead, thank God. What a douche. Phil finally figured out that Colin had forged his resume, except for the part about being a master carpenter. The cabin was ruined, and she felt no guilt there. Nothing good had come of that cabin.

Naomi was healing and anxious to move on. Veronica was still staying with her at the loft. Claire had informed her that she was setting up a trust for Naomi. One that would help her with living expenses and medical bills. Mark was building cabins in Haywood Lake, and Naomi thought it would be good for her to move to one of them and work with Ted Maddox at the facility where they were training therapy dogs.

Sam wasn't sure Naomi had fully forgiven her, but that was okay. She hadn't forgiven herself, but at least she had a second chance at redeeming herself and making it right for Naomi. As long as Naomi felt safe, she could move on with her life and if Sam could help, it was all good.

The police had found and arrested Dwight, the guy Colin

was working with. They were still looking for Roberto, but at least the cops were able to shut down one group of drug dealers. Chrissie had been wounded in their fight and arrested. She was in jail waiting for trial since she couldn't make bail.

"Nothing new, said Sam.

"Well, I have good news. The owner's accepted the offer we put in on the new house

"That's terrific."

They had both decided they couldn't bear to look at the bookcases and window seat Colin had built for Alex. They were beautiful but tainted.

The new house was close by and bigger, with more bedrooms and a large, fenced-in backyard for the dog Alex wanted.

Mark hadn't said anything, but she knew he hoped to fill the bedrooms with babies—their babies.

It was time. Her heart was pounding as loudly as the surf. Her mouth felt dry. She took a deep breath, held it, let it loose. "I ... I want to ask you something."

A question formed in his eyes. Then concern.

"All riiight."

"Mark, you know I love you."

He nodded. "I hope there's no 'but' coming."

She gave him a small smile and shook her head.

"Would you ..." Could she go through with this? Courage, that's what she needed right now. She had plenty of time to think about this. Would Mark even give her a second chance to say yes?

Mark claimed he wouldn't ask her again unless she was ready. But her gran's words kept repeating and rewinding. *Trust your heart. Don't go through life by yourself. It's better to live a life with the person you love than to regret living it alone.*

What was the worst he could say—no? That would break

her heart. Besides, she was a firm believer in second chances, and she needed one right now.

"Would you marry me and make me the luckiest woman in the world?"

Mark stopped breathing. He lifted his brows and cocked his head.

Sam gulped. "I'm sorry. I didn't mean to surprise you."

He squeezed his eyes shut, then opened them. "Sam, you never have to say you're sorry. I can't believe that you asked me to marry you."

She stared at her hands. "It's all right. I shocked you. Forget I said anything." *So this is what feeling like a fool looks like?* Why had she waited? Why had she even asked?

"Oh no, no, no." He took her face in his hands and smirked. "You can't take it back. You asked, and I have to answer."

He kissed her forehead. "Of course, I'll marry you. I love you more than life. You complete me in ways I didn't know I needed. I trust you to keep my heart safe. I trust you with Alex and our future children." He scowled at her. "We are having babies. Right? Lots of them."

Sam laughed. "I'm not sure about lots of babies, but yes, we are having children, just not right away. You are my everything. I'm sorry I said no when you asked me before."

"We've wasted a lot of time." He tapped his fingers on the blanket and squinted at her. "Do you have a ring for me?"

She frowned. *A ring?* Crap. No. Did men even get engagement rings?

"No. But I can get you one. I think."

Mark chuckled. "I don't need a ring. I've been married to you in my mind forever. But I have one for you."

He stood and pulled a black ring box from his pocket, kneeled, and opened it. "I came here today to ask you again to marry me, hoping this time you would say yes."

*Oh my!* This wasn't the way Sam had pictured today in her mind.

The ring was perfect—a square-cut diamond surrounded by smaller diamonds—not too big, not too small.

A tear fell from Sam's eye, and Mark wiped it away. "Can I put this on your finger?"

She nodded and held out her hand as he slipped it on. He kissed the ring on her hand and gave her a silly grin.

Just like that, her world was complete, like the ocean waves that persevered every day, cleansing the sand and bringing new hope.

He was like the sun that rose every morning and brightened the day. She was like the moon illuminating all in its path, so they were never in darkness.

They were the yin and the yang, entwined forever.

# KNIGHTGUARD SECURITY

LOOK for the next book in the KnightGuard Security series, Book 6, Hank and Laura's story ...

## EVIDENCE OF SECRETS

**A bistro owner living her dream**
**A security guard escaping his past**
**Will they find love in the present?**
**Or will a villain destroy their future?**

Laura Clark's passion is cooking and her dream to open a bistro fulfilled. Her mother worked two jobs after her father abandoned the family for a younger woman. Still, Laura craves the loving husband, white picket fence and 2.5 kids. Too bad she has no time for romance or a family.

Hank Peterman doesn't hesitate to face danger head-on. His job at KnightGuard Security fulfills a promise he made to himself because of a traumatic childhood experience. But after watching his father marry and divorce three women, all gold diggers, the one danger he can't face is settling down.

Strange things happen at Salt & Sea, and Laura turns to KnightGuard Security for protection. Hank is assigned to her case. As a villain threatens her livelihood and safety, Laura and Hank fight their attraction despite their opposing viewpoints, but can they work together to foil a villain determined to take everything Laura values?

*Turn the page to read a sample from*
*EVIDENCE OF SECRETS*

*Preview of*

## EVIDENCE OF SECRETS

*Book 6, KnightGuard Security*


## CHAPTER 1: HANK

"Read 'em and weep, suckers," hollered Hank Peterman as he threw his cards on the table. The other guys, Mark Stone, Ben Green, Jake Sommers, Danny Knight and Seth Bowman, groaned and tossed in their cards.

"About time you won something," said Danny.

Hank glanced over at Danny. He was laughing and content. No more worry lines on his forehead. Marriage certainly agreed with him. And Danny's wife, Hailey, well, she was something special. He was glad for his friend. They had served in the Army together and Danny brought him on board to KnightGuard Security.

"Hey, I'm not complaining. I lose more money here than if I was betting on horses."

It was about time, too. Every month when the guys got together, whenever he had a winning hand, he seemed to lose money. Go figure.

Hank stood and started collecting the kitty. "When are Joe and Claire getting back from Connecticut?"

"Oh, they'll be back next week," said Mark. "Claire missed her parents and wanted to see them before she got too big. Joe wasn't about to let her go by herself."

"Can't blame him. I'm glad they took the time off. When's the baby due?"

"Six months," said Mark.

"Joe is making sure Claire sticks close to him especially

after being kidnapped," said Danny. He grabbed his beer bottle and took a long gulp. "Although I'm not sure Claire appreciates having him around so much."

"Hell, if that was my woman, I'd never let her out of the house," said Hank. The abduction of Sam and Claire had shaken the whole KnightGuard Security force. Luckily, they found the women before that douchebag Colin Woods and his girlfriend, Chrissie Thorne, killed them.

"Well, you're in luck. You don't have a woman to worry about," said Seth. He pulled the chips toward him and started stacking them in the box.

"Yeah? Neither do you, asshole," said Hank. He pocketed his winnings and tossed his beer bottle in the trash.

Seth started laughing. "Well, we have something in common."

"I'm off. Big job tomorrow and I need to get up early," said Hank. He saluted the group and left. He'd parked his black Grand Cherokee Jeep on the street.

The drive to his condo was about fifteen minutes away.

Hank plugged in his favorite country and western music and drove the familiar streets home. He relaxed and allowed himself to rehash the night's events. The poker game was the highlight of his month. It was good to chill out and spend the evening with good friends. Several were married and had kids, a couple were looking for their forever mate, and then there was him. He wasn't married and wasn't looking. Why should he? The one thing he had in excess was charm and the ability to pick up a woman. The key was sincerity. He genuinely liked women.

Not to marry, though. He'd been down the route once before and was betrayed by the woman he pledged to spend the rest of his life with. Ugh. Not thinking about relationships right now.

Tomorrow's job required him to concentrate on

protecting a movie star who wanted to buy a mansion in Black Pointe and not have groupies chasing him or finding out where he lived. It would be an easy gig. Not all jobs were. Not that it mattered. He loved working at KnightGuard Security and enjoyed the friendship with the people there. He admired Sam Knight from the moment he met the small, tenacious woman.

Hank parked his car in the onsite garage and walked up to the glass front door to punch in his code. The door opened, and he said hello to Manny, who was on the security night-shift. Manny was a friend from the service who needed a job, and he was perfect for the building. He had a slight build, but Hank knew Manny was more than proficient in self-defense and a sharpshooter. No one would get in the building to do harm to the residents and live to talk about it.

He took the elevator to the penthouse floor. The five-story brick building overlooking the water was his, and it was money well-spent. He could decide who he wanted living there and still have his privacy. He had combined the top two apartments for his own space. There were two nine-hundred-square-foot apartments on each of the other four floors, each with a balcony overlooking the water. Two of the apartments housed single women, three housed couples working hard to get ahead, and the remaining apartments housed three elderly couples.

There wasn't a lot he could control in life, but being able to offer people down on their luck a safe place to live and pay a reasonable rent gave him pleasure. The rents weren't so low that anyone would feel that they were a charity case or too high to keep out people he wanted to help. It was a win-win. They were quiet and good neighbors.

The elevator stopped and he got out and opened the door to his condo. The front door led into a large living room. He pushed the light switch on and felt instantly at peace. He had a little help from a decorator and together they chose the grays, navy blues and browns that created the calm interior. Along with comfy furniture, a big-ass TV, modern appliances in the eat-in kitchen, and three bedrooms, one of which was an office and the other a guest room, the condo was complete.

Hank grabbed a beer and opened the sliding doors to the balcony that overlooked the river. The twinkling lights of town and the muted voices of people at the various Riverwalk restaurants carried over the water. It was a view he never tired of. The building was far enough away from the touristy part of town to not have people walking on the sidewalk all hours of the night but close enough to enjoy the sights and sounds of Riverwalk.

Hank had to laugh. No one knew he owned this building. He'd never had anyone from the company over. He valued his privacy. He also didn't need the money he won at poker tonight, although it was about time he won. Besides, he didn't need to work—ever. Work gave him a purpose in life.

And life was good. The occasional nagging thought that he was missing something in his life came and went. No way was he ever going to let another person bully him or let a woman take advantage of him again. He was content.

## CHAPTER 2: LAURA

A sound like a gunshot behind her caused Laura Clark to stumble and scream. She quickly turned to see what happened. Standing innocently on its hinges, the metal door leading to the kitchen was closed tight. Laura realized the gusty wind had slammed it shut. Her heart thumped in her chest. It didn't matter that she was already on edge. *Damn wind.*

It was one hour past dawn and way past time for Laura to prepare the day's menu, complete the prep work for the lunch and dinner menu and get to the farmer's market in time to choose the freshest vegetables and fruits needed for the day. She'd hoped to sleep in today and was still yawning when the banging door rudely woke her.

Rich Dupont, the pastry chef, had called in sick—again—which meant Laura had to pick up his work as well as her own duties as owner of the Salt & Sea bistro.

Laura sighed, closed her eyes and inhaled. The faint scent of garlic and a whiff of last night's meals, accompanied by the antiseptic cleaner they used, comforted her. Some people hated all the different restaurant kitchen odors, but they didn't bother Laura. To her they were a sign of success.

It wasn't as if she hadn't done all these jobs when she first started out, but ten years later? She'd hoped that the restaurant would be running more smoothly. And it had until six months ago.

The problems started with a crank call to the health department about food poisoning and a number of cars getting scratched in her parking lot. It cost her money that she didn't have to make up the difference that the insurance hadn't covered. KnightGuard Security had installed additional cameras around the parking lot. Even though her best friend, Sam Knight, owned the company and had only charged her for the cameras, not the installation, it still cut into her profits.

The damage to the cars had been the work of Sam's stalker, Colin Woods. Woods was dead, shot by his ex-girlfriend, Chrissie, who was serving time for killing him and attempting to kill Sam.

Something else was going on that Laura couldn't put her

finger on. Strange noises, a request to buy the restaurant for more than it was worth, help that didn't stay, missing food items, plus a feeling that someone was spying on her. All little things. Well, not little things, but things she couldn't do much about. She really needed to talk to Sam about hiring a security expert, but there wasn't any extra money in the budget for that.

Bah. No time to think about problems. Laura glanced around the small stainless-steel kitchen. The theme was French country meets coastal Florida. Warm and comforting but light and airy. The theme continued into the dining room and outside.

The bistro was her happy place. Each piece of furniture, every piece of equipment, the paint on the walls, the checkered floor, the plants—all hand-chosen by her. The original secondhand furniture replaced over the years as she made money. The first time she saw the dilapidated brick building with its large glass windows with a view of the water and marina, she knew it was perfect for her dream. Something about the building's character pulled her in. Black Pointe was gentrifying the Riverwalk area and the price was right. The location was also perfect, right off the main drag. People could sit and listen to the water lap up the sidewalk. She loved its history and its unsavory reputation as a speakeasy.

Laura reached for the wooden recipe box handed down to her from her grandmother. She gently rubbed the painted top but not too roughly. It was already peeling. Reaching in, she pulled up her grandmother's fruit tart recipe. Just looking at the handwritten recipe on yellowing paper brought a tear to her eye. Laura had never met her grandmother. She died shortly after Laura was born, but her mother kept her alive in Laura's mind. Her grandmother had owned a successful bakery, and whenever Laura needed a dessert recipe, she used one of her grandmother's.

What fruit would be good this time of year? It was summer, so she knew the market would have a cornucopia of summer's bounty. Berries, peaches, plums, nectarines. The choice was overwhelming. Well, she would have to see what was plentiful in the market.

However, if she didn't make the pastry crust and put it in the refrigerator, she'd never get to the market and there would be no dessert offered tonight. Besides, she promised Jake Summers, owner of Neptune's Navel and her sometimes lover, she'd meet him there. Their routine was to buy what they needed for their restaurants, stop at Beans-to-Go to get coffee and pastry and then sit by the ocean to catch up with each other's lives.

Jake would ask her how things were going, and she had to be cautious about what she told him. He might tell Sam before she had a chance to. Jake was a protector, and while they would never be a couple, Laura suspected that he would step in to help her.

Two things she knew for sure were that she needed help and that she couldn't afford to hire anyone.

---

Learn more at LilaFerrariWrites.com

# PREVIEW: SEALS OF DISTINCTION

*Preview of*

## LIAM

### SEALs of Distinction, Book 1

At 7:00 a.m., the weather was already hot, although dark clouds hovered above, teasing. A storm wasn't due for a few days. Driving down the dirt road, Lorenzo Rossi's car kicked up so much dust, he had to turn on his windshield wipers to find the abandoned driveway he would hide in to wait.

At seven thirty sharp, Joy Maddox left her aunt's house and drove by, oblivious to the danger she was in. The stupid woman never looked left or right for someone hiding in the bushes—someone like him.

He shivered, not just from the chilly air the air-conditioner was blowing, but from what would happen to him if he didn't complete this assignment soon. His pulse beat in tandem to the aggressive beat of the drums in the hard rock music that he favored. Lorenzo caressed the soft leather seat of his fancy Mercedes coupe and inhaled. Nothing like the sexy scent of new leather to get his juices going. Although if this project didn't work, the Mercedes and everything he owned would be lost—including his life.

Lorenzo accidentally hit his left hand on the steering wheel and screamed "mother fucker" as he almost passed out. No thanks to Gino "The Hammer" Castellani, who'd visited him last night and told him in no uncertain terms what he needed to do—and do it fast—then gave him a preview of what would happen if he didn't.

Gino had his enforcer Paulie hold his hand flat on the table. Lorenzo begged Gino not to strike him.

While he was still screaming in pain, Gino had the audacity to make him say thank you. *Thank you?*

Gino only laughed at his pain. "Yeah. You're thanking me for not messing up your pretty-boy face. This time." Well, thank God for that.

Biting back the pain, he reached for a bottle of pills and looked at the label—take two. Pouring four into his hand, he popped the pills into his mouth. Bile slithered up his gut, and he swallowed hard. Now wouldn't be the time to get sick.

He wondered why anyone thought nicknames like "The Hammer" were funny. He wished he had the courage to say "fuck you" to tyrants like Gino. But that's what happens when you lie down with dogs. You get up with fleas. And boy, had he.

The sweat rolled down his forehead, and he cursed the fact that he inherited his father's propensity to sweat profusely in times of stress. One more reason to hate dear ol' dad. He would be swimming in sweat by the time he finished.

Since Joy left a while ago, it was safe to pull his car nearer to the house. Just close enough so he could drive away in a hurry.

Lorenzo exited the car and stepped into humidity that

closed in around him like a shroud—the irony wasn't lost on him. The air was heavy with moisture and it would rain soon. He needed to hurry.

Joy wouldn't be back for a good two hours.

Lorenzo licked his lips, thinking about the slender blonde.

Yeah, he wouldn't mind doing her, but she wasn't his type —busty, lusty women who loved sex like her cousin Denise were more his type.

The couple of times he and Denise had visited Joy, he realized she had that annoying bubbly personality he hated. Joy didn't like him much either—tough. He wasn't on this earth to have people like him.

A dog barked in her house.

He didn't bother to look around because the nearest house was empty.

Actually, no one had lived next door for a while. The recent development across the cornfield was too far away for anyone to hear the beast who had worked himself into a frenzy of high-pitched yowls.

Lorenzo walked around back.

The patio was as he remembered it: small pavers, a lounger, two patio chairs, a table, and a firepit.

A coffee cup sat forgotten on the table. Joy had mowed the lawn, and overall, it looked like a well-maintained house.

He wasn't selling the home—it had no value to him.

He was here for the land, the hundred-plus acres of prime real estate close to town, perfect for the facility Gino and his friends wanted to build on it.

He'd been schmoozing the president of the proposed medical center for over a year. It helped that the man was Gino's friend—well, not a friend exactly. Gino didn't make friends. The president was in the same predicament as Lorenzo was. Damned if you do, damned if you don't.

Lorenzo took pictures of the development across the

street and the neighbor's house. He tried to remember who lived next door. Oh, right—the McBrides.

A couple of years ago, he had approached the family, but they weren't interested in selling.

Something about family, home, peace, and quiet—blah, blah, blah. Perhaps the family would feel differently after they built the medical center and saw all the traffic and people it generated.

Right now, he had to concentrate on taking the pictures he'd promised Gino.

It was challenging holding onto the camera with his left hand and pressing the button with his right. The pain was a constant reminder of what would happen if he didn't get control of the property.

Trekking through the overgrown, wooded path, he tripped over some roots and sent the camera flying.

Lorenzo's arms windmilled until he put his left hand out to stop his fall, and then he screamed—again.

God damn Gino. Why had he ever gotten involved in the mob?

He'd taped the three middle fingers on his left hand that Gino tapped—Gino's words, not his—with the hammer. But he couldn't stop the pain. He was sure his fingers were broken, but he wasn't going to a doctor or the hospital.

The scumbag had laughed at his pain. Then waved the hammer around, threatening to do both hands and feet the next time.

His stomach clenched. Lorenzo prayed there would be no next time.

Ignoring the pain, he searched around and found the camera in a pile of pine needles. Sweat soaked his freshly pressed custom-made shirt and attracted all sorts of biting insects. He swatted at some. The bastards died on his shirt, leaving a blood trail, and showed no sign of letting up. Another thing ruined. He hurried on with his work.

Lots of underbrush dotted the pine tree forest. He saw some live oaks and different palms. All would be cleared.

Damn, he stepped in some mud. The expensive Italian loafers he wore were ruined.

He let out a yelp and jumped after pushing aside a branch when a bird squawked close to his ear. He hated birds, hated the outdoors, and hated wild animals—hated animals of any sort.

Wasn't it funny that Joy had dogs? He had to suffer through her petting and cooing over them when he visited her with Denise. The universe was conspiring against him.

He snapped his pictures quickly and then looked at his watch. A few drops of rain landed on his head—time to leave.

Lorenzo followed the path back to his car and drove toward town.

So many plans still had to be made.

He needed this land, needed it now, and needed it cheap. No one was going to stand in his way.

However, time wasn't on his side. Control of the property was imperative before other parts of his body got hurt—or worse.

The banknote was due in a month.

The rest of the money Gino had lent him for his last project was overdue, hence the personal visit. He'd given Gino all the money he had set aside for a rainy day, plus interest. It wasn't everything that he'd saved, though. The rest was hidden in an offshore account, and he wanted to live long enough to enjoy it.

The bitch who owned the house was taking too long to die. Lorenzo thought about how he could speed up Aunt Shirley's demise. It would take a little planning, but it was doable. His current love interest, well, convenient love interest, Denise Franklin, was Shirley's niece and only living relative. She thought he cared. Wasn't that a hoot? The only things he gave a shit about were money and prestige.

Denise would inherit the land when the aunt died. Her plan was to build a few upscale houses on the lot and make a killing on them—not happening. He needed big money, not bits and pieces of money, and sharing wasn't in his vocabulary. He had to dump Denise in more ways than one as soon as he got control of the land from her. She was a good lay, a distraction, but business came first.

Well, his life came first. He could keep both if he were smart.

## BOOKS BY LILA FERRARI

### KNIGHTGUARD SECURITY SERIES

Each book in the series is a stand-alone and can be read in any order. Reviews are greatly appreciated.

*Evidence of Betrayal* — Book 1 (Luke and Grace's story)

*Evidence of Murder* — Book 2 (Ben and Marlee's story)

*Evidence of Lies* — Book 3 (Pete and Julie's story)

*Evidence of Deceit* — Book 4 (Joe and Claire's story)

*Evidence of Revenge* — Book 5 (Sam and Mark's story)

*Evidence of Secrets* — Book 6 (Hank and Laura's story) - available soon

*Evidence of Evil* — Book 7 (Logan and Maddie's story) — available in 2022

## NEW SERIES

SEALs of Distinction – Book 1 available in 2022

Haywood Lake Mysteries — Book 1 available in 2022

# ABOUT THE AUTHOR

I've been writing forever. Poems, plays, short stories, cookbooks, grants, newsletters, newspaper articles and now full-length novels.

Growing up in New England where summers are sweet but winters are long and cold has given me lots of opportunity to expand my creativity.

I have enjoyed: basket weaving, spinning wool, quilting, canning, teaching cooking and traveling.

I have been a recipe tester, sailor, farmer, shepherd, cattle-woman, chick herder and Master Gardener.

Like many women, I have worked full-time, raised two children, and helped my husband's career. Finally, I get to make my dream come true. After all, dreams never die, and new doors open every day.

Today, I live in sunny Florida with my husband enjoying paradise. In addition to writing novels, I recently took up birding and photography. My photos have done well in local contests.

My stories are about courage, redemption and second chances. Everyone deserves them, don't you agree?

---

For more information on books by Lila Ferrari, visit her website at lilaferrariwrites.com where you can subscribe to her newsletter to get updates on releases, bonus content, fun facts and enter contests.

**As always, if you enjoyed my books, please leave a review.**

Made in the USA
Columbia, SC
07 February 2022

54836751R00207